SUMMERING

Books by Joanne Greenberg . . .

SUMMERING

A Book of

Short

Stories

by Joanne

Greenberg

Holt, Rinehart and Winston

New York   Chicago   San Francisco

Some of the stories in this volume were previously published in the following magazines:
"Two Annas" in the June, 1961, issue of *The University Review;* "Summering" in the Summer, 1963, issue of *The Hudson Review;* "You Can Still Grow Flowers" in the Summer, 1964, issue of *The Virginia Quarterly Review;* "Lullabies" in the May, 1966, issue of *Hadassah Magazine;* and "L'Olom and White Shell Woman" in *The Denver Quarterly.*

First Edition

Designer: Ernst Reichl
83274-0316
Printed in the United States of America

To My Grandparents

CONTENTS

SUMMERING

TWO
ANNAS

There were fearful times: the few minutes before sleep came, and the few minutes after the morning bell when her mind had not fully come from sleep. To the other routines of imprisonment she submitted, this breaking of her own will was rewarded with the numbness which allowed her to walk through the days without suffering. They were days of loneliness without solitude, organized and crushing boredom, cruelty (more verbal than physical, more silent than verbal), routine ugliness and a paradoxical sense of her own isolation. In the daytime she dressed, went to the toilet, worked, ate, sat, walked, and waited in the geared wheel of the schedule. She had learned to be faceless and so to come to no one's attention, and of this only she was proud. The other prisoners respected her because the covering seemed perfect. In spite of their respect, she didn't enter into any of their intrigues, because intrigues in a prison have to do with alliances, and she wished to have no allies. She wished only for a deepening of the numbness. She was still subject to momentary chills of dread when her mind happened to skip over the defenses erected to stop it and touch on the terror bounding night and morning in the narrow bed.

Once or twice she had been brave enough to try to question

and probe for the meaning of that terror, but there was no test of meaning that didn't depend on the inner response of emotions which had been purposefully and relentlessly deadened. What hadn't been killed by her of sorrow, guilt, yearning, indignation, or compassion had been worn away on the wheels of the routine. Only at the rims of wakefulness did the long and patient defenses against the day pull apart and ravel to nothing, leaving her vulnerable, a naked, frightened victim, gritting her teeth in the unexplainable terror.

When new prisoners came, she sometimes remembered how frightened she had been of the others when she was new, and how long it took her to win their respect. It had finally come in spite of her college education, the absence of which excused so many of them, to their own minds, of failure. They respected her at last because of her strength in not-caring, invulnerability, and hardness; and in tribute to it, they called her Sunshine. She wore the name proudly. The namers wished to be as hard as she, and in their caustic way were admitting it. It was the cardinal virtue of the prison, to be hard. Everyone knew, secretly and beyond illusion, that outside, they were the weak ones.

There was a great seam of difference between Outside and Inside. When things tear apart, it is usually at a seam. It was the new prisoners who were at the seam between the worlds.

When the new prisoners came, Sunshine would let them know what their new world expected, pulling her eyes across their faces as if to leave a scar, and silencing any thought in herself that one was young or another scared. The first-timers were the hardest to take. You could pick any of them out in line: their issue clothes fitted differently somehow, their eyes wandered restlessly, trying to pull futures out of the faces of people who passed by. First-timers were so frightened that nobody could tell what they were going to do.

She had come out of the warden's office that morning and stood looking at the line of them. Silly Anna was mopping her way down the hall toward them, and as Sunshine passed, she gave recognition with a nod to Silly Anna, against the new ones, showing them that they didn't belong, that old and crazy slattern sloshers of dirty gray water were their betters. Anna's vacant eyes didn't flicker. She knew they wouldn't; Silly Anna was one of the dead-living-rote, and when you were in a room with her, you were alone. Anna lifted the mop and let it out, and a tongue of the gray water threw itself across the floor and rode up over one of the issue shoes in the line. A New One swung out of place and threw herself on Anna, cursing and kicking so that the bucket tipped and the mop threw rain, and the line broke and guards and prisoners were scrambling in the hall. Sunshine had just kept walking, but when she was ready to turn the corner she looked back to see if she had won her bet. Easy. The hall was empty, the New One getting it, nice and quiet, behind a door, witnesses told off behind another door; and there was Silly Anna alone in the corridor, pushing the spilled water ahead of her in slow, regular arcs. She was holding herself oddly—they must have broken something inside her. Suddenly Sunshine was aware of a little flicking of the tongue of the Terrible Thing, the night-and-morning fear. It was moving experimentally to explore in the raftered skeleton, finding, finding. Somebody should take Silly Anna to the doc—it wasn't fair—and Sunshine closed off the words from her mind and went on down the corridor. The Terrible Thing tossed a coil and grew into itself and began seeking upward, flickering its tongue as it moved behind the rib-beams.

Under her faceless face her mind was arguing with itself as Sunshine ate. Anna was too crazy for justice, why worry? Somebody should have been told. . . . Hell, their justice is beating the attacker, not comforting the victim; their justice is to level the attacker until he is as hurt as the victim. Who cares? Let the ones who can afford diversion care. Caring is for Them. God, don't let me lose myself now, winding injustices. Just a few months; just a little bit longer—I could list a hundred people in this Can who died of hope. . . .

Because she had been in the warden's office to discuss the possibility of parole—that morning, before the New Prisoners and Silly Anna, there had been proud moments for her. The hardening had gone so deep that she hadn't even counted her days or months or years, or, like most of the others, tortured them away, desperate and fearful that the last days would lengthen into infinity. Sometimes it happened, too, that prisoners got sick and died or were in fights which they didn't start,

but which doomed them anyway. Hopers. Fools. She had submitted all the way, guards and walls; let them do what they
would. Now the warden was talking about reviving a skeleton,
fleshing a corpse and sending it out into some springtime far
distant from the one in which the living being had entered
prison and death. From the window of his office she had seen
the light cloud of leaf buds on a tree down in his garden. Let
him dare her to hunger for it! And the pride had surged up to
answer. She didn't even need to resist. Go ahead then, let them
raise the dead!

There was a rumor between the sheet folds at the laundry the
next day. People licked thread ends at the sewing shop and
words went out with them through the needles that Silly Anna
had died. The causes were sewn in and out, sorted, folded, and
piled. Sunshine heard it in the bookkeeping office where she
worked. She shrugged and went on about her day, knowing that
the corridor guards who had been outside the warden's office
were shrugging too as they heard.

The spring requisitions were coming through—it must really
be spring, then. The Terrible Thing, night and morning, was
growing, feeding itself on her moments of rest, to swell and coil
in the great space inside her, the space that she had emptied of
every memory of preference that could give pain. Could there
be a fear big enough to fill it? Lately she seemed to sense a
sound too, like the sound of wind blowing through her as if she
had no flesh, as if it blew through the skeleton of herself, whistling occasionally across the hollows of her absent eyes. Sometimes, during the day, a wind would whip across the stone front
of the wall of the billing department and make its peculiar
fushing sound; and she would stop, frightened for an instant, to
imagine that it was blowing inside her. Then she would turn
back to work and laugh uneasily. This was what they were
going to parole! She tried to keep the time full, something
against the wind. She had read and written letters for some of
the illiterate ones, and now she spent all the time she could
listening to grievances on pages and copying grievances onto
pages, staying away from her own. When they asked for an
opinion, she gave it; and her judgments were respected because
they had neither sympathy nor mercy. To outside they would

have seemed inhuman, because they were savagely just. Inside, the askers nodded. Savagery was familiar to them; they trusted it.

That spring wasn't just, only savage. It brought longing like a tide over the walls; it brought everyone's Terrible Thing; and it brought the visitors. People who had never come at any other time came for the trip, and as a little reason for gratitude, once out again into the fortunate sunshine. They would come with children and picnic baskets, and there were brief moments when the inmates could be fooled into believing themselves members, sharers in the species which called itself by so many noble names. Sunshine was sure that it was the parole hanging over her head that made her so sensitive this year to the visitors and her imagining of their lives. She watched fathers and husbands and brothers coming. What would it be like to wake up in some sunny, littered room next to someone whose life was yours and to whose life you belonged? Would it be safe to weigh trust so heavily?

She saw a mother walking with her children. What would it be like to tell a child the name of something and have him repeat it, in the grave and self-important way of children, with your own inflection? She let herself stand at the window looking at the mother in her flowered dress, the children with their little brightnesses, and all the baskets and bundles of prudence and concern—the possessions of a private life. It was a trap, a deceit, like the warden's tree. . . . Suddenly she had a terrible envy of that woman.

Something was happening down there. One of the children had run around the mother and hit the other one, crying and shouting at it. The struck child stood stunned where it was. The mother put down her purse and basket and took both children in her arms, comforting both of them as she separated them with her body, holding them close to her and thus also to one another. Then she kissed each one and rose clumsily, and picked up her bundles and they went on. It was so simple an act that Sunshine would imagine it happening often during the day, maybe at bedtime and at awakening. In the very smallest writing there was a dissenting opinion to the curse she had written on the prison wall. It wasn't only baskets and children and flowered dresses that separated the hated prisoners from the hated free, the evil from the good, the damned from the elect. It was a distance perhaps too great to travel in a lifetime. Sunshine turned from the window, and a spring of scorn overflowed to defend her. Oh, what a fool! How many dozens are there, flowered dresses and all, masquerading as members, givers, sharers! It isn't an enemy bristling with guns who comes conquering; it's the masquerader, and I could be as competent as any of them.

Silly Anna hadn't wanted to live. She was trying death anyway; and she would have stood there, watching me from deep inside her safe deadness; and if I had tried to comfort her, she would have mocked me, laughed or answered with something her madness had taught her, something that might feed the Terrible Thing, might know about it, might use it. . . .

"Go to hell!" she said to Anna and women with children; and then she had to look around the office and see if anyone had heard her. It was a fine time to go crazy like Anna. No, nobody was going to cheat her out of getting up and taking that parole and going out in a flowered dress, lilies and roses, and screw you!

> Whan that Aprille with hes shoures sote
> Meeteth Parole Board with its two-thirds vote;
> And I will clean my nails and beg for freeing,
> And masquerade me as a human being!

It made her laugh for a while.

Her card had been pulled. Sunshine heard it from the grapevine; one of the gratuities with which fellow prisoners can keep a person alive or kill him. The Board was going to consider her case. All at once she was frightened. Was it like the old Prisoner of Chillon, the caged man so reconciled and now so estranged from the Outside that he hung back, half-wishing not to leave? No. Not for her. It wasn't fear of the Outside, but fear of the prison now, after all this time, and of what she would say to that Board, and of how she couldn't hope to outrun that coiling fear and that hollowness. Because now she knew what woke the Terrible Thing and what caused it to go seeking in the empty framework of a once-living being.

With every passing day the hollow feeling was growing in her. Daily the sense deepened that a cold wind was blowing through the rafters of her body, through the gape-face-bones.

The sound spread into her dreams; it crept upward from the
night and downward from the morning and across the dead
plain of the prison day. What could she tell those earnest faces
on the Board, sitting at their sensible table? God knew, she'd
heard the answers enough. Someone always asked: "Have you
any remorse for what you did?"

(And what did I do; what did that young girl do, whose life I
used to use. I don't even recognize her any more. What was it
she did?)

In the mold of every candidate before, she put the well-
known questions to herself, answering them as she knew the
Board liked them answered; but coming to the one about the
remorse, she found herself blurting: "The wind drives out everything; don't you hear it all day and all night blowing through
a bone house?"

Parole was a big step and the authorities knew it. A candidate could put off his hearing if he didn't feel ready. Her mind
played with the idea once or twice, but in the end she couldn't
admit so great a cowardice to herself and, however scrupu-
lously she avoided confessing it, to her fellow judges. So few of
them wanted to have hearings postponed that questions would
be asked. Maybe it would even be noticed how she'd changed,
how the rigid strength of her body and spirit had somehow
begun to give back a hollow sound. . . . No, it had to be done
now. The Terrible Thing was growing, not diminishing, in the
hollow place. The Terrible Thing was terror of having nothing,
of being nothing but a forest of bones. No, now. She would play
it out full dress and clean fingernails; the masquerade to the end
and out the gate and down the road and home free all.

Sunshine was coming out of the warden's office again after
another of the short "rehearsals" that would culminate in her
debut before the Board. There was another batch of new prisoners standing in a line outside the door, and again she swept
over them with her eyes and registered them in her mind: all
safe; all two, three times around; maybe not here, but somewhere; all toughened with scar tissue. No one was dying of grief
or youth or shame—hard old pros, every one, with flat, untell-
ing eyes and faces of studied anonymity. She was proud of
them. They were backed-off, strong. Hit any of them and they
wouldn't bleed; do the worst and they would stand and spit in

your eye. She was one of them, belonging, flat-eyed, impersonal as wind, scornful of pain as rock. Wind. It came again, blowing with that chill and rush of sound so familiar that she suddenly had to look down at herself for assurance that she was still flesh, that she was not combing the wind through frail rib-hoops that could not hold it.

The problem was not to panic. The problem was to stop the vital numbness from leaving her now. The problem was to find out why she couldn't master it now as she had when the first days fell like separate mountains on top of her. The gaining of such a necessary strength to reject her whole life of memory and preference hadn't been easy. The pride in it, for which she had learned to scrape advantages from dust, had saved her from madness and from suicide all those years ago. Now, why was it leaving when there was rote-code to talk to the Parole Board and a chance that they might not . . .

She turned from the line of prisoners, walking, then running down the hall, and behind her she heard someone's laughter.

She saw the new prisoners in the line that marched to supper, and one of them had the place next to hers, a big woman, about forty, and tough as nails. New prisoner didn't eat much, and when coffee came, her hand trembled as she reached for it. New prisoner picked up her cup, and the trembling became violent so that she put it down quickly before anyone noticed. Fear like that could ruin a person. If anyone saw, there would be nothing left for her except to be classed with the crazies. She put her hands out of sight under the table, but they continued to shake, and now her face was working in fear that anyone should see.

Sunshine took her hand under the table and held it. She was as frightened as New prisoner, but she wanted and then she had to repudiate her scorn. The pain in New prisoner was almost unbearable for Sunshine. It was transmitting itself through the trembling hands, but Sunshine could not take her hand away. Maybe it would be all right if no one saw.

For a while the two of them sat staring ahead, and then New prisoner said, "Yeah." It couldn't have been "thanks" because thanks is a curseword, one of Their words, like "guilty" and "remorse." "Yeah" acknowledged it all—shame, hopelessness, and wonder, because they both knew that New prisoner wouldn't have helped if anyone else had been drowning in her terror and she safe and wise on the shore. "Yeah" branded her not only as hardened, but as maximum—security—hardened, a tough old con. The word was just loud enough for Sunshine alone to hear, and the lips hadn't moved. "See, uh, it's life, this time, life. . . ."

The hand jerked violently every time she said "life." She was trying to excuse herself by giving just cause. Sunshine let go of her hand and New prisoner reached for her cup with only a slight tremor. "My name's Anna," she said, still looking straight ahead.

"Sunshine."

An imperceptible nod.

The bell rang and they rose; and, hearing it, Sunshine knew that now Anna was hearing it too, as if for life, every day to the end. Her tremor came again, taking the arm too, violently, and not of its owner's will. Anna was scrambling desperately for not caring, the dead level; and it was life-and-death to get it, to outrace her Terrible Thing or be destroyed. Sunshine didn't care any more about anything but the pain she felt with Anna. It was as if she could no longer afford the symmetrical, sterile anonymity of all her years and of this place. She took hold of Anna's arm to steady it.

For a single moment in balance every face she saw was the face of a person, all around them, looking at them with amusement, with scorn, with disinterest—persons. With a curse Anna flung off the hold and turned to her, growling, "Get your paws offa me, ya lousy dyke!"

Everyone heard. It didn't matter. Sunshine was alive. Cradled between the wind-sounding bones were cells, valves, veins, organs, membrane, and muscle woven with the intricacy of something that had a meaning. For another instant she stood, all those cells, nerves, and systems one soul, a single unrepeatable and mortal cry.

Very quietly she said, "I'm sorry."

"You're crazy, you know that!" Anna's fists were ready and her face was working, hoping that Sunshine wouldn't spill anything, wanting to stop her mouth with a fist, but knowing that loonies weren't fair game.

The loony said, "If you hit me, I'll bleed. All over the floor." The loony was smiling.

A letter to the Parole Board. She had torn up three already. Everyone knew what you said, the usual blab tested and proved by ninety-nine percent of satisfied convicts, some without changing a word; but now that she was alive, she was afraid to harm anything, cell or sinew that was filling her body, fitted in so closely and so carefully between the accommodating bones. Lying would hollow her; she had to stand with her truth as protectively as the flowered-dress mother did with her children.

Dear Sirs:

The wind has stopped blowing through me without hindrance. If you listen, you will not hear it whistling among the empty rafters; but do not think that because I am quiet, I am dead. By no means imagine that I am dead. To end is to begin.

Dear Sirs: . . .

YOU CAN STILL GROW FLOWERS

"I have given you what help I can," said Reverend McNeith, and he lifted his hand a little way from the table. "Indeed, I would be more than happy if I could be of further assistance."

The old way, slow and measured. Run the tape recorder, Ann-Mary thought, but there are gestures with the old words, and the words and gestures have another meaning here, where life is very hard, the old language is dying, and the young people leave and the wind blows all day long. "You have given so much help already," she said. A long summer spent with the Islanders had shaded her own speech to match theirs. "I am most grateful."

Sometimes she felt uncomfortable with Island custom, because for a stranger the courtesy was so one-sided. She had come in June to do a series of language studies and take transcriptions of Island speech. Its dialect of Scots Gaelic was dying with the dying old of the Island. At least, she thought, as she shouted into ear trumpets, it can die into a tape recorder where it will be caught in its last accents, as it was spoken. Even here, to this tiny colony of persons separated from Scotland by a wild and treacherous stretch of water, and looking westward on an endless ocean, change was creeping, seeking its levels with fine fingers, the way the high tide sifts and combs, etching caves for itself.

The isolation of the Island had kept the ancient tongue from change, but the old ways were going. In 1934 a generator had been built, and now there were two radios, and at the midwife's house an electric light. The packet boat came twice a month now, and it had begun to bring magazines and newspapers as well as tea and flour. With the new ways and the Second World War had come the new language. Few but the old spoke the Gaelic any more, and the young, who had learned from grand-parents net-mending songs and love songs, the dirge and the lullabye, were ashamed and would not speak.

"It is ourselves, rather, who should be grateful," the Reverend said. "You have come a long way. Few come to our Island." His courtesy could not mask the raw Island sorrow, not that so few came but that so many left, and none returned.

"There are some little sidelights I would like to investigate before I make my final notes," she said. "I wanted to ask you, for instance, if you have in Gaelic animal imitations?" He looked up quizzically, but with interest, so she went on. "For example, we say 'bow-wow' for the sound a dog makes, 'moo' for the cow, and so forth. Does your dialect also have such sounds? Something which perhaps is taught to children?"

His eyes widened and she realized her mistake and began to blush. "It is those on the mainland," he said with a touch of asperity, "who use a dialect, young woman. Our speech is the pure Gaelic, the correct Gaelic, the true Gaelic." Then he went on in a slow, tranquil tone, measuring the chastening with forgiveness. It was the Island way. "As for the animal sounds, I do remember being taught something of them when a child. . . . I shall telly-phone David McCloud by Bride's Hand and inquire if he or any of his acquaintance knows aught of them."

Two "telly-phones" had been installed the year before, one at the Reverend McNeith's home on the eastern side of the Island, Green Rock, where great boulders stood against the surf-covered sea moss, and one at Dr. David McCloud's at Bride's Hand, six miles away over the rocky pastureland. The Reverend cranked for a while like a man possessed. Island courtesy was a desperate, vital thing in this hard place, and it was mandatory that he wear himself out to answer a request.

"Hallo!" he bellowed.

Ann-Mary smiled. She could hear the answering bellow. From then on the conversation went into a "Standard" Gaelic, wildly howled and interspersed with cock-a-doodle-do, bow-wow, and cut-cut. The Reverend explained the problem in detail. When he replaced the receiver, his face was red with his exertions.

"It is, though I mean no discourtesy to you, an unusual problem with which you confront me." He sat back in his chair and committed himself to thought.

"There is one man who might be of help. He has the Gaelic as perfectly as it was ever spoken, and surely he will know if what you seek can indeed be found."

Ann-Mary wondered if she knew this perfect speaker. She had asked words and compared speech patterns with dozens of people all summer, faithfully plodding with the tape recorder to one family after another, being introduced by the Reverend and, slowly, half-accepted. She had searched out all the old, feeding their words and the ancient sounds and rhythms of their speech into her machine. Now, summer was ending. When the next packet boat left, she would be on it back to the mainland; and the sounds at sunny doorsills and the inflections of worn voices at the turf hearths would become a certain weight in the university's dusty archives. Surely she had heard them all.

The Reverend smiled and said. "It is old Ian Graeme McNeith. He is a fine man, but now without close sentiments of family and therefore living more than a little in the past. Mind you, he is not a recluse, but—perhaps some might find him outspoken."

"Living in the past"—"outspoken . . ." That was the last tape for which she had been looking, a tape on which the voice of this Island would speak the thoughts of the Island. How astonished the keepers of the archives would be if someday one of them would idly flip a switch and come uptide of the chilling Island wave, to hear the voice of a man telling in his own words what it was like to bear the raw, real wind of life and death in this hard place.

She thanked the Reverend eagerly and went out into the bright daylight. Her mind was busily making its plans. First, the animal sounds—it might ease him into memories of his own boyhood. Perhaps next, an autobiographical . . .

She was walking down the single short street that edged the quay. Nine houses stood facing to sea, all dry-stone, low, like crouching fighters, wary, grim, and determined. Before them the sea milled, rose, whispered, and fell back, waiting. It was a beautiful day. The wind was clear and late summer sunshine was warming the stones. Everyone was out, sewing at the doorsills, cutting vegetables, or chopping fish.

The young girls were out, singing over the clustered washtubs. Their sound rang sweetly down to the sea, and Ann-Mary thought that the flavor of life here—salt tears, salt rime, and sea—had its sweetness too, maybe more treasured because of its rarity; and it had an ancient rhythm: seasons of fishing and farming, wash slapping against buckets, and laughter now and then, and women singing. She recognized the tune then; it was American. It was the long dead "Don't Fence Me In," twisted and tortured into rises and falls more comfortable to these singers by ever and ever more uncomprehending groups of Scottish pop combos on the radio. The song was a translation into "correct" Scots Gaelic.

At the last house the street gave out, and Ann-Mary went around it to where the rutted sheep road led around the Island. Starting out, she thought about the Reverend and his ancient Gaelic blessing at parting. He spoke English well, but the rhythms of his speech were all old language. Each word seemed to come singly to Islanders, and one paused between each as if to give the listener time to take the full meaning from it. That was custom, too. At first she thought it ponderous and stilted. Even the English vocabulary had never left the 1880's. Its formal, pedantic weight hewed thoughts as if from granite. But before long she began to hear the measured talk with a keen pleasure and to envy the pride that each man took in the simple act of speaking.

Islanders were isolated and remote—by any evidence of the senses they were the only speakers in the world; and language, the sacred trust of mankind, was theirs alone to preserve. Walking between a capricious sky and a mad sea on their barren and wind-beaten spot of land, they had taken to themselves some of the dignity of their adversaries, and some of the patience.

She was almost at open hill pasture when she conquered her ambitions enough to think about what she was going to do. If there were two things disapproved of on the Island, they were

haste and strangeness. She knew it had been the skillful inter-
vention of the Reverend which had modified these qualities,
both of which she had in abundance.

Now the knowledge came with a twinge of embarrassment.
How many times had he left her with her elderly speakers,
giving them some message with good-bye in their life-giving
"true" Gaelic? (Forgive her if she pries; be gentle with her;
America is such a young nation.) It suddenly dawned on Ann-
Mary that it was strange for the Reverend not to offer to introduce her to this last inheritor of "the pure speech."

She decided to go and talk to Miss Alice Graeme, a widow
who lived back near the western side of the quay. Miss Alice
had been one of Ann-Mary's best speakers, and they had
seemed to hit it off right from the beginning. There might be
some softer way of approaching old Ian McNeith, some friend
or topic of conversation that would move her easily into the
language study and animal sounds. She smiled, remembering
the polyglot howl over the phone. It was the only time she had
seen Reverend McNeith laugh. When he had hung up she had
told him how the Chinese imitate their dogs' barking: "hwo!-
hwo!" It had delighted him. A rare thing here, delight.

Miss Alice greeted her with the elaborate courtesy that was
custom. Ann-Mary accepted the visitor's chair and sat listening
to the silence. Island houses were all very quiet. The electrical
hums and switchings on and off, which Americans think they
do not hear after a time, were all nonexistent. Outside, white
sea birds wheeled and screamed over the quay, but because
Island houses had to be storm-tight and wind-tight, as storm
and wind were enemies, the closed door shut out all their
sounds. They went through the pleasantries in the carefully
threaded way of Island people, and then Ann-Mary explained
the problem, mentioning Ian Graeme McNeith, and watching
Miss Alice's face.

When she had finished, Miss Alice said slowly, "Where do
you belong to in America?"

"Utah," Ann-Mary said, "but I went to Massachusetts to
study."

"Is your home near Memphis, Tennessee then?"

Ann-Mary told her that it wasn't.

Miss Alice's hand moved with the barest hint of impatience.
"No matter. Perhaps you will understand nevertheless. I shall

tell you about two brothers." She looked carefully at her guest. "And do you make such brothers over ten times, and even more in your mind. These two brothers were young and strong and proud. Now, you have been here a summer with us. You know that they who have little yet have their children. The young men were kin and friend to all. But the packet-boat's coming made them restless and soon they were to Mull to see the place from where the boats came. When Mull was passed, to Oban, and soon nothing would satisfy their hunger's urgings but Glasgow and then London, and then yet further, on strange oceans; and the young men were lost at last to Winston and Salem in Northern Carolina, and to Tennessee." She rose and went to her cupboard and came back holding with painful care, The Picture.

Ann-Mary took it and looked at it gravely. In the sunlight of that foreign place two blond strangers in khaki pants and leather jackets posed proudly beside their new motorcycle.

Miss Alice looked at her as she handed back the picture— (What have you done to me? What have you and your people done to me?)—the surprise and pain could only be seen in a very small gesture, as she took the snapshot and turned to put it away.

"Are they your brothers?" Ann-Mary asked into the silence of the room.

"They are nephews. They are his sons, Ian McNeith's sons."

Of course. She was a widow, not a spinster, and wouldn't have had the same name as her brother. Ann-Mary saw Miss Alice perceiving her embarrassment at trying to remember if there had been any cause given to be insulted for that brother. Then, Ann-Mary caught the meaning of the pictures to Ian McNeith, a man with the old ways and the old tongue, whose own flesh and blood and future had become exiled from him forever.

"It is not our sorrow alone, as you know," Miss Alice continued. All the young—all—and the girls now as well, that have none to marry to."

They were sparing of gestures, Island people, but her hand almost imperceptibly formed the fluttering sea bird which was the departure, and Ann-Mary saw for the fraction of a second the noise and life and vigor of the sea bird-children, and their departure and the silence after.

"They do not send letters any more. At first the letters could make us eager with the boats, but the letters became few, and now there is only perhaps a picture and a name at Christmas."

Whatever elaborate words an Islander might use, when the thing went deep, the words were bare and plain. For a moment Ann-Mary thought she saw lights striking off a tear, but Miss Alice was standing so straight that she thought she must be mistaken, and when Miss Alice sat down again her eyes were clear.

"I think it is the word Miss that confuses you," she said, pulling them both away from the source of her pain. "It is custom that they without living husbands be called Miss. The rocks are sharp here, the boats small, the sea treacherous. In older times a woman might marry three husbands, or four. It is, as one says, custom."

"It is said of your brother," said Ann-Mary, "that he has the best Gaelic that is spoken."

"That is so," she answered, with no show of pride or a putting down of pride. That seemed to explain why Reverend McNeith had not introduced him, Ann-Mary thought. "He has the English, but he does not favor it. If you wish to go to see him, I will not dissuade you. It would be better to go to him alone, as he is not a man given to inducement."

Which of them was the Reverend protecting?

She sighed and rose. It was going to be a difficult thing to walk into a man's house with no introduction, no way smoothed, to tell him briskly that his people and custom and language were dying, and to hurry up and think, feel, speak before the light went; and just a little louder, please, right into this little box. Perhaps he would ask her about her country, and she could tell about the tropical opulence of Tennessee, where trees grew. Perhaps the exile of his sons could be opened to him to admit one tiny shaft of light.

She said good-bye to Miss Alice and left, taking the sheep track of a road that led to the Bride's Hand side of the Island. Perhaps she could help him more than simply to preserve his thoughts for the days when no one made nets and some automated fishery spewed fish guts into Green Rock channel.

The land grew more and more rugged toward Bride's Hand. Great toothed boulders stood as if they had been set on purpose to mark the landfall; and the sheep, untended, wandered about picking over the scant ground cover.

"Poor," she muttered, "so damn poor, and they wonder why the children leave! Stubborn as rock. They have to send their kids to school on the mainland, so they are only parents during the summers! Stubborn, wind-worn, water-worn—what a winter anyway, that dulls, only dulls the edge of starvation!"

But the muttering had as much awe as impatience. She didn't really want them to change. Why not be afraid of the ridiculous "telly-phone" and the ridiculous ethnolinguist with a tape recorder? She knew that her very presence had made them aware of the imminent death of their tongue. She had heard all summer about the young going and the old ways dying. People usually don't deal with their great sorrows by telling them to one another, giving them to strangers. Her presence had told them that they were doomed.

About an hour and a half later she reached the Bride's Hand side of the Island. Jutting from the hand was a small finger of land on which stood an old Celtic cross. One of the women had told her that it had been put up in the "papist years" to commemorate a fishing accident in which three-quarters of the men of the Island had lost their lives. Around the point, about half a mile beyond the cross, stood a low, thatch-roofed cottage. It was his. The weight of the box was making her arm feel dead. She began to wonder what she would say—there had always been someone before, explaining, assuaging. But seeing how resolutely alone the old house was, she understood why Miss Alice had spoken against an "inducement." She went over the wind-beaten furze slope to the cottage.

The door was open, and sitting just inside, as straight as a soldier, was the old man facing the adversary sea. He was dressed in very worn gray clothes, and chickens ran in and out at the door about his feet. Ann-Mary stood near the doorway, confused and wishing she had some right word from which to start to him. He was perfectly still, and his erect posture on the plain wooden chair gave him the look of a figure carved or molded in stone. He and the three-century-old cross seemed of the same substance.

"You are welcome in the house. Do not stand aside then; come in."

For a moment she madly supposed that she understood him

in the Gaelic, and it took a moment before she realized that it was his grudging English. Still he did not move, but motioned her with his eyes to the visitor's chair that was just inside the door. She was inside the purview of his hospitality, the custom, but only just inside. He had been forewarned then; not induced, but forewarned, a protection for his pride—perhaps by his sister.

"Fiona!" he called. From somewhere inside, a woman's voice answered. "The woman will make some tea," he said.

"Oh, please don't go to any trouble for me," Ann-Mary answered quickly.

He stiffened, if possible, and looked straight ahead, and she raged at herself for being put off by his preparations, and so forgetting everything that she had learned all summer. Damn the styles in politeness! Her almost automatic "American" demur was an Island insult, a ridiculing of the host's manhood, and a scornful cut at his age and strength.

"Tea will be brought," he said. There was ice in the tone.

Of course they had warned him, and sent the girl to permit him the added dignity of leisure; and she had come with insults to his house. Part of the trouble had been that he was a man and she was used to women's hospitality. Well, there was no help for it now. There was probably no use in sitting back and asking him what he thought of things in general. It was better to start with the animal sounds. After a while she introduced herself and the reason for her visit, which, of course, he already knew.

"I have been speaking with Reverend McNeith, and he has told me that you might be able to answer some of my questions about the Gaelic."

"Have you got the Gaelic?" he asked her in Gaelic.

"No," she answered, "but I study the structure of languages, and my university has sent me here to study and record the Gaelic."

He didn't speak, and his utter silence was unnerving, so she blundered on alone, drifting into an explanation of what she wanted of him. She knew it seemed strange to him that the "student of Gaelic" didn't speak it, and she couldn't explain why this should be.

She sighed and moved on into the bit about the dogs' barking —how it really sounds the same, but that each language hears and interprets the sounds differently. A study of the differences would be significant then, as to how each language trains its speakers to hear its sounds. When she had finished, he waited a long time, and then he spoke.

"Are you telling me that you spend time studying this?" His face was full of an incredulous wonder. "Do you tell me that universities consider this worthy of study—the sounds of animals?"

"No, not the sounds the animals make, the sounds the people hear. . . ."

He was searching her face with great intensity. "Surely, young woman, surely you are joking." He spoke slowly, letting the words weigh one at a time.

She said she was not. His astonishment made her defensive. "Of course this is part of something larger. I've been recording examples of all phases of Gaelic. . . ." She saw his incredulity deepen. Was she equating animal howls with his mother tongue?

"Your university—where does it belong to?"

"It's in America—one of the best ones. People come to our language department from all over the world." To her it sounded sententious.

To him it was perhaps another of the cruelties of the conqueror. Her world had already taken his sons and transformed them beyond recognition. Was she now to come with news that the victors were mad and the victims also to be given to useless, purposeless insanities?

He rose stiffly, giving her a long, quiet look. His voice had become gentler. "Come out here, young woman, with me."

He led her out the door. For a moment they looked out at the great, brutal sea and around them to where the gray-green land stood against it. Then he led her around the house. Growing low, clinging to the ground at the cottage wall, as if for dear life, were eight single cries of defiance against the beating wind, the beating sea, and the years, and the barren, rocky soil. Flowers, eight of them: a brilliant red, a yellow, orange, crimson, purple, magenta, violet. After the eternal variations on the sea theme of gray to blue, blue to green, green to gray—they shocked her eyes with light.

She looked back at the old man in wonder. "The care, the patience . . ."

And what else from an Islander to whom patience and life are tested to the limits of a whole ocean. Islanders seldom touch one another in public, even to shake hands, but she saw his hand come up as if he would touch her shoulder.

"It is hard work," he said, "but it is well done. The house shelters them, you see. Listen to me, young woman. You are still young; you are strong. There is still time for you to grow flowers."

He had to have it then, the Voice of the Past, a man so rooted in yesterday that he disdained to speak English. Even his neighbors thought so. The past burned heretics, chained the insane, broke argument on the rack; but in return for the kidnaping and estrangement of two sons, this Past was offering all it knew; and for the enemy's aberrations, pity and then hope.

They had tea—courtesy demanded it—but every so often the old man would look at her in her terrible insanity and the insanity of her world and he would sigh, partly in sorrow, partly in awe. When Ann-Mary said good-bye, he rose again and went to his eight flowers and broke off one of them and gave it to her; and the breaking of it from its stem was as if he had broken one of his bones. She took it, in the Island way, with formal reticence but no denial; and she left him sitting in his chair, straight as a soldier.

She walked down the road carrying the flower in one hand and the tape recorder in the other, still feeling his eyes upon her. She tried to walk straight, even under the burden of the now heavy machine. An Island wind would never riffle papers in the linguistic department of the university archives now. The voice of the dead would not speak of dead dreams to astound the living. When she presented her spools of tape at the familiar conference room at school, she alone would see him looking out at the green waves; and only for her would the room be made strange by the stern, keen look of his wonder and the slow abiding look of his pity.

THE
UNNAMED

My grandmother's grandmother lived in a small peasant village in Poland. Her sorrow was of the quality of peasants and of the quantity of kings. Her sorrow set her apart. Everyone in Zoromin suffered cold and hunger, poverty and sickness; but every year or so the young wives would groan and bring forth a child, and the children that struggled from the urgent wombs grew up around their mothers like protecting thickets of warmth that twittered with laughter as with birds.

Every year Hannah also labored with child; and every year bore a child and sang to it as all mothers had sung from the beginning of voice. She sang of the heart's desire, of raisins and almonds, of the warmth of eider quilts, of leisure and softness; and as each child left her breast or clung to her skirt, it sickened and died. One by one all of the twelve children went, still in its little gown, to the cemetery. Now, Hannah's twelfth child was being buried and the mourners were standing in the mud.

When this child had died, Hannah had screamed like a woman possessed, torn at her hair, pulled at her clothes, crying over and over again, "I am cursed by God!"

The villagers standing mute in the cemetery believed her. They were frightened of what mighty lightning had used this Marked One to come to ground. Whom God curses are His; it is better to be overlooked. Might not the whole village be seen in her lightning? So, when the prayers were ended, the mourners left without a word or touch for the childless mother, and they left going by the far side so as not to pass her. She stood alone by the new grave, muttering. Reb Eli had been weak and ill lately, and could not bear his own weight of walking to another funeral. She thought of herself standing there in her black clothes by the long row of her little stones like a skinny crow in the autumn field. The mud was cold. What had she done to be noticed by the Lord?

She spoke with familiarity, the privilege of the cursed: "There they are, my twelve. What have I now that you have not also?"

Even as she stood clutching her hands against her grief, she felt something stir within her. It was a thirteenth stirring. Screaming, she threw herself upon the stones of her children and beat them with her hands. She cried in the mud until the villagers came and took her, still moaning beneath the enormity of the curse, to her house.

Zoromin was an average village, poor and small. Summer came with plagues and boils, winter with starvation and cold. The rains fell and the wheat grew, but often the sun only smiled upon the wheat so that the last whip of the winter's anger could catch it and freeze it on the stalk. If the world outside had found easement for some of the anguishes that beset man's life, the villagers did not know it. Springtime was the cure for winter, death the cure for illness, and God's will was His own. But the village did glory; with side glances and muttered magic, the village gloried in life itself. Every spring each old man would congratulate himself that he was yet alive, yet alive. Each mother would revel in the laughter of her children. The winds blow warm—we have conquered death yet again!

For Hannah, this glory was a light put out. Marriage bed and birthing bed, she heard in her mind the other women making their bittersweet complaints: "Who can feed such a son as mine? He eats like ten!" "Shoes are wasted on my youngest; she dances all night to the fiddle!"

Hannah had carried, groaned, and borne as they did, and

had hoped for a few short months, giving her breast into the little hungry mouths and covering tiny arms; but the summer fevers would come and the autumn coughs and the winter pestilences, and Hannah's house was never spared. When the last child had shuddered and whitened beneath her hand and she had cried that she was cursed, and her neighbors had turned away, they did not see themselves as cruel. Were not their little ones vulnerable, as vulnerable and fragile as hers had been? Better not tempt Death's angel with that lightning knife of his. So they clucked their sympathy, fearing, and turned away, fearing, and ran to their homes, fearing, and slapped their children, fearing that so much was the love, as much would be the betrayal.

In Hannah's house there was always betrayal. Even Reb Eli had weakened as if feeling that he was being blotted out relentlessly from the Book of Life. When the last child died, he had taken to his bed, too weak to eat or talk or mumble his prayers. When the women brought the moaning mother from the place of her children, he was lying in the same position in which she had left him. When she stopped her wailing they left her alone with Reb Eli in the cold room. His face was to the wall and he did not speak.

At last she said, "I am going to bear another child."

He made no sign. Pulling his breath in and out, he consented to death, and in a week he died.

All during the long, familiar months of carrying, Hannah wondered by day and dreamed by night how, only how she could turn the anger of God. The snows fell and the cold wind shrieked around the huts, and still she tormented the question. Some said that if a woman changed her name or moved, Death's angel could be tricked into believing that his mission was with someone else; but from this long-standing, constant, intended malediction, Hannah knew that she could not hide. At last, in one of the burnt-out nights, it came to her that God's vengeance was with her and not with the dwellers in darkness.

The winter left in its time, not sooner and not later. The spring came; the air warmed; and the women sang at their washing. In summer, on a day of no particular omen, Hannah gave birth to a daughter. The child came on quickly as she was working in the garden that had now to feed but one soul. She barely had time to call to her neighbor, and lie down before the born one pushed free of her and into its own beginning. As the neighbors took the child and wrapped it, screaming with life, in the bands that had held twelve others, Hannah cried to them: "Take her, I am cursed!"

The women looked about in confusion. If the mother would not take her own newborn child, it would surely die. Every time they offered the bundle for her to hold, she would scream at them like a madwoman. At last they left the baby at the bottom of the bed and went from the house.

But the child lived. Almost by habit Hannah nursed it and bathed it. In a kind of haze of madness she changed and tended it; but when she rocked it, she held the child far away from her body; and when she nursed it; she closed her eyes and averted her head so that her cursed eyes would not light upon the nursling, nor her cursed breath touch the little life and wither it. She knew she must send the child away before the last lightning of the curse should fall. Twelve, twelve had already perished under her bewitched hands. As she went about the house caring for one she dared not name, she spoke to God incessantly: "Who is this child? Who is this without a name? Out of charity I tend it, for it is a waif; no one claims it; no one says—this is mine. I, a pious woman, from charity tend this child." After months of turning the question how to avert the awful oncoming, Hannah saw a way.

There was a third cousin living in another village. The woman had children of her own and Hannah had heard of her that she was kindly. If she could be entreated to take the child, perhaps God's wrath would not follow. That very evening Hannah sat down and wrote a letter to her cousin, stumbling and worrying over the crude marks on her paper until the candle burnt to wick end and false dawn was over the village. When she had finished, she ran to the house of the postman.

Days passed, Hannah waiting, fearing moment by moment the lightning of God; and at last the answer came. Then Hannah wrapped the little girl in a blanket and took her to the landing where the farmers weighed their cattle and carts left for the city. She gave the baby to one of the drivers, who promised to take it to her cousin's village. She paid him every copper she had. If she was sad, she did not show it, turning from the landing without a word and never looking back. If the Unnamed lingered in her mind, it was never spoken of, and the people soon forgot that there had ever been a daughter.

Life went on and it carried Hannah the Cursed with it, uncomplaining, like a stick in the water. Every month on the child's birthday, she would go to the postman with some money —a few pennies or a broken coin, and she had a ritual with this money. She would give the postman the coins and he had then to take a like amount from his box and send his money to the distant village. It must be coin that her hands had never touched. For the feasts when children have sweets and little gifts, she would sell one sack of goose feathers, or what she had woven, but neither goods nor money did she send that bore the mark of her hands. For the rest, she consented to grow a bit skinnier and a bit odder each year. She often visited the cemetery to walk among the stones of her children. Her own house was bare, and as the years went on—the snow, the sun, the crow, the nightingale—she often forgot which house was hers: the thatched hut at the edge of the village or the stone city in which her children rested. Sometimes she would find herself confused about which turn to take, and she would stand, muttering her answers to the God who waited above her: "Does one elude You? Seek in my house. Behold, even You are mistaken. No shining eyes follow; no arms reach out; no small fingers touch. Where is my home now, Almighty? Husband and children are waiting, husband and children are waiting."

Years turned. The rains wore down the stones a little more and Hannah the Cursed muttered forgetfully on as the thatch darkened and rotted on the hut and the sun hardened the mud walls until they cracked. The children of her neighbors grew, married, and bore; but she did not mark them. Her children of the stone city were still very young.

Then one day the postman stopped at her door and delivered a letter. It was sent from her cousin's village. It must concern that one who was Unnamed, whose name could not even be thought of lest it be lighted for the eye and the hand of her curse. Had the Angel of Death at last torn down her hiding place? Day after day the letter stood, like doom, waiting, until at last the distracted woman could bear ignorance no longer. She ripped the covering from it and read.

The letter was about a woman. It was about a woman who had lived and grown and married and borne six children. The husband of this woman had gone to America of the golden streets, and now he was sending for his family. They were leaving, the letter said, but before they left, desired to see, for the first and the last time, mother and grandmother.

At the bottom of the letter was a name, but Hannah did not dare to read it lest her lips form the word. She put the letter down and, clutching her head with wonder, addressed the Lord: "Children and grandchildren! Child and child's children! How beautiful they are! See how the sun shines on them in my vision! Look, they are full of laughter and small pranks, and she—how fine and strong she is. Surely she sings at her work. Oh, the treasures she has to kiss to sleep at night!"

As Hannah stood, turning this way and that, unable to contain such joy in her thin body, in her tiny room, the terror took her again. What a harvest He could reap of her now! What a taking! And her mouth opened with wonder and awe at the power she saw gathered over her. It was too late to keep them from coming; if only she had not held the letter so long! Now there was only time to sweeten the house and give a last few pennies for a handful of raisins and a handful of almonds. Then, dressed in sabbath clothes, in which she had stood at many funerals, she waited.

And they came. From her place, stiffly, at the open door she saw them; and the sun shone on their white shirts and dresses and gleamed upon their shining hair as if they were angels in a vision. They came walking through the village from the station, a blaze of burning white in the noon. They seemed not real at all. They moved closer and still closer, but they did not disappear: a mother, strong and rosy, and six little children, vain and careful in sabbath clothes. Nearer and nearer and then they were before her.

"I wonder who these people are!" Hannah cried to the Lord, her face brilliant, her voice ringing with the towering pride of a grandmother. "What do they seek of me?" she cried, twisting her hair.

In their whiteness they lit the path to her house.

"Mother?" the young woman asked.

"Who hears such a word in this weather?" The mother was jesting with God. "Who imagines white doves coming?" She looked at the little children, the clear, vulnerable flesh like that of her own dwellers in ground; and she seemed to hear over her house once more the rustling of the wings of the dread Angel.

As the beautiful Unnamed stood there with her children, Hannah went slowly toward her, and standing before her, began to draw with her hand her daughter's image in the air. Almost touching but never touching, she traced each curve and line of her daughter's face, rise and ridge of neck, pulse throb in the hollow of the throat. Then, on the mouth of her image, she drew a smile of love; and then she kissed the image that was drawn in the air. Before each child she paused and over each small head, never touching a single hair with her cursed hands or breathing upon a single cheek her cursed breath, she traced each face. She averted her head and caressed each little image, and then she turned again and breathed deeply of the fragrance of each warm neck and smelled the sweetness of each soft head of hair; but she touched none of them, not even with her voice.

"Behold, O Lord," said Hannah the grandmother, reckless with love, "are they not rivals of the angels? Are they not beautiful and clever; are they not vigorous and full of laughter?" And her pride soared above the house, the town, the world; it was like a great bird crossing to the sun.

"Old Hannah has gone mad completely," the villagers said. "The visit of the strangers has unhinged her." And they all went to look at her, for there were few distractions in the village and any distraction was a holiday.

She was in the cemetery, dancing and making wild gestures among the graves; and when the villagers, mocking, asked her what she did, she replied with a brilliant smile that she was but drawing the images of her living to show to her dead.

SINGERS

☙☙☙

There must be big happy families, all with The Gift; children who would never remember any old Thursday afternoon when it wasn't there for them, and a handful of aunts to say, "lovely, lovely!" and pat them on the heads. What vanity I must have had then, not knowing anyone with The Gift. I was like a blind man dreaming red and believing that he had created it. I thought I had invented The Gift, borne it, begun it on the afternoon of September 9th at the stop for the Perry Avenue Crosstown bus.

I'd been going back and forth on that damn bus for weeks to visit Aunt Louise, who was dying in the hospital. At every visit her world would be narrowed closer and closer around her. She was haunted by her own body, her pulse that beat and paused, the patterns of the pain, the awful unconcern of her heart and veins to her own wishes. Week after week I would leave her, promising to come back, and walking to the bus with resentment, confusion, and love weighing on me like a stone dress. And that day it was raining.

A mean and constant and nagging rain that I had to stand in with cowlike patience to wait for the bus. Pain, my psychology course had told me, warns of a dysfunction. All right, she'd

been warned! We had all been warned. Why should a frugal
body, carefully re-circulating its store of blood, saving the good
years' fat for future famine, be so spendthrift-reckless with its
pain? It could not warn her any more; it could only grind away
all her courage and all my memories of a witty, loving, gentle
favorite aunt. When the bus pulled up, it splashed mud all
over my shoes.

I was going to get in—I had my quarter in my hand and my
foot raised for the step, but the driver (whatever was corroding
in his darkness) was wrinkling his face over his irritation.

"Fer crissake, girly, move!"

Then I couldn't. I couldn't move at all; I could only hang in
that minute, foot up, hand in front of me like the photograph of
action in being.

He shut the door in my face and drove away, leaving the
fumes for me. I thought of laughing because my foot was still
raised, although the reason was gone, and my hand still held
out its incentive quarter. I thought of running back to the impersonal deadhouse to tear away the professional, self-preserv-
ing smiles. I found myself moaning, moaning words. I began to
listen to them:

Dr. Rafferty, Dr. Lafferty,
A pill, a puncture, too bad.
Tube-winders, where is Dr. Death?

I was moaning words, moan-singing, and a woman in a raincoat and umbrella passed me and let her eyes widen and her
mouth cinch up, taking me in. Two thoughts tripped over one
another: watch out for the curb, lady, and I don't give a damn
what you think. My foot went down and my hand went down
and I found that I was singing. It was raining hard by then, a
heavy, cadent beat. We lived all the way across town. I sang
all the way home.

It was a harmless heresy, that singing, but the rules were
built up all around me, and heresies, no matter how gentle,
were not in the code. I knew what Mother and Dad wanted
for me: a year at a harmless job after college, a nice marriage
and nice children—no questions, no passions, certainly no calls
to Dr. Death to end the forbidden, barbaric suffering. These
hopes for me were so possible and reasonable that I'd never
learned a style in going against them. It was a comfortable

life, except for feeling the chain so much. Reasonably, the chain was lengthened at suitable times—my summer in France, choosing my own job after graduation—the control was very civilized and kind; but sometimes the chain would catch on something invisible and I would be pulled up strangling.

In a way I couldn't explain, Aunt Louise's dying made me feel the pull more keenly and more constantly. Except for that afternoon, near home and all sung out about her, wet through with rain that was beating up from the street and down from the sky and somehow consenting:

> Let the rain come down,
> Let it wear away stones
>   and blur away the carving and the stone rose.
> Fire will hiss to death;
> Anger will splutter and drown.
> Right now, I am content,
> Just and unjust, and let the rain come down.

I didn't sing any more until Aunt Louise's funeral. She lived on for three months more, her agony leaving me nothing of her but remorse and pity. It was a large family funeral; it brought out every old member who could still warm gnarled hands before the ceremonial glow. Everybody was happily genteel—how natural dear Louise looked, death was a mercy, and so on and on. And did the Allens come? No? Shocking! And did the young Henrys come, the cousins? Yes, of course, check. Everyone comes. I feel the chain again. "How do you do, Reverend. Very well thank you." The chain tightens. "Yes, we're all resigned; she was a wonderful woman though. Yes, quite close."

On the way home I kept hearing mother's comfortable lament, as if it were being played as counterpoint to another voice, softer but wilder, that was groaning in me. It's coming up, long and slow, some song. Greek women bay and shriek and the Irish keen—ritual wails. Why are we unlucky, without The Gift? The Gift is coming up in me; it's going to burst true and rude, right out of my mouth . . .

Mother was saying, "Christmas won't be the same this year, now that poor Louise has passed away. . . ."

"Mother, let me off here, will you. I forgot I was supposed to call Roger about tonight, and he'll be leaving any minute, and I have to pick up something at the drug store. I really need . . ."

"All right, but I wish you had done these things before."

"I won't be long."

It was only to walk the seven blocks home, singing a good-bye before it burst from me in a howl.

> "Passed away"—too easy.
> Who looks "natural" dead?
> Not you, Aunt Louise, without the lip twitch
>   and the knitting.
> Knit me up remembering
> Before the song dies.

People looked, not too many. It was just a keen, not too loud; and when I got home, instead of the efficient elevator, I climbed the steps.

> Numbering
> One: I sat on your cake when I was seven.
> Numbering
> Two: The blue-bottle lamp, thirteen lost fountain pens,
>   thirteen at least,
> Four, number for four:
> Sudden laughter, threading the summer days.

I was crying when I got to our door, but I knew that what I had was a Gift, because between steps four and sixty I had her back, pulled from the self-despising months of bitter dying to where the sorrow was clean and strong, where the love had been given and returned.

So my Gift came home and I accepted it. I sang greetings and gratitude to all the miseries from Late at Work to the Essential Loneliness. Soon I was singing out pleasure, too. I didn't sing high and I didn't sing loud, but it was mine, not dum-de-dum set to a recognizable tune. No one who passed my songs on the street could rhyme them out of his anxiety; my songs rang.

> No death, no death like Saturday night,
> When the cool cynics case the dances
> Like lots of second-hand cars:
> (Smile with the teeth-teeth) "How'll she run?"
> (Show the dimple) "Is she sleek and shiny?"
> Who wants a faithful Packard touring car
> 'Stead of a low-slung souped-up Jag?

Sometimes they were jazzy and sometimes formless, but I found myself walking a lot, to sing out; and twice I rushed away from that bitch at the office, MacNamara, not to escape but to get into the street where I could see what my Gift would make of it.

College was over and I'd had my year of "independence." Most of mother's friends had seen their daughters married and were finally beginning to wear their faces in repose. My acquaintance, on the other hand, was getting less "suitable." I took Adam and Marie to lunch after I met them kidding each other gently in beautiful flatted blues on a line at the post office. I met Little Charlie, a bus boy who addressed his load of dishes in low, staccato rumbles (strange, powerful voice from such a small man); he nearly dropped them when I answered, singing in their name. I met Lucina, who worked in an office over on Maylan Avenue and had a brilliant litany about the time clock, her tyrant.

I suppose if it hadn't been for the knowledge of other Singers, I would have been less sure of myself and I would have listened with more attention to the sharpening words of the family. They offered to have the chain set with sapphires if only I would come to my senses.

"Go out more."

"Be more interested in your future."

"Why not think of starting a serious . . ."

I told them that I had never been out more and that the air and exercise were doing wonders for my health. The family didn't know in what way I was withdrawing from their plans, only that I seemed to be doing it easily and gaily and without remorse. It must have hurt them, but I was too busy developing my Gift to notice how much, until Mother rallied her forces to mount to counterattack.

We began to have dinner guests. Three times a week one of Mother's friends, or friends' friends, or a remote but suitable acquaintance of friends' friends, would appear at our dinner table accompanied by the appropriate son. Mother suddenly became a student of corporate law, tax law, kidney surgery, insurance, land development, and the soap industry. She began to seek advice on all of these subjects from the appropriate sons. I suppose she had to—I never drew any of them into my hope. I felt only a quiet, abiding disinterest, which was all I shared with them. More than a few, I found, were being chastened with me for having fallen in love with other, less "suita-

ble" girls. I began staying away during dinner. Mother began
mortgaging my Saturdays and Sundays.

I had always gotten my way by dissembling, by gently un-
dermining the family's arguments or subtly advancing my own
under the safe cover of some authority—usually their own. It
was too late for that now. My need was as crude and honest as
a skeleton, but my reasons were none that they would recognize. They had made their statements and I did not have the
courage or experience to stand and fight. So, because I didn't
know what to do, I gave up.

I promised Mother and Aunt Selma and my sister, June, and
To Whom It May Concern that I would take it all seriously and
submit to the remaining bachelors of our "set." I promised that
the next young Appropriate that any of them brought home
would be shown my smile, my enthusiasm, and my Best of
Show ribbons. I knew I was agreeing also that after that I
would go fashionably blank about the eyes and eventually be
a well-dressed matron who only occasionally locked herself in
the closet to wail out her pique at the judges of the garden
show.

On the evening before another Presentation, I was sitting in
the living room and watching the rain come down. Mother had
just been comforting me by reminding me that these young men
were not monsters, after all, but fine and future-seeking; and
the boy that Daddy was bringing home was fine, fine, fine. I
dreamed up another errand and got out, taking my raincoat and
umbrella dutifully and throwing them in the hall. How many
nights could there be without The Gift?

It was beautiful outside, especially with no destination. I was
singing, loudly now, because I had lost.

> Good-bye, sweet-sounding—
> Now I have to grieve Official Griefs.
> Virgin joy, good-bye;
> Little joy, into a breath unbidden—
> Their joy must be approved
> By the Committee.
> A metronome will mark my days—
> The time clock on its nail.
> Who needs the nightingale?

Almost no one was in the street. A few people were hurrying
out of the unpleasant rain, scattering it from their bodies as if it

were not a treasure. I heard someone behind me and I listened
as he came to pass me because he was singing. It was not tum-
de-dum set to a recognizable tune; it was a drawn-out heave of
sound; and there were words.

That Max Kleber is a lousy bastard!
Two new dance steps and he makes like Robert Taylor.
Where are her eyes? Has she no eyes?
That girl, that sweet, small-waisted . . .
What do I do to make her see me?
How do I ask her to come trembling to me?
How can I ask to shield her from rain?
Max Kleber—break a goddamn leg!

It was my last night in the rain without an umbrella, because
my hair would soon have to be set, and it would have to stay
for the young men and the parties. So I sang to him as he came
closer.

Don't you worry, mister; he goes over,
Over with the sun, like you and me.
He does the same up-ending.
Whatever life has got a shortage of,
It ain't banana peels.

The last two lines were sort of lifted from Little Charlie of the
dinner plates. It stopped him, so I didn't feel guilty. Then I
sang:

You get the gift from cradle-singing,
Listening to the pain at the crosstown bus stop;
The rain can keep a beat the best of all.

He did a beautiful slow cadenza on "I thought I was alone,"
and its last high was so nice that I just nestled a sigh of a tune
under it, to let his note weigh a little on my tune, the way an
easy wind does to a resting bird.

Hell, no—
Sing is laugh and cry; we make a sound
That carries far
enough so that the Lord comes to his door
And opens it, and looks out on his high front stoop.
There's a Singer. (*The tone flatted blue, like God's
disappointment.*)
Tired and hungry,
Weak with wanting. "What is it?"

> Because he is still leaning
> On that mean, loud bell.

Well, there's no egotist like a humble man with a little rise in him. He turned and took a breath, stopped and took another.

> And part of that sound
> Is *mine* . . .

Trumpets and drums and a full chorus on the mine. No doubt at all where the weight of that message was. I came up light as I could against the pouring rain.

> Mighty hearty for a dying man.

He began to laugh, and then I sang with all the tune I could manage while the rain roared around us—a song of welcome to him—and we stood in that rain together laughing as if we had invented laughter.

HOW
BEAUTIFUL
WITH FEET

"The world is a hard place," my Grandmother says, and she should know.

She came to the Golden Land when she was sixteen and pretty enough to have been misunderstood several times in her own country. She was fired from her first job as feather girl in a big mass-production millinery near the Brooklyn Bridge. In those days only prostitutes and actresses wore rouge, and the black-haired country girl had two burning red spots over her cheekbones. The more she tried to squeeze the fashionable pallor into her cheeks, the redder they became.

"We do not employ *that* sort of woman!" the boss told her, and so she was out of a job before she ever learned what sort *that sort* was.

Imah was a Category B immigrant. Now, Catagory A immigrants come to the Golden Land and make it into a new kind of Dubno or a Zoromin with paving. They live in the old ways and will not change. Category B immigrants race out into the new land, flinging off their old clothes as they run. All the ways of Chelm and Vilna must go.

"If you call me that sort of woman," cried Imah to her accuser, "call me at least that sort of Yankee woman!" Whenever she would tell of her adventures at the feather factory, she would add, "That man! He was himself wet-footed from the boat!"

So Imah dove from her boat into America, and later when she married and had children and discovered that they spoke their English with good, sharp Brooklyn Bridge accents, her love got so mingled with awe that she could never speak harshly to them. But it was we, the grandchildren, who were her crown. All of us, even the girls, were going to college. By this time, love, awe, and misunderstanding had reached splendid, vast, truly American heights. Perhaps she felt that she wouldn't be misunderstood if she did the misunderstanding first.

Tales of her early uproarious blunders in the Golden Land had fed us from childhood, and we lived Imah's perils over and over, out the door of the factory and off down the road through the intricate and perilous ways of American law, social usages, customs, and language. These exciting adventures had a feeling of great importance and antiquity because of Imah's strongly biblical style. "Now it came to pass in those days," she would say; and the policeman, fish peddler, tax man, and landlord would take on some of the formal grandeur of the Book of Chronicles.

For us, however, Imah was frightened if the slightest trouble or confusion marred one of our days. Adventures were all very well for a greenhorn of humble background, but they did not fit at all into the lives of American-born-and-raised citizens of the United States and English-speaking college people. We therefore began more and more to shade the unpleasantness from anything we told her. Since humor and discomfort seem to find themselves so much in one another's company, the funny things also faded away and finally disappeared from our days as we recounted them. I thought this a great shame, since she had given me so much laughter and excitement, and once, only once, did I make the mistake of trying to change the way it had become.

"Imah, it was a wonderful summer!" I said. (*I had spent it working on a Navaho reservation in Arizona.*)

"Don't call me Imah; it's a greenhorn name. Call me Grandma."

"Call me Bubbles," I said. (*It was a very old argument and by this time only form.*)

"You really met Indians?"

"Oh, yes. For a while I was the only Anglo girl on the school staff."

"Oy! God protect us!"

"I was treated very nicely by everybody," I said.

"But it's dangerous out there in the desert!"

I objected. "Did you think I had unexpected things happening to me with the Indians? It just so happens that the most outlandish thing that happened to me this year was just this Tuesday, right here in the city."

"What could happen? It was Yom Kippur Tuesday."

I told her about Yom Kippur morning and I tried to bring it out at its best to repay her for what she had given me with the rich webs of cross-current circumstances and strange turns of fortune that gave excitement to all her stories. I even started as she would have. . . .

"Who knows in the morning where he might be standing at noon? There I was on Tuesday morning, walking to *shul* with Mama and Papa, and I wasn't even hungry for breakfast. The only trouble was my feet. All summer in Arizona I had worn a pair of Navaho moccasins. They are very soft and you shape them in damp sand until they follow every curve of your foot. The new, stiff shoes that I was wearing to the *shul* were hurting worse than my sins for the whole year. As we got there, I noticed that my feet had swollen and had begun to puff up over the rims of the shoes. As the service went on and on, getting up for responses and sitting down, up and down, I realized that the skin on my heels and toes and at the top had broken open, and that my feet were beginning to bleed. I asked Mama if I could go home and change and she said yes, so I crept out, and I had to grit my teeth to keep those shoes on. When I was out on the street I knew I couldn't walk another step. There was nothing to do but take the miserable things off.

"Because of the holiday I wasn't carrying any money and I didn't feel right to hail a cab and pay later, so I just started to walk the ten blocks home. I was feeling pretty good by then. I had to keep my eyes on the street so as not to walk in anything, but the day was so nice and I was all dressed up, and the tormenting shoes were off. Then"—and this I did in imitation of her own Bible-born style—"then, I was brought low. I passed by Bunthorne's bakery when someone was just opening the door to go in, and a blast of warm bread-baked air came out at me. It was so good and of such a sweet savor to me, Imah, that my mouth began to water and my stomach began to urge for a bite of that bread. I was standing, hypnotized, at that bakery, a girl in a black silk dress, holding her shoes and looking as if all that the world held was as nothing compared with a fresh poppy-seed roll. Before I knew it a man came up to me. 'Miss, are you in trouble?'

"Imah, I was so embarrassed, I could have crawled away. I thanked him—'No, thank you very much'—and walked away, trying to hold my head up and yet watch where I walked and keep my poise in my stocking feet."

Then we both laughed and saw her again in our minds, a girl whose breath and bones, on that day, went crosswise to the flow of the world.

A day before I was supposed to go back to school, Mama came home and saw me sitting in the kitchen, reading.

She greeted me, "You idiot! I could wring your neck!"

"Hello, Mama."

"Hello nothing! What on earth can you be thinking of when you go over and frighten your grandmother half to death with your adventures in Arizona!"

"What adventures? I told her that Arizona was wonderful."

"She told me that she stayed awake all night wondering how we could have let you go into the desert without any money."

A gleam, a semblance of a remembered phrase came to me. "Mama, gently, slowly and gently, tell me what happened to me there in the desert."

Mama began, remembering the years of prose which had illumined her youth as well as mine. "God sees us and He weeps. There she was, penniless and hungry in the desert. Miles and miles in the damp sand until every curve of her foot was swollen. Every step was torture. (*I was beginning to feel sorry for her myself.*) As the sun rose higher, her feet began to bleed. Hungry, starved, and with bleeding feet in the desert, she walked!"

"God, help us!" I cried.

"At last, famished and exhausted, she came to a bakery."

"In the desert?"

". . . to a bakery. The man took pity on her, standing so pitifully outside his door, where she smelled as sweet savor, as sweetest savor, the baking bread. The man went up to her, seeing how fine she was, and how innocent and lovely her face was, and how gentle her manner . . ."

"Only a Jewish girl from a good family could be lost in the desert and stay refined-looking."

"He offered his help. 'Please, miss, you must be tired and hungry. Come in and take some of my bread. . . .' But she was very proud and she knew that she had no money to pay him. 'No, thank you very much,' she said, and walked on into the burning desert alone."

"A dark day!" I cried out. "Was she lost? Was she lost?"

"Very funny," Mama said, but at last she consented to listen to the first theme of this brilliant fugal variation, and when it was over she said, "Well, then, what will you tell her now?"

"I don't know. We can't leave me dying in the desert like that. I have to go back to school."

"Tell her the Indians found you."

"I'll tell her how they put me on the plane so I could come home."

"It wouldn't work for anyone else but you or me, you know," Mama said. "Only we are armed with innocence perfect enough to overcome a tribe of savage Arizona Indians."

"Or the charge of being an actress in a feather factory."

ELTON'S STRANGERS AND OUR STRANGERS

The hard part of leaving Severn Mountain to take up in town wasn't the new ways they had to learn, but that neither of them understood the reasons to those ways. For years Rutheen and Carl had planned and saved to come out of the hills and better themselves. At first, when it was new, they stared and giggled at the goggle-eyes of oven gauges and the fury of water that surged in the flush toilet. Outside their house there was the pole and traffic light glowing all night in an empty street, making it look more deserted than if there'd been only the simple darkness. They saw their kids getting town-sassy, they abided. They worked at trying to talk like "town" in front of the kids' new friends, but it was a difference in thinking that dazed Rutheen, a difference she had not expected and couldn't prepare for, and which always showed her the terrible distance between herself and the cold new neighbors in this cold new place.

Even the simple thing of eating outdoors brought out her strangeness and Carl's. Town people were always packing up food baskets and going off to sit by crick banks and look at the water running. When the boys asked if they could go with friends to one of those basket-things, she and Carl had laughed.

It seemed silly, people with money enough for cushion chairs and all the hot food they liked, going out on purpose to suffer hard ground and cold food, chigger's maybe, or the snake-bite.

There was bitterness in Carl's laughter, too. She heard it and suffered, knowing what it meant. The boys went out disappointed, not looking at their father's face, or, as they might have once in Severn, staying to bear a shadow of his pain. He looked at her and said quietly, "I didn' leave my daddy's land to come down an' work for somebody else just so's my kids could go eat in the fields like sharecroppers!"

She told him it was town's way; he said he knew it; but she saw that his sorrow and anger wouldn't be eased by any word of hers, no matter for comforting or loving.

"Don't you see," he answered her, "we ain't been town long enough for our young'uns to go back like town-folks go!"

For a moment they were both afraid of what they had done —bettering themselves. Carl yearned for what they had left. He saw in his mind the house, gape-windowed with shock. What would the roof-shakes do when the wind upcut Brye Hollow? The fences were sagged inward; the chipmunks already noising in the bins, and circling closer, like rapt and careful wolves; the first raiders—weeds, vines; then the forests. In all their hoping and planning, working and saving to get into town, no one had calculated the ache of a man for owning something that was forever in back of him and his children, and forever in front of them.

In the beginning, their first weeks in town, Rutheen used to go down the main street almost every day, into the stores to look and wonder at all the colors and the plenty—ribbons and paper and work dresses in the dime store. Even the work dresses were no two the same. Up home, she thought, you farmed. Here in town, the boys and girls both would be able to have colors and choices in their days, and like the pretty prints she saw, no two the same. She told Carl that her fancy was a mercy, because whenever he needed anything, she would know where it was to be found and glad enough to have a reason to go for it.

So he sent her to the hardware store with a list. She smiled and shrugged; it was one of the few places she didn't like to go because it hurt her so much for remembering home. How much

easier it would have been with one of the light ladders that
leaned against the wall at the back of the store; how much
quicker than that ratchet posthole shovel. . . . And farmers went
to the hardware store, not hill men, but the complacent flats-
farmers that hill people always laid scorn to. There was one of
them in the store when she went in. He was a lean, boy-faced
man waiting by the nail cases. As he stood quietly, another
farmer came in and walked up behind him, a coarse, thick,
quick man, red-necked with windburn. Here, as home, Rutheen
thought, there's always men fill up a room so's there no space
for anyone to breathe in. And she smiled to herself, because
she was working so hard to make town familiar. When the big
man went over to him, the other one seemed to pull himself in
so that he shrank in the space he was taking.

The big one walked close and slammed a hand on the other
man's back as if it could print on him. "Why, how-de-do, Suzy-
Lee."

The store went quiet. The only breathing seemed to be the
big man's, and it was heavy with his fat.

The quiet one said, "You know my name."

The big one was getting ready to say something when Mr.
Rivers came up, quick and keen as if he knew it was trouble
and feared it, and the only way to ease it was to sell it something, like throwing a bone to a strange dog. "What can I do for
you, Elton?" he said to the quiet one.

Elton said ten pounds of roofing nails.

All the time he was waiting, the big man kept mumbling
small, sharp insults at him. No one of them was bad enough to
strike out at, but they added, like wasps.

Elton just waited quietly, not even shifting weight, and his
face was as still as if he were asleep. Somehow the people had
gathered in around them, and yet it was all in silence. The only
sound was the nails being weighed and the big man's mumble.

Mr. Rivers gave Elton the nails and asked him if he wanted
anything else. Elton shook his head and then turned to go, and
Rutheen, from where she was standing, saw the big man put
out his booted foot in Elton's path.

Elton hooked on it, reached, pitched, buckled, and came
down splat. And the bag split and there went ten pounds of
roofing nails broadcast all over the floor.

The big man pulled up his stomach and rocked back laughing. The others laughed, too, but their laughter was strange to them.

Rutheen saw a kind of shame; they were brushing their fronts for bits of tobacco or scratching at stains with a thumbnail. Mr. Rivers went down beside Elton and they started to pick up the nails. There was still a shame-feeling in the store that Rutheen didn't understand. She thought in older words: Flat-head flatters! Squnch-eaters! Flatter don't know livin' from dead; ain't a man in a roomful. Hill man let another make a fool of him, why, he'd be shunned worse'n a dog!

Elton never looked at the big man. He got his nails and left, and after a while most of the others did their buying and drifted away.

She asked Mr. Rivers about the two farmers when he was wrapping her things. "I seen that foot come up sure as judgment. That wasn't no mistake."

He looked around the store. No one was there, so he leaned on the counter to ease his feet and started to tell her about the two farmers.

It began, he said, when they were kids, Elton and this big one, Tolliver. Tolliver was one of those joke-makers with no way to laugh but at a rump-thump to the floor, ice down the back, travel on a banana peel and a week in bed. That big laugh used to go after everyone, because he tricked everyone: nailed Bob Coster's shoes to the floor, got Amon Merrin's old Ford to shake a wheel. There was nothing cunning or finespun about Tolliver's tricks; his humor ran to the sound of falling and the crack of bones. But people laughed—some because they thought it was funny, some for fear, some because they knew that laughing when the joke was on them took away from the fun of it to men like Tolliver. Some had to fight free of his pranks. Anger is a way of answering to a thing, too, taking note. After a while when the jokes went dull there was only Elton left. Elton abided. He would take his stove-in hat or his busted fishing rod and go off without a word or a look. Tolliver could stand laughter or anger, but not that abiding. The tricks began to come more in anger and less in fun. Elton never mentioned them or Tolliver. When he passed Tolliver in town, he would always say the same good morning in the same even voice. That good morning was an apology for not seeing Tolliver at all. That was Elton and Tolliver.

Mr. Rivers said, "Ain't that somethin'?"

He was asking Rutheen for wonder, not an opinion, but she read wrong again. "I don't hold with a man lets another man wound him in his pride." For a minute she saw herself as hill, purely *and forever*, answering proudly, hill's way, in scorn of all flat-head flatlanders, towns, and the cruel seasons that had toughened her. "No hill man would take a day of that hurt without puttin' hand to weapon. . . ." But what could be said after all? She didn't live on Severn anymore; its house was falling in by now, and the storekeeper's look said that she couldn't expect to judge the way town people went about their living.

She took up her packages and went back to the house they lived in now, and looked at all the new and clever things that were in it. They had the plastic curtains that never dirtied, and the "color integrated" ash trays, and a house number that glowed in the dark; but they weren't town. She thought: Carl an' me are pictures, just pictures of towners. She didn't go to the stores so much after that.

Autumn came with trees turning, leaf fall and chilly mornings, and harvest fruit piling high in the stores. Not the strange, foreign things she was ashamed to ask about but new apples and the late grapes and brown-skin pears—familiar. Rutheen got a terrible hill-hunger. The memory of every autumn in her life was walking still warm and golden hillsides for berries and nuts and wild apples. She had had a pride in shelves of jars with preserves from the abundant gifts of the wild places: ruby, purple, yellow, and amber. She made some jelly out of restless habit, but it wasn't the same, and buying fruit made it costly, so Carl had to tell her to stop.

The kids had been laughing at her behind her back, mimicking her intensity as she wrinkled her nose over the bubbling pans, because town fruit didn't smell the same. She didn't realize that their laughter was ridicule. It was subtle, town-learned. Her eyes still saw friends and allies in them, even though they laughed at her more and more since the new ways had come to them so naturally and she had been left behind.

Winter came. She joined the Ladies' Guild at church and went for three meetings before she quit.

"You ain't given' 'em a chance to be friendly," Carl said.

"Minister's wife an' them in the choir—they're likely-lookin' women."

"They're all nice an' that, but I don't want to go to those meetin's. I don't know. It's all them little teeny sandwiches. They get me nervous. You can't tell what the taste is goin' to be. They talk about people I don't know, an' things I don't understand. They got all these changes of *hats*. . . . Oh, Carl, they didn't really want me there. They was glad to see me go."

It surprised her that Hollow Time came in town as well as on High Severn. She knew that hill people were bound to the hill's seasons, that for those on Severn, even love and hate are geared in with the turn of the year: springtime means work and courting; June is time to marry; and in late winter the spring brides come mother. But there is a special season before the ground thaws and when the winter's work is finished that's Hollow Time. Flour whitens low in the barrel and the apples are scant. Women bitter-up and smolder with cabin fever, and the men take insult at the wind on their faces.

On Severn, where Rutheen had been listened to, she had once said, "If the blood-feuds was to be tracked to their beginnings they'd be, near all, birthed in that Hollow Time." And the old men had nodded, that's true.

The brief season came less cruelly in the flatlands, people being less bound to their weather, but it did come, and it came to the farms outside of town, making men dark-minded and their unease as keen as pain. Elton and Tolliver had to live through that time.

Tolliver's pranks got more desperate. Of course, they had to come where people could see his laughter and Elton's loss as he sat on the sawed-off chair or was foot-noosed and wrenched upside-down.

One night, Tolliver got over to the washline where Elton's long winter drawers were hanging. His neighbor-wit gave him to know that the clean drawers would be for wearing to church under Elton's stiff Sunday blacks. Tolliver opened up the seat of the drawers and put in a handful of devilweed burrs. They are gray and very, very small. It would take some time before they worked themselves into Elton, and when they did, he'd be standing in church scoured with fire. When Tolliver crept away, he must have been choking back his big laughter at the picture in his mind: Elton, screaming and clutching his pants, tearing at them in front of a churchful of people all Sunday sweet and sanctified.

Sunday came and Elton was there, best blacks and all. Tolliver spent the opening prayer staring at him, waiting. The hymn passed, the doxology. Nothing. Elton's mother remembered later that during the sermon he was breathing hard, and she thought he was falling asleep, so she turned to whisper him up. He was looking straight ahead and there were beads of sweat gathered in the runnel by his upper lip, and he was breathing like a horse in August, though it was still wintering cold and the heat in the church mostly promise. She was turning back to the preacher when she saw two small tears rolling slowly down Elton's face. She whispered, "Praise the Lord!" And gave herself fully to the sermon because something the preacher was saying had surely taken to home in her son's deep and secret mind.

Church was over and they were leaving when Tolliver stopped Elton and his mother, blocking their way on the steps. People remembered that look of hate for years after, a hate that twisted Tolliver's big features and trembled along the arm and hand that he stretched rigid to point at Elton. "You ain't a man; you ain't a livin' man—you're a devil-born ghost, a ghost dead a hundred years and risen to haunt my mind! You ain't real! You ain't alive! Risen dead is playin' with me, but I won't scare; I won't scare!" Then that Tolliver laugh, for a minute more of a scream than a laugh, and Tolliver walked off.

Elton didn't make a sound or move or blink.

All the Sunday-dressed farmers and their wives walked carefully around him.

On Sunday afternoons the young men from the farms usually went into town to sit in the lobby of the Matson Hotel or smoke on the street corners talking loudly for the benefit of the town girls who had come cautiously downtown to avoid them.

Elton came into the Matson, at about two, but he was dressed in his work clothes. Tolliver had been sitting with the Lennart boys, cutting up, but there was a strange tightness in him that made them uncomfortable. It seemed as if he was trying too hard to imitate himself, generous and loud, wide-handing his laughter around the room. When he saw Elton, he carefully doubled the laughter and shaped his mouth for a joke, but the sound of his laughter was strange and tight, and people turned to look. Elton only raised his arm very quietly. There was a shotgun with that arm. A moment's dead silence held everything: breathing and words. Tolliver's mouth held the shape of his word. The shot roared. Tolliver fell. Elton turned and went up the street to find the sheriff.

His trial emptied the town. Stores closed; women packed lunches and went to stand outside the courthouse for the words of testimony to be passed out to them. Carl's boss was on the jury; and Carl, Rutheen, and the kids were at the courthouse every day along with everyone else in town. There was no doubt what people thought of the case. Nobody really liked Tolliver enough to miss him. The state's lawyer tried to make that stand against Elton somehow, and he was jeered at when he left the court. When Elton's turn came to speak, his lawyer asked him to tell how it had been between him and Tolliver starting back at the beginning. Hollow Time was long gone by then. The air had a spring grass smell and the little rain that was carried on the wind wasn't the cold rain of winter's vengeance but the warm awakener of seeds and hungers.

Elton stood in the courtroom in his puzzled, mortal mistakenness, and everyone remembered in a little blurred and softened way, the sorrow of being young. Standing shyly in the dust mote light, wearing that same good black suit, Elton told in his slow voice about his years of ridicule and shame at the hands of Harkin Tolliver. He put name to maybe twenty things that Tolliver had done, hurtful, humbling things forgotten by everyone but Elton and now recalled in the telling.

His plain voice, the blacks he wore, the way his large, bony hands worked the rail of the witness stand—all of it seemed to plead for him as victim and not killer. He told how in the beginning he had tried to make peace; and when he knew there would be no peace, how he tried to ignore Tolliver. He told of growing up yearning after a girl but afraid to speak with her on account of what Tolliver might do. He told of a keen, drawing loneliness, of never daring to befriend. What friendship could last in shaming and hurt that never ended?

His lawyer asked him why he didn't fight Tolliver as the

others had done, or laugh, or trick back. Elton looked at him with the friendly seriousness he might have used when speaking of life's simplicities to a small boy.

"A person's supposed to obey the word of God. You know that God says that hating is a sin. Didn't they ever tell you it was bad an' sinful to fight? Didn' your ma ever tell you to mind the Bible an' not fight, an' to love your neighbor?"

The room was still. Witnesses and jury, judge and spectators hung silent in incredulous wonder that Rutheen saw and held a little bitterly to herself. He's no stranger, that Elton; he's one of your own, and he can't make out your criss-cross ways. Many of the women in the court blushed, and the men coughed and looked away because they knew Elton and that he had spoken without irony or wit. All the Sunday-School ideas—and he had listened, actually listened and believed.

In the stillness his lawyer asked, "Elton, the Book says: Thou shalt not kill. Why did you break that law?"

Elton dropped his head. He said he hadn't ever thought of killing Tolliver, never till he was sitting in church. He turned to the Judge. "Sir, the hurt come; it come so bad." And he looked down at himself. "I knowed somehow it was him doin' it, doin' somethin' to hurt my—my. . ." And he blushed. "I knowed he wouldn't leave me be—ever."

The court was very still; people outside listened as the word was passed back. The jury didn't even go out. They went into a huddle and the foreman spoke to the judge and the judge blew his nose and gave Elton seven years. "Out in five," he said.

The town cheered Elton when he went from court; and when he went to the train for the state prison, he had a whole crowd to see him off and wave. Rutheen and Carl had stood in the cheering courthouse crowd and looked at one another like mourners at a graveside.

That night she cried to him, "We're strangers—strangers!"

On the day of the train, with Elton in handcuffs being cheered, Rutheen stood at the edge of the crowd wondering if she could ever find the warp strings to lead her into the cloth where this pattern was made plain. Her mind was unused to searching its own easement. It moved numbly to thought. Thread doesn't have to know what the pattern is. A red strand crosses, then a green. Thread doesn't have to know there's a plaid, clear and plain all around it. The thought gave no comfort. She felt tears beginning to blur across her eyes. What am I doing in this place with these strangers, not knowing their minds or their ways! And then she looked at Elton. He doesn't either, that poor fool off to jail. He's lived with these people all his life, and he doesn't know. That made one neighbor. It eased her a little, but she couldn't stop her mind from searching and wearing over the trouble as she walked home.

Years worked themselves away. The girls went on into high school; the boys into junior high. Carl joined a bowling club and Rutheen took her turn inviting the women over. She greeted her neighbors and they greeted her, but there was no comfort in their laughter, no sharing in their sorrow. Men's wolves are fear; women's loneliness. Men fight with their muscles; women with their tongues—a hill saying. No one would know it down here.

Rutheen's girls were happy in their ways and freedom now. All the things she had saved to teach them were useless to them. What they needed, she had no knowledge to give. Carl was bitter about the boys, but he kept his pain to himself except when he and Rutheen were alone in the darkness.

"Millis sassed me, Rutheen; did you hear him at supper?"

"What's come on them boys; they don't take no pride!" She would only sigh quietly. "Up home, I knew many a woman hoped to herself her daughter wouldn't marry. Daughters was company up home. Here they ain't even like blood. They're— they're *secret*." Up home.

When the girls began to go to dances, Rutheen would listen to them talking on the phone endlessly to their friends. She tried to catch anything she could predict or understand in the secret, meaningful code they spoke to one another.

Sarah—she was Sandy now—sounds like a dry crickbed, Carl said. She had easy laughing conversations with so many friends, but Rutheen couldn't ever get a hold on any single part, nor could she tell in all the welter of names if there was any particular boy who stood well with her out-land daughter.

Cleaning one day, Rutheen picked up one of the movie magazines the girls were always bringing home. She thought, *This is what has a meaning to them. I wonder what it tells them.* She hoped it wasn't in that code of theirs as she sat down, half-guiltily, and began to turn the pages. A picture caught her eye. It was the picture of an older woman, a familiar-looking, smiling woman. Under the picture it said, "Mrs. Wilson Answers," and under that there were letters from people all over the country. She began to read. The first was a letter from some girl in Idaho. Needs her bottom spanked, Rutheen thought. Is this where Sandy comes for what she wants to know? Then there was a letter from a boy about kissing girls, and then another. Reading on, Rutheen saw in amazement that it was about her and about Carl and the kids. She never knew written words could be set down so truly. A woman was writing from Minnesota. So far away, Rutheen thought, but she was here. The letter said how lonely she was, moving to a new place among strangers. What should I do, it said, to neighbor these people, to come to be friends with them? Rutheen went to the part where Mrs. Wilson gave her answer. She read and studied the words, following with her own lips what Mrs. Wilson had to say. Then she read it again, and then went over it point by point.

Making friends is largely a matter of turning your thoughts away from yourself and toward others. You have to take the initiative and make the first move. Get out and be a joiner! Church groups are a good start, and for widening social horizons, nothing beats getting behind some good and helpful civic or community action. Neighbors who seem reserved are usually waiting for you to show your own eagerness to know them. Remember that an invitation to a little get-together can make friends out of nodding acquaintances.

That night, when Carl came home, Rutheen rushed at him like fire to paper. "It's the most sharin'-close, homed-in thing happened in this town. What is it?" They were hill words and he answered them Hill.

"What's raw-new in your mind is quick out of your mouth, Rutheen. Sharin'-close: privy-holes. Sociable is that shavin' mirror upstairs."

"Oh, Carl!"

"Well, then, o.k. I reckon it was that boy Elton's trial."

She smiled and nodded, lighted with the brightness of her own new hope. There had been that look to the town, all sure in its way, all sharing in its way, everybody at the courthouse and the train. Rich and poor were there, farm and town, even the ladies of the Ladies' Guild—all of them sympathizing Elton off to jail. She and Carl had been the only ones who weren't gladdened by Elton's justice—too late and too much. Well, town had its own ways; it knew it's own; and it had had a wholeness then. Only those unwise in the way had read it wrong.

"We're gonna start it, Carl, we're gonna start *bein'* town."

She called the sheriff; she called the Ladies' Guild. She called Elton's preacher and hers. On the 17th of April, two months off, Elton would be free with something called a parole; and she and Carl, the strangers, were going to give him a welcoming party. Anyone who wanted to come would be invited, and all the folks from the trial.

"We're goin to *do* somethin' at this," she told Carl. "Our party for Elton will heal him an' heal us an' get all these neighbors together. We're goin' friendin' good an' hard, like we was sicklin' off a rocky acre."

"The people you been callin'; they been helpin' you any?"

"Well, they act kind o' surprised when I tell 'em what I got in my mind, but they been real nice."

She worked long and hard. There were invitations to be sent, punch glasses and plates and chairs and tables to be planned for and borrowed. She invited the mayor and the sheriff and all the main people at the trial, her neighbors and the Ladies' Guild. In a thousand later nights of bitterness or shame, picking over those two months like the survivor looking for what could be saved from a gutted house, Rutheen could never remember one single voice, not one, of all the voices on her telephone, that told her she was wrong to have the party. Maybe it was only town-wrong, but it was wrong enough to widen the lonely hollow of the night between a neighbor's house and hers. Fools that are small, humble, and modest at their foolishness are told to come away from it, like children; but the cathedral fools, the earthquake fools are awesome, and their mistakes are magic from which people draw back as if they were witnessing wonders. Even the kids said nothing. They were town people: secret-keepers.

So Elton was released; and that evening Carl and Rutheen stood in the light of their open door and waited. The house was festooned with streamers; punch welled red in the borrowed bowl; chairs stood ready; music played. Time came; time wasted; time was past. The street outside their lighted house was very dark and still. They sat stiff in their party clothes, vastness and silence all around them. In all the spaces and long falls of Severn, how could they have come to such a little room and still feel so alone?

In the end the little Bruno boy walked innocently to their door. "Hello, Ma'am," he said formally. He was collecting again for his bunch of initials starving in Europe.

She dropped the quarter in the can he held without talk, as she had learned in more than one hard lesson. Yet, he was someone inside her doorway, someone who could explain. "Oliver, why ain't no one come to a party for Elton Rand that's been away?"

It confused the boy to be asked such a thing, a genuine question by a grown-up, one who, after all, made the rules. He checked quickly the nearness of outside and safety. "Heck," he said, "nobody's glad *he's* home. You know where he was? In jail. He's a jailbird!"

"But, Oliver, a man stops bein' a jailbird when he's out of jail, don't he?"

The boy's eyes whipped from one of them to the other. What kind of people were these? "He's a *jailbird* an' nobody is *ever* gonna forget that!" And out the door and gone.

They sat in the garish, lighted silence for a time, and then Rutheen looked around and sighed. "I never thought they had it in 'em, townfolks, to judge so hard. Elton Rand won't *ever*—have an easy day. She laughed. "Well, I got to get these cups back tomorrow, an' the chairs. . ."

Carl put a hand to comfort her, and by that hand, she knew the degree of ruin they had suffered; because Carl was not a man who showed tender ways. His hands had always been scarred and work-roughened. She had never been able to remember a time when there wasn't some gash angry and some healing on his leathery, calloused palms. His hands hadn't changed. Those hands were here in the lighted house, among the party things. She began to cry. "It runs in us so true. . ." She tried to stop crying because he was always embarrassed by it. "Carl . . ."

He turned his patient face toward her. "What?"

"We ain't the only strangers, at least. I got hill wit enough to know what's goin' on in that house over west. I'll tell you. I see the house, the only one lit. The curtains are shut, though, an' there's a woman pretendin' to sleep in the room upstairs. Settin' late in the kitchen is the man. He thinks he's through with his pain; the woman knows it's just started. What a hard road these town folks mark for a man! I can feel that pain for now an' for tomorrow too, like it was mine, come by in the blood."

He looked at her and then down at his carefully cleaned fingernails. "We did think these here folks was soft, didn't we." And he nodded with the awe of it. "Is it a mercy you knowin' and feelin' the pain of that stranger-woman? God, if it's a mercy at all, Rutheen, it's a hard mercy—a hard mercy."

LULLABIES

It had started simply with a trip to the planetarium because Grandpa loved to go there anyway, and he said it would be nice to take Jane and let his son and daughter-in-law sleep late. When they went together into the strange Sunday morning quiet, they looked up and down its deserted streets, taking pleasure in noticing small things and discussing them with great seriousness on their way to the planetarium.

"Open Sunday," he said. "The directors of *this* place have good sense, because there are people working during the week who want to see how the sky looks from China."

They stopped before the great, grimy old building, and combed-up and straightened their clothes. The Grandfather was a small man with a badly-pocked face, but he stood gracefully erect. The little girl was plain-looking and bone-thin, with straight brown hair that was tied up with a small cluster of white ribbons.

"Shall we go in now?" he said.

They took hands and went up the steps. It was a little past nine when they started inside, and they stayed till twelve, stopping often to look and talk about the displays and to observe the other visitors. Then they had lunch, sauntering past a dozen restaurants and coffee shops which one or the other turned from loftily: "Too dark inside . . ." "I don't like the name . . ." Until they found exactly the place they wanted. They went in and ordered with great formality.

"This is Sunday, Miss," the Grandfather said to the waitress. "The day of rest for us. My granddaughter here is against injustice of any kind. She wishes to order food that has all taste and no vitamins. My granddaughter is giving vitamins a day of rest."

That was the first time. On Sundays after that they went to the zoo and the city tulip garden; they had their chests x-rayed and their horoscopes read; they went to a convent to hear the nuns sing and to the penny arcade where they took pictures of themselves that looked back at them like resigned suicides. Dozens of places opened to Jane from the Sunday sun, months and years of Sundays, finally stopping only when she got to high school and the boys began to ask her to go ice-skating with them on Sunday mornings.

When she and Rudy were going together, Jane kept remembering the beginning of those Sunday mornings with Grandpa. Perhaps it was being in love that brought back echoes of his gentleness and pride, and she found herself talking about him more than anyone else in the family whom she wanted Rudy to know so easily and like so well.

"Going through the city with him was like learning myself in a way," she said to him. "We've lived in the city all our lives and gone all over, shopping and to schools and doctors; but when Grandpa and I went—well—do you know, for instance, that there's a Buddhist Temple here? It's on East Fairfield. We went to a church social once and they served little chinese pastries. And there's an apiary. Where in this brick-and-stone-works do bees find flowers to drink? I don't know, but they do."

Rudy smiled at her. "He sounds like a wonderful guy," he said. (Guy because it made them more like equals.) "I'd like to meet him." They were walking down the street then, on their way to pick up Jane's dog at the vet. "In all your ramblings," he said, "did you ever go through my old neighborhood?"

"Where was that?"

"South of Van Hoven. I grew up on 8th and Vandalia." A silence was where her casual answer should have been, so he went on. "It wasn't as bad as people say. We used to kid about it, and the kids who grew up there feel kind of a—well—a camaraderie now that it's over and they've moved away. We used to say about my block that with all the wash they always had on those lines, the buildings looked like sailing ships. People would yell up to us: 'You see the big wave yet?' "

She looked at him sharply, having heard no bitterness in his voice, to see if it would be in his expression; but his thin, slightly irregular features had not changed.

"We never got around to—uh—Vandalia." Embarrassment seemed to have made her voice thicker, and she knew the words were false and stupid. Who takes his carefully raised granddaughter on a Sunday morning outing to a skid-row slum?

For a moment they stood there in the brilliant June sunlight, and then Rudy put his head back and laughed. Rudy's laugh was so big and plain and whole that people passing looked and then laughed too as they walked, and soon she was laughing.

"Janey, I'm going to broaden your horizons. We'll do Vandalia one of these days in style. We won't even wait for the big wave." The took hands and walked on, shining down the street.

But it was a while before they went to Vandalia, or before they met Jane's grandfather. For a time it seemed easier and happier to learn to know one another first among interesting but not intensely personal things. After a while Jane's parents began to ask more about Rudy. She told them that he had just taken his Masters and that they had met at the university, and her mother and father both nodded unconsciously because of the university and the Masters.

Then they said, "Why don't you invite your young man for dinner some time next week, and we'll have Grandpa also. You used to be so close, and now he says he hardly ever sees you."

That week she got an invitation for dinner with Rudy's family. So it was their parents, almost at the same time, who began to talk about them together.

When Grandpa came late and smiling and with two little bunches of wild daisies that he had gotten heaven knows where, Jane felt a sudden urgency in his meeting with Rudy. If they could like one another, how wonderful it would be. Fathers and mothers have to stand off a little; Grandpa could come closer. Parents were too frightened and too careful, and it was natural because of all the years of manners and school reports and dental work they had always had to worry about. She knew they could never be free of her as something of a responsibility; but with Grandpa she had always left that weight of obligation behind her, and they had gone simply and happily through their city. On those trips he had taught her how to look, really to look, and to think about what she saw; and with his gifts she had seen Rudy, and been able to see deeply to where his joy and strength lay. So she introduced them and watched with tenderness for both of them, as they shook hands somewhat stiffly, each unknowing what a rare and special person the other was.

When Jane rook Rudy to the table, she knew that her mother hadn't been telling the truth about its being just for supper so we can get to know him. They had the blue dishes and the best silver and some sort of French dessert loaded with brandy. It was all very pleasant and uncomfortable. When Daddy got down to the Questions, it seemed as if the whole dinner had been made simply to loosen Rudy's tongue.

"Janey tells me you have gotten your Master's degree."

"Yes, sir," Rudy said.

The sir was good. Jane could see it.

"But she never told us what your profession was."

"My degree is in clinical psychology."

"Oh—uh—that's working in the—uh—mental places."

"Well, the hospitals have clinical psychologists, but there's a lot more to choose from. Psychologists work in personnel and research and teaching." He was being very formal, but that was appreciated too, as a mark of seriousness and the importance of getting to know Jane's people.

"And do you know which of those fields you will go into?"

Rudy was opening his mouth to answer, but Jane saw that he was trying to do too much. It was good to impress them with seriousness, but he was also trying to allay their fears and be honest at the same time.

"Daddy," she said, "why don't we let Rudy relax a little."

Rudy came back gracefully saying that he would answer the question as well as he could, but finally Mother caught Jane's eye-signal and suggested that they all go into the living room.

As they went, Jane stayed close to Rudy and whispered,

"Oh, Rudy, can't we wait to tell them; they're all too nervous and uncomfortable. I never knew Daddy to be so . . ."

"Look," he said, "if they ask, I'll have to tell them. We know how we feel about it, and if things work out and we go on (he still couldn't say marry, Jane thought), "it'll just be worse when they do find out."

"Well, I'm proud about it, and I know Grandpa will be too, but . . ."

"You know I'm a psychologist. Why argue when I know everything there is to know about human behavior."

It was from their small but growing store of private jokes, and she answered it. "Wraps 'em around his little finger—show 'em the finger, perfesser!" And they laughed and went in.

"There are psychologists writing articles in the magazines I read," Mrs. Simon was saying. "Marriage counseling. It's helping people with their problems, not crazy people, just people who need advice."

Jane thought she saw a fleeting incredulous look on her father's face, as if he was asking himself if he would seek any advice whatever from the unformed, unlined young man, Master or not, who was standing in his living room with his pale and fragile and trusting daughter.

The look angered her, and Jane answered it. "Rudy has some exciting plans for his future."

All the eyes came up. She had begged him to wait until the family could see a little of what she saw, and then she had made waiting impossible.

Rudy was beginning, looking toward the Grandfather he had been told would be his ally. "Jane has—uh—Jane has told me about the trips that she used to take with you, sir, and how the trips helped her to love the city . . ." (So Rudy, too, had seen the need to cushion the idea, to give it slowly and in a context of possibilities so as not to shock them with the raw thing all at once.) "One of the areas you didn't visit was south of Van Hoven Boulevard." Dead silence. They were feeling some sort of appeal in his voice, and why does a stranger appeal unless he has something shocking to show? "I—uh—I grew up in that area, and when I began to study, I realized how much really sensible could be done with youth groups and so forth down there."

(She had heard these words so often—all kinds of ideas

about child care centers and adult education and various kinds of classes. She tried to think back to the first time she had heard them, before the language of it became hers as well as his—had it shocked her? No, it had seemed faintly amusing, as she remembered it. "Living among the poor"—it had seemed not so much frightening as quaint. But these were parents. . . .

He had heard her thoughts again as she had begun to hear his. "I'm not going into this alone. One Against the Slums," he said. "There are new and old programs already working down there, and the pay in most of them is quite reasonable. Then, I hope to be writing after a while, and, later, private counseling on the side. When I know that I have something important to say, I might go into teaching, but . . ."

(She held her breath. Don't say any more, please. Leave it there—*teaching*. It was the last thing you said, a thing they might be able to hold on to.)

But he hadn't heard her that time, or didn't want to hear. "But the thing I want to say about going back is that I think I'll be happy because I'll be living and working where I know I'm really needed, and Janey . . ."

The utterance rose from the mother with the thin gray smoke of her cigarette. "Living?"

And the father, antiphonally, "Living?"

Their carefully constructed "casual" evening fell apart around them. Jane saw them looking into the ugly world that they were sure would be her future. She tried to smile and be graceful with them.

"We've been down there, Mother, and sure there are tenements and and all the rest of it; but there are nicer places too, two-family houses that will just take a little fixing up. People always talk about Vandalia Street, skid-row. You get a picture in your mind, but you've never really been there. You don't *know*."

And then Grandpa stood up and looked at Jane and for a moment she was shocked that she could barely trace the resemblance between the proud, gay sharer of all those Sundays, safe and well-loved, and this present, trembling, bitter-faced old man. "What do you know, my clean—smart—smiling . . . ! Look at you! No bruised hands, no rotten teeth. *I was born on Vandalia Street!*"

In the end they smoothed things over. Rudy came to dinner soon again and they ate without special fuss; and Grandpa "stopped in" for something and stayed to dinner. He was patient and polite to Rudy, the way one is with someone whose face is familiar but whose name and contact have been forgotten. When he spoke to Jane, he seemed restless and vague.

He came over the next day in a kind of frantic hurry to see Jane, and the next. He began a kind of desperate badgering to convince her of something whose wavering, oblique outlines she could barely trace.

"I was reading this morning in the paper about a couple with a baby," he would say, pausing as if waiting for her to break a code in it and see to a reality under the "innocent" fact. "The kid was born with club feet. Isn't that a shame. They had to have special things to keep the feet straight after the operation." Then, as if coming to the most important thing, the crux of it all, his voice would rise and quicken. "Listen, the parents can't go out unless they have a trained nurse for the baby, and when this trained nurse goes home at night, she has to be *where she is safe so she won't be afraid to walk home at night!*"

". . . I heard your mother say that your friend Beatrice got married. A surgeon, she said. I wonder if they are going to stay here. Parkdale is very nice, so green for the city. Or he could commute. It's not too far from Tyler, really. Remember when we went there? It was only an hour on the bus, and the advantages . . ."

Jane's mother was no help. Mrs. Simon only shrugged. "I never knew about your grandfather's having come from that section. He was always very well-spoken. They lived on Perrer, I remember, when your father and I met."

"He acts as if my going there with Rudy would be like— dying. He won't see the wonderful things that Rudy wants to *do*."

Her father said, "I was born long after your grandfather moved out of that section. I never heard him mention it. Marriage is a big step, Janey. Of course we're happy that you and Rudy will be near us, but are you sure about the *boy*. This— idea—of his . . ."

But the date was set and they looked for a place near the Settlement House where Rudy had found a job counseling delinquent boys. Rudy's parents had scoured the neighborhood and found them an apartment on the roof of a building that housed some moribund wholesale places. The place itself was pretty shabby, but Jane saw potential in it, wonderful potential with a little fixing up.

The best thing of all was the whole roof of the building surrounding them, like a huge, light patio. There were no other tenants except for the businesses during the day. When Rudy was there, he seemed happy too. Jane thought it might be mostly gratitude for her joy. She had put her arms around her new parents and kissed them both in a spontaneous rush of love. The Wilenskis only smiled, seeing her and their son planning and consulting and laughing together as if they were some kind of strange, exotic visitors to the known world. Jane went home full of eagerness to tell her parents.

"Mother, it's *wonderful!* There's plenty of light and air and privacy, and it isn't like being poor at all! I want Grandpa to know it. Neighborhoods and classes of people and rich and poor are different now, and there are other people at the Settlement House to be our friends. Rudy said so, and I'm going to meet them next week. And I found out that the Eilers—you know, those medical students; I told you about—they live right near the apartment."

The mother only smiled a little vaguely and said, "Right now, helping the poor is not what I want to hear about. I want you to try to help your grandfather. He's coming to dinner tonight, and I want you to reassure him. I think he has a little gift for you that he doesn't want to give in the confusion at the wedding. He's an old man, Jane, and you are his favorite." She looked up from the salad she was fixing. "I know that at this time in your life you and Rudy are both very honest and very brave and full of painfully proud integrity. I don't want that from you at this moment. Your grandfather is coming; Grandpa, who loves you so much. If he wants you to give him a pleasant lie, you do it. Tell him what he wants to hear. As for the principles of it, you can charge them to my account." And she went on chopping with short strokes of unnecessary vigor.

Jane went in to the living room to wait for her grandfather.

He came like a mourner and spoke a few soft words to her mother at the door, and then walked into the living room and addressed her with the courtly sorrow of old people who have been to so many funerals that they know the etiquette of them very well. When they sat down together he said, "Janey, I have a wedding present for you, and I brought it here because I want to forgive you."

She sat quietly and smiled at him, not knowing what to say.

"Open it."

She took the envelope from him and opened it. There were five twenty-dollar bills in the envelope, and nothing else. "The silver things," he said, "your grandmother's silver things, that ladies like to serve tea in, those you will get with all the rest at the wedding. This—well—this is for when trouble comes. Maybe it will be secret trouble. You can put it away and forget about it until the time. . . ." He patted her hand with a strange rapid spasm, as if he wished to strike her. "Janey, do you know what you have done to me?"

How could one lie pleasantly to that? "Oh, Grandpa. Rudy is a wonderful man, you'll see. He reminds me of you in many ways. You think I'm letting you down, but we aren't even leaving town, and we'll be able to visit and so will you."

He hadn't heard her and she knew it. He was thinking and speaking again out of that bitter stranger's face that she had seen at the awful dinner with Rudy.

". . . all the years and struggling. You can't even know what you are destroying. You don't know the man, Siemonowsky, whom you have killed so easily, whom you have betrayed for—for nothing." He had been whispering the words, crooning them like a lullabye. Suddenly he seemed aware of her sitting next to him. "Who is that Siemonowsky? Why, I am that Siemonowsky. Simon is not the name of a boy and then a man and then me. My mother had Siemonowsky in an alley between the laundry and the tailor on 10th and Vandalia. She couldn't climb the steps to the flat and she didn't speak English to ask for help. Two generations of struggle, and you take us right back to that—that . . . You know, when I was ten I told my father I wanted to be Simon, an American. He beat me and threw me out of the house. I went to work at Berrigan's saloon, cleaning up and running errands. I worked for a bed under the bar and tips, and during the day I went to school. Could you even know a man who grew up in the stink of cheap whiskey? I lived only because I knew I would gain back everything I lost and more.

"If not, Janey, how could I have gone to school and even through college, clean and decent and—*human*—and been a bouncer for Berrigan at night? I did things on that job, such things. And I saw such things, that—there on your precious Vandalia Street. This was me, your grandpa, whom you love so much. My sisters and brothers are still Siemonowsky somewhere, I guess. I had to lose them too, when I left that place. I went to Jerome Street and then to Benton and then to Perrer, an educated man, an American; and I married a lovely American girl and had a son who was born decently in a hospital, and he didn't go to the City College but to a university where all the best people sent their sons. And he married a lady, a lady! And they had a lady too, and I sang to that sweet, clean, laughing little girl, lullabyes. And I never knew."

Jane sat on the couch and thought of the pearls she was wearing and the cashmere sweater and tweed skirt, and thought, a lady. One of their Sundays in a distant springtime reminded itself to her. She had come running to answer his special knock, and had been surprised to see him gasp a little at the sight of her, and then stand for a moment while his eyes filled with tears. He had passed it off as a joke, and she had been too frightened to ask him about it again. What had frightened her was not his tears, but the realization of the power she had over him. Because she was small and timorous and because she loved him, she had put the thought of using that power out of her mind; but she had never forgotten the sight of him standing in her doorway. Why on that day and not another? It could have been the way she looked: the new light blue dress with white petticoats and ribbons, little embroidered forget-me-nots, a long white sash. It was the innocence and the idealizing portrait: America's Little Sweetheart. For the first time she tried consciously to use the power she had once had in her smile.

"Grandpa, you gave me more on those Sundays than walks and looks around the city. I would have been so much less alive if not for you and those Sundays. But—I don't know what it will be like, living on those crowded streets and sharing all the things that Rudy will want me to do with the people he'll be helping. I'll need you more than I ever did, when I can't stand the noise or the pain or the trouble down there. I'll need to know that I can call you up and you won't judge Rudy the way Mother and Dad would—would *have* to. I'll want to call you

up so we can go off some afternoon to some nice place where
we can sit and talk and drink something without any vitamins. . . ."

They had been so quiet and so polite. She found herself
wondering if the unknown, ancient, estranged Siemonowskys
had cursed in their anger and screamed in their despair.

He said, almost in a whisper, "They have a smell, those
streets. The smell of Berrigan's saloon has filled every corner.
After I had been at Berrigans for a while, and seen—I began to
notice that the stench of the place was starting to creep into the
street outside. I noticed it beginning to spread up and down
the whole street, and then out through the back door where the
toilets were, and then it began to pour out of the windows, until
you smelled it on Bisher Street and Moody and on and on all
the way down to the avenue. I love you, Janey my darling, my
little lady. Always so delicate—you were always so clean and
innocent. But I couldn't live with one of mine, smelling of that
smell, smelling of it and bringing the taint across the boulevard,
and going back to live in that awful—that awful . . ." And he
turned away from her and rose and left.

Jane sat on the couch looking down at her pearls as they
enlarged to great globes through her tears. She had forgotten
that they had been his gift to her when she had started college.
"Perfect pearls for a perfect granddaughter," in his beautifully
legible script. A perfect granddaughter was shining and innocent and gentle and quiet, and the cold, pale opposite of
Siemonowsky. Very quietly, she began to cry.

GLOSS ON A DECISION OF THE COUNCIL OF NICAEA

The major schisms of the Church. A list of the Bishops of Sarum. She knew a great deal about medieval church politics. With luck and God's help, knowledge would save her. Because the jail was so terrifying.

She had seen the demonstrators out there in front of the library, and she had watched them for a few minutes, unemotionally, and then she had gone into her little office and scratched out some words on a piece of cardboard for a sign. Then she had walked out of the library and down the steps to stand with the demonstrators. She had made no conscious decision to do this. Her heart was exploding its blood in rhythmic spasms of panic, but she paid no attention to it; and this frightened Myra, because she had always weighed her choices carefully and measured feeling against propriety.

Now she was standing in a jail cell. What was there to be afraid of? Jails haven't changed much since the Middle Ages; the properties of a jail—the dirt, discomfort, lack of privacy, and ugliness—were the same. Being a student of history, she had pondered many imprisonments. Except for the electric lights, Tugwell's county jail might have been anywhere at any time; and for Myra, who had always respected fighters for a cause, prison had meant Boethius' great hour, Gottschalk, the Albigensian teachers, and John of the Cross. She now understood that the worst, the most horrifying feature of their imprisonment had eluded her; and in her own moment, its sudden presence was almost too much to stand. Captors hate. How could she have missed so plain a fact? Captors hate. When the sheriff had come to "protect" them from the hecklers, she had started forward, trying to get to him. "These Negroes and I are protesting an unjust . . ."

But he had turned, reaching to take her and the girl next to her, and he had looked at them with a look that stopped the words in her mouth. At the jail, as they went past him into the cell, she saw the look again, a loathing, an all-pervading contempt. Before the wave of fear and sickness had passed, the door was closed and he was gone.

There were no statements taken, no charges made. She had wasted the first hours mustering answers from an array of imprisoned giants, the brilliant, searing words of men whose causes, once eclipsed and darkened, were now the commonplace truths of our civilization.

After a while Myra had looked around and counted. There are eight of us. The young men had been taken somewhere else. Eight girls, two beds—an upper and lower bunk—one spigot, two slop buckets, one bare wall, and two square yards of floor to sit on. That was all. The girls had gone to the bunks in an order that seemed natural: two rested or slept on the lower, four sat on the upper bunk, leaving the floor for the remaining two. When anyone had sat or rested enough, she would move and a girl on the floor would take her place.

She had expected choices. There were none, not even a list of rules that they could obey or refuse to obey. It underlined the sheriff's look. One doesn't give choices to an animal; the sheriff, giving such choices, would be recognizing the humanity of his prisoners and their right to make some disposition of their own lives. So, Miss Myra, the careful librarian of Tugwell, who walked in the crosswalks and did not spit where it said *No Spitting*, was forced to put her own boundaries to her day. She decided to spend the mornings mentally recounting history, braiding popes and synods and the heresies they sifted. Perhaps they would shed light on the evolution of secular law, in which she had done a good deal of reading. In the afternoon she would have to find a way to get some exercise, to get a letter out, to wash her clothes. . . . The girls talked a little now and then, the random exchanges of people waiting. Myra sensed that they didn't have her need for formed, measured bits of time, for routines and categories. They seemed to hang free within the terms of imprisonment, simply waiting.

On the evening of the second day Matilda Jane asked her, "Miss Myra, how you come to be with us?"

The others looked over at her, some smiling, no doubt remembering the scene of themselves as they stood and sang in front of the library, hoping they could keep their voices from quavering. They had watched the door, certain of the nose of a gun or the tip of a firehose as it slowly opened. Instead, there had grown only the tiny white edge of Myra's quickly lettered sign, giving them a word at a time: OPEN LIBRARY TO ALL! IGNORANCE IS NOT BLISS. Then, Myra herself had come, slowly, very much alone. It was as if in the expectation of a cannon, they had been shocked by a pop gun. Some of them had even laughed.

"I'd never thought about it, I mean about colored people not using the library, not until Roswell Dillingham came. After that, I had to—well—to protest."

"Roswell?" And the other girls sat up, surprised, interested, waiting for something rich. "Heber's little brother?"

"Hey, she mean Sailor."

They laughed.

"What Sailor done now?"

"I didn't know his nickname," Myra said, and Lalie, who was sitting on the bed beside her, guffawed. "Lord, yes! Great big mouth, blowin' an' goin' all the time, two big ears a-flappin', ma'am; you be with Sailor, you ain' need no boat!" And they all wanted to know what Sailor had done now. They were all eager to hear Roswell's latest, all except Delphine, who was stretched out on the bed dozing.

"Well," Myra said, "there's not much to tell, really. You see, when Mrs. Endicott left and I took over as county librarian, she simply told me that you—I mean that Negroes—just didn't use the library, but that when a Negro needed to look something up, why he would come to me and I would take the book out myself. I know it will seem odd to you—it does to me now—but before that it had never occurred to me that there were no Negroes coming into the library. Anyway, one day this spring, I was locking up and Roswell came and asked me for a book. I just followed Mrs. Endicott's instructions—I got it for him on my card. In three days he was back. Soon he started asking me to recommend books for him to read. Two or three books every week. I started combing lists for things I thought he would like, and the more he read, the more foolish it seemed not to have him come and browse around and pick out the books for himself. When I told him to come, he looked at me as if I had told him to fly like a bird. Negroes were forbidden to use the library.

"*The library!* That business of my getting the books for him had been designed to make me ask him why he wanted them, and then to decide that he wasn't responsible! I wrote an inquiry to the county commission and never got an answer. I never dreamed of demonstrating. I have to be honest and say that, but *the library*—well—I just couldn't consent to that. So, I suppose it was Roswell who got me to come out."

M.J. looked away and there was silence while everyone groped for a new, less dangerous subject.

Loretta whistled softly and said, "Kin you beat that damn Roswell?"

No getting away now; there it was. "What's the trouble?" Myra asked.

"You in here with us, Miss Myra," M.J. said, "so I'm gonna tell you truly what Roswell been doin'. He been makin' money offa them books."

"I don't see how. They were returned on time and in good shape."

"Ma'am, he been liftin' offa them books."

"I'm sorry, M.J., I just don't understand . . ."

"I'm in here in this jail, an' I got to be ashame' for that bigmouth! He takes them books, an' he reads 'em, an' then he take an' make 'em into a play. Then he go an' puts up a sign down to Carters' store an' he an' Fernelle an' one or two of 'em, they acts it out, see. Ten cents a person. He get almost everyone to come an' bring the kids an' make a night out. He ain' stop there. I know there's whole parts of the play that he have just graff right out of the book. I could tell it. Don't shake your head, Lalie, you know good as I do, ain' no words like that come out o' Roswell bigmouth! He lays them words down so nice—an' *powerful!* Miss Myra, he been gettin' maybe five, six dollars clear every Saturday, just showin' *your* books in the meetin' hall of the Hebron Funeral Home!"

Echo of Boethius, calling out of a sixth century cell, "Come, Goddess Wisdom, Come, Heart-ravishing Knowledge . . ." Roswell Dillingham, bootlegger of knowledge, echoed that day when knowledge was an absolute and its conquest as sure as the limits of a finite heaven. Myra wished she could tell them about Boethius, broken and condemned, and crying in his agony: "Earth conquered gives the stars!" It would only embarrass them. She said, "Do the people like the plays?"

"Well—yes, they do. See, Roswell's plays—they're about us, about colored people. It's a' interestin' play, an' folks don' have to go all the way in to Winfiel' Station, sit in the balcony. My granmaw say, she gets to see a play she understan', an' they's nobody drinkin', swearin', runnin' aroun' in they underwear. Roswell plays—I mean *your* plays—they about what happen to our people. Like las' week, he had one call *Oliver Twiss.* Everybody cry in that one. Before that he had one call *Two Cities.*"

Myra heard Dickens' story about how Sydney Carton gave himself up to the sheriff, back in the thirties, when the K.K.K. rode patrol out of Tugwell.

"Kite my books, will he . . . I wish I'd known. There's a fine one about a Civil Rights worker who got too rich and comfortable, name of Julius Caesar; one about a girl named Antigone, the freedom play of all time."

There was a snort from the bed. Delphine stretched and then swung her legs over the side and grunted again. "*Miss* Myra, we don't need white stories made over for black people."

"I wasn't patronizing. The books I gave Roswell were good books. They weren't 'white' stories. They were about people— any people . . ."

"No, *ma'am,* Miss Myra, *ma'am,* not while you got 'em piled up and stored away in the white-only library."

"That's why I was glad about Roswell." Myra looked down at Delphine. The two girls on the floor shifted a little, ready to use their bed places. Delphine got up slowly, and Myra got down, and they stood together in the cell.

From the beginning Delphine was the only one with whom Myra knew she could have no more than an armed truce. Delphine knew it too, probably. They seldom spoke to one another directly; when they had to speak, they used an agonizingly elaborate etiquette, which Myra noted had just gone over into parody. Delphine had a hard, absolute way of speaking that Myra found irritating; but Myra knew that Delphine must find life in the cramped cell more difficult with her there. Delphine was their leader. She had been in protests and sit-ins, and jailed four times. She spoke with hard-won, frightening knowledge.

"Next time, wear pedal-pushers like I got on, plaid or check. They hold up good an' they don't show the dirt."

"When they're going to hit you, the muscles by their eyes cinch up. You can always tell. Never take the smack, let the smack take you. Go with it."

If she had been an Albigensian under the Question, Myra knew that Delphine would wake great admiration in her. She was strong and intelligent; she could duck a blow, parry a question, and make her silence ring with accusation. Somehow, the heroine was also an arrogant bitch. Myra wondered if some straying grain of her own prejudice made Delphine's virtues seem so much like faults. As the pressures built up in the shares of water, slop bucket, and stench, Myra could see, from her neatly labeled and scheduled mental busy-work, that Delphine was trying to separate her from the rest of the girls.

They waited for three days. On the morning of the fourth, the sheriff came around with his notebook. As he stopped on the other side of the bars, Myra spoke to him. They had been arrested and jailed without being given their legal rights, she said. Would this be remedied?

The sheriff looked up slowly from his book, feigning a courteous confusion. "Why you're the little lady works over to the library, ain't you?" Then he let his gaze sift slowly over the others in the cell and come back to her, the expression now one of sympathetic reproof (Now, look at what you have caused to happen to you.)

She had a sudden, terrifying vision of him in all his genial Southern courtesy cutting away their justice, their law, their lives.

"Oh, ma'am, it's a shame! The commissioners only decided last week that we got to do Comminists the same as we do niggers. Comminist wants to live with niggers, why we ain' gonna stop 'em. But, ma'am, I seen you over in church on Sunday, an' all the bazaars, an' you was servin' donuts at the Legion parade." He looked at her earnestly. "It must be a mistake. I'm sure you ain' one of them Comminists."

Myra had never thought of herself as being a perceptive person. A narrow and careful life had never made it a necessity. Sensitivity can be a frightening gift. It was better to depend on more tangible things: hard work, reasonableness, and caution. Now, in the quiet, fear-laced minute, she suddenly knew that this contemptuously play-acting man was offering her a way out. She had only to weep and tell him how confused she was, to ask for his protection. (Lonely spinster-woman—everybody knows how notional they get. A woman, being more took up with the biological part of things, why, if she don't get to re-lize that biological part of her nature, it's a scientific fact she'll go to gettin' frusterated. Women, why they're *cows!*) It was as if she heard his mind form words. When he did speak, the words were so close that she was dumfounded.

"I guess you kinda got turned around here, all this niggers rights business. I guess you just got confused for a bit. I sure hate to see you in here like this. It sure is a pity." White women are ladies, the code said. You crush ladies not with violence but with pleasant contempt.

She didn't want to leave the girls in the cell. She looked at the sheriff, but she did not speak. The "lady" dealt with, he turned his attention to the others, and his voice hardened and coarsened as the code demanded when speaking to Them.

"We got a list here. You answer to your name when I call it." Then he read the names, stopping between each syllable to allow for their slow black wits to apprehend his meaning. The girls answered in the way Delphine had taught them: their voices cool and level, their eyes straight on him. Myra had been in Tugwell for only three years, having come in answer to a wildly exaggerated ad in the *Library Journal*, and staying because she had liked the town. She had never had any dealings with Tugwell's Negroes, except for Roswell; but she knew somehow that this was not the usual way for Negroes to react

to authority in Tugwell. She couldn't trace this knowledge—she
had never seen it directly or heard mention of it—it was just
there, a certitude that their look was treason and would damn
them. She also knew that from that judgment anyway, she was
exempt. She might face down the sheriff and be called an old-
maid eccentric, but she wouldn't be hurt. Another line of difference had been drawn, excluding her; and for a long moment of
the sheriff's passing by, she was overwhelmed with a loneliness
so keen that she found herself shivering and on the verge of
tears.

She tried to close this separation. To do it, she had to appeal
to Delphine. "Four days!" she said. "There must be a way we
can get hold of a lawyer . . ."

But Delphine stepped back from the line that the sheriff had
helped to set between them. "You aren't Miss Myra here; you
aren't ma'am. Not with us. Not for giving us white-man heroes
or white-man lawyers either. *You* get *your* lawyer. Let him get
you out."

"Look, Delphine, I don't know anything about the struggle
between the races. I know about the library and the books that
are in the library; and I know that it is wrong for the library to
deny its treasures to those who want them. I know about books
and reading. That's what I know about, where I am strong and
where I will fight."

But Delphine had turned her back and gone toward a space
on the bed which Myra realized shouldn't have been there. It
was there for Delphine. She was the complete leader now. She
would always have a seat on the bed or a space to lie down on
the bed when she wanted it. Having measured the sheriff, the
others had chosen his adversary—tyrant for tyrant. Delphine
went to rest on "her" bunk, to claim her compensation. "Her"
places would now be offered to others only at her discretion. It
was wrong. Myra saw it denying the very equality for which
they were risking so much; because Myra now knew that her
cellmates were facing the sons of the men who had broken
Gottschalk's bones. If only she could give them some of his or
Boethius' passionate and simple poetry to have when the time
came. They might be strengthened by the words of great prisoners whose causes had been so much like their own. They
would need grandeur. That sheriff was one who, to the end,
would follow the Customs of the Country.

Later, she was sitting next to M.J. on the floor and they were talking quietly about wonderful food they had eaten. After Myra had dismembered a large, delicately broiled lobster and dipped the red claw carapace full of its vulnerable meat into a well of butter, M.J. leaned close and whispered, "Hey, Myra— uh—you ain' a Comminist or nothin', are you?"

Myra turned in wonder from the fading lobster. "What? Whatever gave you that idea?" Some words scurried across her mind in a disorderly attempt to escape being thought.

"I didn' mean to hurt your feelin's," M.J. murmured, "but, see, Delphine don' trust you, because if you was another kind of different person—well—it wouldn' be like it was one of the regular whites comin' over to our side; it would be like you was arguin' for your own difference, see?"

"M.J., you tell Delphine that all I want is to have the Tug-well library open to everybody, regardless of race, creed, color, or national origin."

"I don' think Delphine is really agains' you."

"Where does she come from?" Myra asked, and M.J. said quickly, "Oh, she from here . . ." And then she looked down. "It's the schoolin' make her talk so much nicer, that's all. Her folks don't live but a street away from us. Her daddy work on the railroad, though, made steady money."

"It's not the way she talks," Myra said, stumbling over that other barrier between them. How could she have read the sheriff so well that his predicted words followed like footprints, and yet not be able to show herself to this girl who had the face and voice of a friend? "Delphine is different from you other girls, she . . ."

"It's the same with us as with the white," M.J. said, and she fingered her torn sleeve in a little nervous gesture that Myra had seen her begin to use after the sheriff's visit. "Some people, you fit 'em in with the rest; it don't bother 'em none. Some, they got to be just one an' the mold broke. Delphine, she like that. She always did feel sharp for things that was done wrong to her. I think she felt hurts more, say, than me. It's cause she's smarter; she got more person to hurt. You know, she went up North to the college."

"I didn't know that."

"I can remember her sayin' all the time how learnin' and

education was goin' to get her free. Our grade school here in Tugwell, it ain' hardly one-legged to the white school; an' our high school ain' but a butt-patch to the white. Oh, Myra, an' we didn' know it! Delphine come out of Booker T. Washington High all proud an' keen. She made the straight A. Then she went up North to the college. An' all of a sudden, here she was, bein' counted by white folks measure—an' put down, put way low. It shamed her. The white-school diploma she got cost her a extra year just to fill in on what ol' Booker T. High didn' think a Negro had to know."

"But she did succeed . . ."

"That's what I wonder at—why she come back afterward, here to Tugwell, where she ain't no different from any of us that never done what she did. I can't see how anybody that got the college degree would come back here to be put down low again."

"The fight and the fighter have to be close to each other," Myra murmured.

"What?"

Myra felt a gnawing in her mind that was strange to her. She had to wait until it became plain, and then she recognized that it was her mind moving, feeling blindly toward one of its own motives. It came bumping against something, won the shape from the darkness, and with the shape, a meaning. "Not pretty or smart or gifted, but I had one thing that was mine. The pretty and smart ones had the future; the rich ones had the present. I had the past. In a way, in 'having,' I 'owned.' The history and literature were mine to give when I opened that library door every morning. . . . When Roswell told me that Negroes couldn't use the library, I was mad because the town had no right, no right to deny what wasn't theirs to give or withhold. In a way, Delphine and I are alike." Then she said to M.J., "Delphine has a calling; there's no doubt about that."

Why can't I like her? Myra looked at the leader over the soggy bread in her dinner plate. She has everything I've always reverenced. Watching Delphine at the spigot. . . . not running away, standing, as Boethius stood, and Gottschalk and John. The courage is in knowing exactly what will happen, where the wound will gall most cruelly, and still, standing. . . . But the arrogance in Delphine, who was beginning to posture like

Savonarola silhouetted by the light of his own fire, made Myra wince. Delphine's arrogance reached into Myra's thoughts and began to move toward all of the heroes Myra had stored there. She began to worry for the giants she venerated, for years of her pity and love. Was courage only the arrogance used to an enemy?

The next morning the sheriff began.

Tactical blunder: He took Delphine first. She came back sick, the brown color of her face grayed. She was bloody and puffy-faced and harder than ever. Now, anyone who followed would have to come to Delphine before and after, and would be judged. When Loretta went in the afternoon and returned still retching, she was greeted by Delphine's wry smile and the slow unfolding of Delphine's bones, one by one, to make a place for her on the bunk throne of honor. The next day Dilsey and Lalie went. They came back trembling and exhausted, embarrassed at where their hurts were, and with a rumor that things were going to be speeded up because the legal machinery was slowly lumbering in to help. In the night, counting the heretics she knew, burned between 890 and 1350 in France, Myra could hear M.J. quietly sobbing with fear.

It had been hardest for M.J., who had seen all the hurts and heard the accumulating voices in their nightmares. Now the untried ones had the floor all the time. Myra crawled over to M.J. and put a hand on her thin back in a forlorn gesture of comfort. M.J.'s back stopped heaving and the crying stopped or, rather, retreated inward. Myra began to feel that someone was observing her; another silence was there, one that seemed to fill its space instead of being there by default of sound. She turned and saw Delphine looking at them from a seat on the top bunk, her face showing nothing in the dimness. She was awake, all right, watching, listening, as if she were waiting to pounce. It made Myra feel guilty of something. She looked down at M.J., who hadn't moved and was pretending to be asleep, and then she stood up. It was painfully slow; she grunted with the effort and the pain; her legs had been bent against the concrete floor for a long time. When she finally stood, her eyes were at the level of Delphine's kneecaps.

"Help M.J. You know, Delphine, we can't all be as tough as you." She realized immediately that such a plea for M.J. was wrong and stupid.

Crying weakness to Delphine was like asking sympathy from a tornado. Were all heroes so frighteningly impersonal? Damn her! Why couldn't that precious martyrs' firelight extend its warmth and radiance to cover M.J., who had waited all these days while the terror grew?

"Listen, Delphine, I know something about you."

Delphine's impassive face did not move. Damn her, I'll make it move.

"I know, for instance," she continued slowly, whispering a word at a time, "that whatever you took from the sheriff, it didn't hurt as much as theirs did . . ." And she gestured around the cell at the sleepers who were shielding their ugly dreams from the forty-watt light that burned in the corridor outside the cell. "Maybe you didn't feel it at all."

"How come?" Delphine said, fastidiously disinterested.

"You knew it before you went in," Myra went on. "It's a nice secret, too, Delphine, because the welts are real and no one can prove they didn't hurt. Maybe they don't even hurt now."

"No!" Delphine hissed. "Nothing hurts! It's the black skin. Makes you immune. Tougher than the white! Less sensitive!"

"Come off it. It's the anger or the hate that makes you immune. Your anger and hate are better than morphine for shielding you from pain. You were dressed up to the eyes in hate, and you walked in with it to the sheriff and took your licks and came back bleeding. You didn't even have to lie. Did it make you feel superior to the other girls who had to take it raw, without hate?

That hit. Myra could see it going in to burn behind Delphine's slowly blinking eyes. She was standing close to Delphine, whispering, but they were both aware that M.J. and maybe others were awake and would hear them if their voices got any louder.

Delphine began to negotiate. "What are you going to do about it?"

"You help M.J. to take what she's going to have to take or I'll tell what I know about you."

Delphine laughed, a silent mouth-laugh, whose mirth died long before it reached her eyes.

"I know they won't believe me," Myra said, "but maybe

there'll be a minute of doubt, just enough to force you to come right out and claim that bed space and that first drink in the morning."

Delphine sat there, surprised, and Delphine's surprise was a source of pain to Myra. She had no style and she knew it. Her courage looked silly. Nevertheless, she had gotten to Delphine, and Delphine wasn't used to being gotten to.

"I don't want you here!" she hissed. "I don't want what you have to give us! Get your white face out of this cell and let us, for once, do something all by ourselves!"

"I'm here and my white face is here, and you can either like it or lump it."

Where had the words and the strength come from? She had always been a sheltered person, and three years as Miss Myra, the toy librarian in this toy white town of antimacassars and mint tea hadn't done any more than confirm her opinion. Who had she been a week ago that she could be so far from that self right now? Like a rocket, she thought, that had veered a millionth of a degree from the center of its thrust. She had, on the 14th of April, asked a question of a boy named Roswell Dillingham. It was only the smallest shift, a millionth of a degree, and that smallest change was measuring her path at tangent, thousands of miles into strange darkness, to end lost, perhaps, in uncharted spaces that she could not imagine.

Delphine was muttering curses, and Myra turned back to her place on the floor and sat down. Delphine didn't want her, and she had said so. Why not? What did Myra, and by extension white people, have that Delphine couldn't accept? If Delphine hadn't been to college up North, it might have been a falsely exalted picture of American history, a Parson Weems history that no Negro in slave-holding country could take seriously. It wasn't that. Delphine had read enough and learned enough to know that white men also searched their souls occasionally. Myra knew that she had to get at it, whatever it was, because she needed everything she could use against Delphine's arrogance. She found herself staring at the slop bucket, riveted on it. Exhausted, she thought.

Hard floors and groping, needs and angers, mine and hers, and barely knowing where to separate mine and hers. Why is *she* in this cell? Then she found herself staring at Lalie's back

as if to bore through it, and Lalie shifted and moaned so that
Myra pulled her eyes away. I have the past. . . . I have the past
and two enemies, who both seem to say "nothing personal." It
really isn't, I suppose. They are enemies to my history. What a
couple they would make: the sheriff, with his fake past, and
Delphine, with her fake . . .

It was there, somewhere near, elusive but near, in Delphine's
idea of a future. She became alert, groping to more purpose
now. It was in a future of which Delphine dreamed, a world
that made "white" history irrelevant and Myra a danger. She
looked over the sleeping girls. Delphine had given up too, and
was curled in a ball, her arm protectively over her face. The
only ones who merely pretended to sleep were the two whose
turn it would be to go with the sheriff tomorrow. Myra knew
that she would not be beaten, and that the law was slowly
lumbering toward her. If only Delphine had let it happen, she
might have given them a thousand years of prison humor and
two thousand years of resistance to the tyrant, eloquent, proud
resistance, face to face, as Delphine would have liked it.

And *I* wanted to be in the history too! she thought. Oh, my
God, it was as simple as that! I wanted to be in the history even
more than I wanted to fight over Roswell's reading. I wanted to
come forward where the fire was, feeling that in the fire, I
would not be so alone. . . . The thoughts that she had sent out
walking for Delphine's weakness had found hers instead. Does
it hurt and sear and shatter, that thought? Is it as hard as the
sheriff's blows? No, not so hard as that. She wasn't going to be
in the history, even though she was in the fire. In the fire, but
no less alone. Delphine had fixed that. A segregated fire. She
would have to work at not hating Delphine. This cause was
right and the cause should take precedence over its leaders.
Heaven knows it was an old argument. It showed up as the
Montanist Controversy; and it was put to a rule in 325 A.D.:
Decision of the Nicene Council, valid sacraments by a lapsed
bishop. Very good. It was a comfort to know that the early
Church had ruled on Delphine's case.

M.J. rolled over, but her eyes were closed, and she was still
pretending to be asleep. She was a nice girl. If Delphine had
allowed it, they could have been, all of them, friends together in
this cause. Her mind yearned toward M.J. in the night. There

were thousands of men and women before you in that room, a thousand rooms, acts, moments. Don't be afraid. You are neighbored all around by people who have screamed or been silent, wept or been brave—all the nations are represented, all the colors of man. Don't be afraid of pleading, of weeping. You are with some shining names.

At the window there was a little gray light coming. The window was almost hidden by the bunks which had been pushed against its bars, but from where Myra sat on the floor, she could see up into a tiny square of the changing sky. The cell looked even worse in the muddy yellow of the electric bulb.

I suppose I shouldn't stop at the heroes of the Middle Ages. There are more recent slaves and conquerers. Dachau and Belsen—they, too, had men who stood in their moment and said, "I am a person; you must not degrade me." Her eye wandered around the cell and fixed on the slop bucket again, and she tried to ease her aching body on the floor. Dachau and Belsen.

In 1910, technology was going to make everybody free and freedom was going to make everybody good. The new cars had rolled up to the gates of death camps. Dreams of the perfecting of man ended in the gas chambers and behind the cleverly devised electric fences. Didn't everybody dream that dream? Didn't we *all*?

Maybe all but one. Is man imperfect by nature? Maybe only white man? There it was. Delphine was answering to everyone who had ever told her that she and hers were outside the elm-street-and-steeple dream of democracy. If the black heroes weren't in the history books, then they were also not included in the Albigensian Crusade and the ride to Belsen. The possibility of perfection—that was being girded, all right. If Delphine took her blows in hate and in the belief that *her* people could be perfect, not in some millennium but soon, and by her own good efforts, what would be, could be given her, what pain could she endure that wasn't worth it? Not for freedom, not for friendship, certainly not for the right of ingress to the Tugwell library. Oh, God, who will help M.J. take her hurting now, when all that M.J. wants is to include in her God-blesses before bed all the misery-running, sorrow-spawning world of white and black?

It was morning. M.J. was trembling quietly on the floor. She looked exhausted and ill, and she hadn't even gone yet. Myra got up, and the aching numbed to her every bone. She went to where Delphine was perched, sleeping.

"Delphine?"

"What-do-you-want?" It was the too-clear enunciation of an educated Negro to a white who will call him Rastus if he slurs a letter.

"You've got to do something to help M.J."

"I bet you're happy, white gal. If it wasn't for your people putting us down, she wouldn't *be* scared now!"

So it was true. The blind would see and the halt would rejoice. No cowards, no sinners, no wrongs. In the jubilee. In the great jubilee. "Help her, Delphine. The sheriff is looking for weakness. If he finds it, he might kill her with his hands or with her own shame. Help her, or I'm going to start talking about you, Delphine. I'm going to start asking questions that the others have never asked."

Myra could see the gains and losses ticking off in Delphine's head. Her eyes were clinical and her expression detatched as an Egyptian funerary statue. Delphine, at the height of her concentration, was intensely, breathtakingly beautiful. She stayed in her place for a minute, two. Then she stretched and the odds and possibilities arranged themselves before her. With elaborate, lithe ease she swung down to the floor, yawning, and bent to where M.J. lay. They began to whisper. Myra was glad she couldn't hear them. For a moment her eye strayed to the vacant place, Delphine's place on the bed. She had a sudden urge to climb up and take it and make Delphine fight to get it back. The place would be comfortable for a little nap; she was sore all over from the floor. The place would be dark against the back wall; she could sleep for a while.

No, Delphine was the leader, the place was her place. Only Delphine, however fanatical and blind, could lead the girls through all the questions, the licks and the lawyers. She found her eyes fixed again. What was so fascinating about that slop bucket! We're both on the floor, she thought.

"I wish to record an opinion," she said to it quietly. "In 325 the Council of Nicaea decided that sacraments at the hands of a lapsed bishop were valid where the intent of the communicant was sincere. The baptisms of these bishops stood. I always wondered about that decision. It smacked too much of ends justifying means. I hereby make my statement to the estimable theologians of the Council of Nicaea: 'Avé, fellas, Salvé, fellas, Congratulations and greetings from the Tugwell jail.' "

A PASSION IN EDEN

I spent one summer as a tree, standing out in the garden spreading my fingers and feeling the wind go through them. It wasn't that I wanted the body of a tree instead of my own; I wanted to think like a tree, stable, rhythmic thoughts, with no social arguments, physiological confrontatons, or psychic wars. I was someone in whom a great deal had been invested—in expectation, music lessons, dentistry. I was tired of not believing in what was hoped for me, and so I planned a summer of green peacefulness and of sifting nothing more subtle than the rain.

At first—in school. My behavior annoyed the family because they had to make excuses to the people who visited. They gave all kinds of reasons for my standing out there in the garden with my arms spread wide. I was surprised, pleasantly, by their wit and inventiveness in this regard. Mother was both scholarly and artistic: "It's some kind of dance they teach them in school . . ." My sister, Sharon, who had never been the type for pastel whimsey, rose to the occasion. "She's feeding the birds." My brother, Luke, the pragmatist, was typically succinct. "She's scaring away the birds."

But the summer leafed out and the sun cooled to green through my leaves and the leaves of the other old maples in the garden.

I held my arms up, catching the breezes under my branches, thinking. By the beginning of August the family began to accept, almost as a fact, that I was a tree. When they came into the garden they wouldn't notice that I was there. The maids, too, used to sneak out of the airless house for a few minutes of respite in the garden, and they would talk, quite freely, of their own lives and events. It was the first inkling I had ever had that the maids lived lives apart from us and the house. I had always thought that on their days out they merely ceased to exist—except for the time they spent in town talking about me. It was as a tree that I learned that living beings kept on living, joyfully even, beyond our street. Many things interested our maids; I learned how busily they planned their days off and with what vigor they recovered from them.

Grace was small, and my mother called her frivolous even without having seen her with Everett, the butler, in the garden after lunch. Louise was tall and gaunt and she separated the entire female world into "good women" and "others." Louise was a "good woman," but she was not happy being good. She plodded on through the housework seemingly without any sense of election at all. Everett, our butler, was a serious man, a rather quiet man, but he had a burning ambition to improve his station and to blot out forever the shame of having been born at Sheepshead Bay in Brooklyn. He proposed to do this by training himself into an English accent. He modeled this accent on Lord Henry Brinthrope's—he was "Our Gal Sunday's" husband on the radio soap opera; and the upshot of all of this was that Everett sounded, most of the time, like a Brooklyn tough imitating a Midwestern radio actor imitating an English earl. Worst of all, when he became excited or was out in the garden with Grace, the mantle of Lord Henry would be set askew and one saw the essential Everett.

"M'deah," he would begin with a twang that could only be Minnesota's contribution to Bedfordshire, "I was wild fer yuh since I first saaw yuh."

When I was a tree, I saw the romance in Everett; his dreams had fire and jubilation. Everett was a fine dreamer, but he was not, as I see him at this distance, too well endowed with brains or he would have realized that while Grace flirted, promised passion, and loved to hurt his feelings, Louise loved him. She would have followed him to world's end and committed suttee on his funeral pyre. Unfortunately, American men do not seem to appreciate suttee, particularly the suttee of an ugly woman, and the pretty ones do not seem particularly inclined toward it for themselves. Everett was more myopic than usual when it came to Louise's feelings for him, and he would probably have been surprised if he had heard the conversations in the garden between Louise and Grace. They would both come out for a breath of air, make a few perfunctory remarks about the weather, and then get down to business. Louise would always start by sitting down—it had a kind of finality to it—and sighing: "Oh, my."

And Grace would be all solicitude. "Oh, Louise, you shouldn't take life so serious!"

Then Louise would pour out her misery and love for Everett, and Grace would swear that there was nothing between herself and that old liar with his honeyed words. (Years later I wondered where she had gotten that phrase, honeyed words. Grace never read; she claimed that reading was bad for a person's eyes and made her squint and lose her looks. What wounded, calf-love suitor had reproached her with these words, and where had he read them? The wine of the muse passes through some pretty strange vessels, but I thought at the time that the phrase had been wrung from the poetic soul of Grace herself.)

With a show of sisterly concern for the ugly Louise, Grace would promise to help all she could. The first thing to do was to make Louise be more attractive. This generally involved some simple change in outward appearance: a different dress, a new hair style, a "newer" face cream, powder, lipstick, eyebrow pencil. Louise would seize on these changes with the naïveté of desperation. She could always be fooled, and Grace would promise to give her *the* cream or show her *the* hair style; and Louise's face would be suffused with eagerness so that it looked almost beautiful by itself. She would go in, revived, full of hope, with plans to make. Grace would stretch gorgeously, and breathe in and yawn widely, exhilarated by her youth or health or beauty or by the power in her lie. So I stood, waiting and burgeoning through the summer.

Everett came out for a breath of air one evening toward the

end of August. For several weeks I had been planning to change color in a grand, early spectacle of dying—perhaps with sound effects. I would have to be completely leafless by the time school started, and I was standing with all my leaves hung at rest in the still night, saving my strength. He came into the garden and ceased to be A Butler. He stretched and scratched and groaned, full of magnificent male vigor. Then Grace emerged from the kitchen door with the slow, silent, langorous tread of being on "her own time," free. How beautiful they were, how beautiful we were—a mature and luxurious tree; two graceful and secret panthers, sinuous female, regal male.

"Have they retar—d?" Nodding toward the otiose employers.

"Soon," she answered with a shrug of her magnificent shoulders. "Readin' and sewin'."

There was a kingly grunt of assent from Everett.

"*She's* inside curlin' her hair." A tilt of the head toward the ugly, skinny part of the house where Louise was ugly and skinny and mourning.

"Yeh," he said, smiling perhaps in the darkening garden. As the night came on I could not discern what was taking place, but there were a few giggles and sighs of contentment, and then they began discussing their plans for running away together.

Woe is me! I couldn't realize then that one day I too would be cautious and thrifty, and that woman's job in life is conserving, that I would one day say to a beloved husband going off to a shattering war: "At least take this sandwich, for the trip." It seemed to me then that Grace and Everett should have gone, just as they were, disappearing into the darkness on their softly padded paws, soundlessly, their steps in rhythm, their tails entwined and quivering with delight. But to my confusion, the main part of their discussion was concerned with how Grace would pack her clothes and *essential* cosmetics—curlers, yew de cologne, ribbons, bracelets, and notions—*and* escape on the day of wages without arousing the suspicions of the alert Louise. I was bitterly disappointed. Was this romance or merely a change of employment. I decided to un-tree, to enter into the foreground long enough to express my scorn at the way it was going. I would write a note to Louise telling her what was about to happen. The note would have to come from some wise and elderly woman who had become acquainted with the entire problem by her efforts at the ouiji board (I had begged my mother to get me one for months, promising to make the family millionaires by betting on horse races.) I would call myself Arbora. (I couldn't resist the cryptic clue, forgetting that most sensible people didn't have time for riddles.) And the note would come from a romantic and mythical place which I knew how to create by altering the letters of our town postmark. I spent the next morning preparing my counterplot.

I wrote the letter in the afternoon, using a handwriting that I had been developing for such an occasion. The elaborate and mystical language did me proud and justified my years of reading. I couldn't trust our gabby postman or Grace, if she got the mail, so I took an envelope from a letter which had been mailed to my mother, blocked out the names, changed the postmark, put in my note, and glued the envelope closed. I deposited it on Louise's pillow. The need for subtlety and mystery was at war with Louise's slight myopia, and the myopia had won.

I awoke very late that night with the sense of someone standing over me. I muttered to the blur of white nightdress that I saw hovering close to my bed, and it bent down very close with a raucous, "Shh—hh," and a white sleeve jerked in the direction of my lumped sister sleeping in the other bed. It was Louise. She bent down so low that her hair brushed against my face, and I could almost see her intense, shortsighted eyes peering hard at me.

"Are you really a tree?" she said. And still closer, "Are you really a tree?" I had been hit with my own arrow. Without making a statement to the reality-demanding world, I could be what I wished. As soon as I said definitely that I was not a tree, I would die as a tree and miss the peace, the invisibility, and the radiant and beautiful death that I had planned for myself all summer. I loved Louise because she was so ugly and had never cursed nature. I was angry at Grace and Everett with their wages and curlers—but myself—not to defend was to repudiate, and I knew it. Even then. If I gave up now, it would never come again. Children can be cowards too. I finally said, "Sometimes I am—and sometimes I only seem to be."

She turned and left the room. She had the step of someone with her mind made up. Arbora's ouiji board spirits had risen and entered the lives of those who walked, whose feeding veins branched in flesh instead of wood. Who faces any issue unless he is driven to it? I hoped that equivocation had saved me. I fell asleep hoping.

Habit holds sometimes, even after the need. That was a great comfort to learn. Because people still saw me in full leaf, as it were, I could keep on standing invisibly in the garden. I wanted to protect my family as well as myself from my hard awakening. The habit held; they saw no change; they were content, smiling and nodding automatically at my branches, which were no more. Everett and Grace discounted my presence; even Louise paid no attention to the change, still seeing me as I was before, still yawning and sighing as she came out for a little respite in the garden, as if she were alone.

Now the talk about running away together began to center around the end of the month. Maybe Grace had submitted to Everett's pleading, realizing that time was passing and that they could go henceforth as a "couple," getting better wages and pooling salaries. Romance—I was sick at heart.

And then, to the Eden of trees and placid leopards, came the king of leopards. As soon as Grace saw him I knew I had been wrong about Everett entirely. He was in the story, but he had the role of the old leopard, the one who claims the prize first and is to be challenged by the young king, strong and beautiful in his pride. This Prince-Errant was the Man to Fix the Stove. He was the true leopard of the Eden, whose Tree of Knowledge I was now pretending still to be.

As he leaned down to look at the stove, I saw the ripple of supple muscles beneath the shirt, heavy neck, great biceps pulling for freedom at his rolled sleeves. Grace saw it also; she too had her ripples and her arabesques beneath the skin. Oh, it was glorious to see them together! Everett floated out of the mind as if he had never been. After this glowing animal, a skinny arm was unforgivable.

Of course, he asked her out—one night and two nights and three—and I held out my false shade in the evening garden for the brokenhearted old leopard and the sympathetic aging leopardess. He sighed and she sympathized, and when at last he spoke, Britain had been repudiated for Brooklyn forever and there was nothing left of Lord Henry Brinthrope at all, only a wounded Everett with thin arms. He was soon praising the love-drunk Louise for her sympathy and kindness.

Woe unto you, oh, daughters of Ypsilanti! Cry aloud, ye virgins of Passaic, if a man loses his beautiful, fickle girl, cries out his anguish against your bony shoulder, and calls you a good conversationalist! For an hour or two in the dusky gardens of those nights, I almost believed that he would see under Louise's hopeless, chronic plainness the soul which held him so high; and that he would love her for it and soon, perhaps, for herself. But the summer had passed, and Eden and my tree had passed. I was too old to be fooled for long. Many are the tawny animals with gleaming pelts and midnight eyes. Since Everett was already packed for freedom, self-knowledge, and the fall of man, it wasn't long before he found a companion. By the morning after pay day he had disappeared. People in town said they had seen him with a girl. It was rumored they had gone away together. There was nothing more.

Lousie was romantic, but she was also practical, and when she saw that even with Grace disposed of, she would have no chance, she told her cousin, the decorative king leopard, whom she had imported all the way from Hackensack, New Jersey, that he could slip free into the jungle night. The hero, a leopard of so many but not one, vanished also, leaving no scent, no print in the soft earth. The thought that he must now be sixty or so makes me want to cry, not for myself but for the world which loses its lithe princes to the old age pension.

So flowered passion in Eden and so died, and Eden also, not for everyone, just for me. When my daughter begins to grow leaves or feathers or practices dying so that it won't be done clumsily, I will not think of the soft wind that once rustled the green leaves of my branches or moved to shield me from the unfairness of growing up, I will think that we'd better begin saving money for a catered wedding, that it's time to start with the orthodontist.

Grace ran away with a Coast Guardsman, and Louise, to everyone's surprise, was seen at last, myopia and all, by the new man on the milk route. They married and settled near here, where they have three children and a fleet of trucks. Edens— only Eve never really had one of her own.

FEINBERG

RETURNS

Abram Feinberg looked at his friends and partners and tried to listen to what they said, but a voice was humming in his mind and the hum drowned out the sounds of life and reality and the friends around him. The hum said: She-is-gone—She-is-gone . . . no more his looking forward to the evenings with her; no more standing at the kitchen door; no more watching her hands serving or taking, moving or still in the rooms of his house, through the years of his life. No more the little deprecating gesture she had, and then the smile. No more. No more. The hum built into a moan inside him until he could scarcely contain it.

Even in the deepest places of his sorrow he knew that it would be best for him to get away for a while from the cold house to which she had abandoned him. Time-car trips were expensive, but they were the very best of vacations, and modern technology had made them safe and comfortable. When he met his friend Isaacstein a week later and mentioned the idea, vaguely Isaacstein was delighted.

"I was foolish not to have thought of it myself," he said happily. "Edith suggested that you come with me, and why not?

Next week I am going to Jerusalem, the Jerusalem of King David when he returned from the campaign against the Philistines. Why shouldn't we share his victory together! We will dance the dances and see the faces of Jews who had no idea that there would ever be such a thing as exile! Come with me!"

"In a week . . . ?" Feinberg had asked, and wavered. He did not want to decide, although he knew he should, and that it would be good for him. "Well—there are still arrangements, and . . ."

"You think it doesn't look good, don't you, to take a vacation now? Abe, we're your friends; anyone with a grain of good sense would understand. Please." So gentle was Isaacstein's appeal, and so moving was his look, the great fat man in his suit so much too tight, the eager, heavy face and lifted hands, that Feinberg said quietly, "All right, I'll come, but not so soon. On Thursday the family is coming to take from the house—things . . ."

"Sunday, then. We will meet there!" And seeing that Feinberg said all right with his eyes, Isaacstein came close and clapped him on the shoulder.

"I will call the Time-car agency and make all the arrangements for you. Ah!" and his face was full of pleasure, "You'll see—it will help; you'll see."

"Good-bye," said Feinberg.

He stood behind a tall, raw-boned woman in a suit. She, Ruth, had always worn soft, feminine clothes. He looked at his ticket, trying not to think of her. Time-car tickets never said when or where the passenger was going, but only how long he expected to be there. The ticket said: FIVE DAYS. Five days with King David and Chaim Isaacstein. There would probably be no others with them, because in the beginning, when the Time-car first started taking passengers for vacations and everybody wanted to go to the same place at the same time, there had been a few incidents, one involving a death; and after that the tourists were only allowed two or three in a group and they were given careful instructions.

When the first molecular transformer made it possible to travel through time, the historians and specialists who had priority to go for their studies wanted to enter the past unobserved. Later adjustments in the molecular machines made it possible to transform people not only in time but in form. Thus, Geoffery Hildebrand went to Cyrenaica in the year 582, appearing there as a three-legged chair; and Humphrey Burden went to the Chicago Fire of 1871 as a ball of light energy. Hildebrand came back with a chair's account of the crisis in Cyrenaica; and Burden spoke of being whirled about, unseeing, unknowing. Both of them had much to tell the scientists about light energy and the structural stresses of wooden chairs, but for events, it was seen that people were necessary.

Invisible people were tried next. The advantage of their being unseen was negated by the disadvantage of their taking up space and acting in a tangible way. They thus accounted for at least two miracles in 1313 A.D. At last the psychologists took up the problem. The true safety, they decided, was in being, and yet not being. They did studies of what came to be known as the Background Man. There are people so inconspicuous that nobody misses them when they go, or notices them when they come. Their names are forgotten. They are the ideal men to be sent on visits into the past without rattling any of the chains which hold reality to its groove in time. From these anonymous ones the psychologists learned how to make time tourism possible for the many. Finally, with the invention of the equifier, men could go anywhere in any capacity. Built and placed like a hearing aid, the equifier translated immediately and with full cultural significance any and all speech important to the traveler, who needed only to verbalize his own responses in his mind and have that speech translated into the local language and broadcast through his own speech centers and out of his mouth.

The woman in the suit stepped forward to the admissions table and presented her ticket.

"Where is this timed to?" the travel agent asked.

"Rome, of course," she said. "Court of Nero twelve days before the fire. Everybody's going."

"Certainly." He wrote out a little coded ticket on a machine that he had in front of him. She handed him some currency which he counted out. "Thank you. Right through those doors." He gave her a stub of the coded ticket. "And you, sir?" He looked up at Feinberg. "Sir?!"

Feinberg had been lost in a formless flowing dream, and at the sound of the clerk's voice, returned from it. "Yes? Oh . . ."

"Where are you timed to, sir?"

"What? Oh, to Jerusalem, to the victory celebration."

"Israeli?"

"No, King David."

"Oh, yes," the clerk said. "Weren't you the man who was going to meet a friend? Wait a moment, I will get his stub."

A tall, thin man had come up quickly behind Feinberg and pushed him aside. "I am Lionel Simmons," he said. "30 A.D.," he said. "Crucifixion."

"You will have to wait your turn," the clerk said.

The man showed his green priority card. "Let me through."

"Sir," the clerk said, "you may have priority, but this passage is uncompleted. Please, pardon me a moment." The thin man muttered and threw his priority card on the desk, and Feinberg wondered why he was doing this at all, why he cared for going anywhere except to be where Ruth was. They knew, these Time Travel people, that the world was full of yearning Feinbergs. No one could meet his generation or the previous two.

The clerk came back and handed Feinberg a coded stub and motioned him through the doors. He heard the thin man behind him beginning his arrangements.

"Right here, sir, in this car," the attendant said. "Will you give me your stub, please. Very well. Here are your instructions." And he handed Feinberg a printed sheet. "Your stub will be run through the calculating machine and your clothes and money will be transmuted into the appropriate ones. Here is your equifier." He helped Feinberg to put it on.

It was strange and uncomfortable, another hum in the mind. The attendant helped him into the car. It looked like some of the ancient carriages that used to be pulled by horses. The doors were closed and the machine darkened. Feinberg waited a long time for it to start. He felt nothing at all. He glanced at the written page, but the material seemed dull and meaningless and his mind soon wandered. The car became somewhat stuffy. He dozed. When he woke, he was still in the car, still motionless, but now the lights were on. He read a notice that was lit up on the wall of the car:

> You will return to this vehicle every 24 hours and
> will press the button marked LD and then the button

marked PBJ and then the button marked S.
In case of danger, illness, or unforseen circumstances, press button marked G and then button
marked PP.

There was a row of buttons underneath. Feinberg thought
vaguely about suing.

He opened the door.

The light was brilliant. Heat waves watered up from the
dusty road. He got out and it was not here; it was there. He
found that he was smiling.

The car sat inconspicuously in a little glade off the road, and
one had to be looking for it to see it at all. The road was not
well-traveled at any rate, and no one was now on it.

"I wonder where Isaacstein is," he thought, and opening his
mouth he began to say, "I wonder where . . ." It came out
something else, something only faintly familiar. It was Hebrew,
ancient Hebrew as a man of his station would speak it. He
looked down at his clothes. Not bad; rough and tied oddly, and
pinching and bunching in unexpected places, but rather pleasantly novel. They were, he guessed, the clothes of a man of
reasonable means. He got out of the car and made for the road,
walking south.

For a while he avoided people and hesitated to acknowledge
their nods, but then, shyly, cautiously, he attempted a question
or two. Stopping a farmer on the road, he asked, "What is this
road? I have left the main way."

"Why, this is a by-road to the city, to Jerusalem."

"Is there a festival in the offing?"

The man gave a snort. "Times are hard for festivals now,
unless for some heathenish thing."

"Heathenish?" And Feinberg began hurriedly to flip the pages
of his mind's eye's Bible.

"Mind, you know they do not forbid our solemnities, but
throttling taxes do better than decrees. No money for wine or
cake, and no appetite for revel, and where is your celebration?"
The farmer shrugged.

A hint of something not right began to dawn on Feinberg
as he stood, somewhere, somewhen, he knew not when, in his
strange garments. He needed to make sure. He pressed on
toward the city.

Perhaps, he thought, he should go back to the car, press the emergency buttons, and be taken back; but now that he was getting used to these clothes, equifier, a being not quite himself, he began to be exhilarated with the idea of an adventure. He was free of care, in a sense, of an identity that was agonizing to him. There was no one to meet, nothing to be responsible for. He thought, I will let my feet take me. The road broadened and became more crowded; but now, since he had the safety of his inconspicuousness and the protection of his equifier, he did not mind being jostled by these strange-looking people. Beggars began to line the road, making pitiful charades of infirmity and disease. Feinberg went over and threw one of them a coin. He was amazed at the imperious way in which he did this, but realized then that his thoughts, read by the equifier, had been translated into words of a cultural value and had been acted upon in that way. And then he saw the city.

He could have wept. It was ancient, the color of man, the color of time. He remembered: "If I forget thee, oh, Jerusalem," and the equifier translated into the indescribably lovely words of the lost language. He stood on the crest of the hill while the others passed him by. He filled his senses with her. "Oh, Jerusalem, if I do not number thee above my chief joy . . ."

He heard a sound behind him. Horses. He moved aside almost automatically and they came thundering past. Soldiers. Pictures in a textbook of a sun-filled childhood. Roman soldiers with their pomp and their plumes—and there was no mistaking now, he was near the Jerusalem of a Roman occupation. Full of wonder he walked down into the city.

Noise, smell. . . . Feinberg, from his world of toilets and sound-proofing, where excrement and excess were dealt with and put away quickly, could scarcely believe his senses. He thought he would faint. He felt ill of the stench, the push, the heat. The narrow street twisted in and out. He turned off it a few times into other alleys and lanes, and at last he came to a square. It was cleaner and more spacious than the streets, so that he was tempted not to leave it. There was a crowd at one corner of the square. When he was somewhat over his dizziness and nausea he moved closer.

"We're in the wrong place; we'll miss it all!" one large man said to his companion.

"The side door can be more informative than the front," said the other man.

From around the corner Feinberg heard a muffled roar. It was a crowd of some kind, but he could not tell whether it was a gay one or violent. He edged closer.

"What is taking place here?" he asked a man next to him.

The man was dressed in a leather shirt. "Oh, we've been waiting to see the heretic. It's fifty-fifty he'll be saved. I say Pilate won't concern himself with this. It's a religious matter, and the heretic has friends here and there. If anybody wants to, a few pieces in the hand would work wonders."

"Do you think they will come out this side door?" Feinberg asked.

"Yes, that bunch of goats out front is blocking the way."

Another roar went up.

"Where will he be after this?"

"Depends if he's innocent or guilty, that is, if Pilate decides to let him go or not. Like I say, it's fifty-fifty, but heretics— they're tricky business. This one, he says he's the son of God. Name is Jesus. Says he's Jesus Christ."

"Oh . . ." And Feinberg, sick again, sick to death with horror and grief, paled and looked about for a place against which to lean until he could restore his own past present. He decided that when his dizziness eased, he would go back to the car and return to his own time. The man in the leather shirt noticed the look of sickness on his face.

"Makes you stop and think, all right. Man saying he's the Messiah. Still . . ."

"Yes, I know," panted Feinberg, "the miracles."

"It puts me a little scared to think of them. Raising the dead. It scares me. If he can raise the dead like some say, can he dress and eat like me?"

A third roar went up from the crowd, and by now Feinberg did not need to be told by the equifier what they were doing. He had a mad impulse to run to them, to say something, anything that would make them stop. At that moment the door opened and a soldier leaned out.

"Get away from here. We've got to have a clear road!"

Another soldier pushed through, and then a simply dressed man came cautiously from behind the door. When he saw that it was a small crowd he relaxed visibly and did not seem to mind the jeers. He was followed by a great brawny one who was obviously enjoying the whole affair. He was going to make his day remembered. As he came out of the door he made a move as if to break away, and as he did so, he gave a low growl, like a dog. The crowd scattered, so many brown and brittle leaves before a wind. Then they saw that he was chained and was amusing them, and they recovered themselves, laughing, and turned the jeers friendly and the insults to a certain gaiety.

Following this great bear came the heretic. The difference was so striking that the crowd pressed forward, laughing with all their bellies and shoulders at it. He was pale and had a look of hunger. A beard, struggling for a hold on his face, won only the jutting cliff of his chin. The crowd knew that he would be no fun for them. Floggings, which would make the second man wild, would only deepen his resignation. As Feinberg looked at him, the thought he detected—in spite of the now bent shoulders, the dirty, ill-fitting undercoat and the resignation—a wiry strength. He laughed at himself. Two thousand years later, who isn't a prophet?

The soldier who brought up the rear followed, and the crowd closed around.

"Where are they going?" Feinberg asked the fellow in the leather shirt.

"Praetorium. (And a spit into the dust.) The soldiers have to strip them and give them their number and get them ready. You look like someone from a pretty big town. Here we make 'em carry the crossbar of their own posts. It saves confusion."

"Oh," Feinberg said.

The interior of the palace was dark and cool, a relief from the noise, stench, and glare of the outside, and, most of all, from the overwhelming sense of too many people. Strange, thought Feinberg, that in our world of time there are so many more people, yet so much less press. Soldiers, seeing the prosperous cut of his garment, let him through. As he walked to the anteroom where a few others waited with their needs and desires, plots, pleas, and rumors, the petty politics of this ancient day that here at least was so much like his own, he began to be frightened for the first time in many years. The instructions he had gotten from the Time-Car agency were all very specific on one point: We will equip you, clothe you, and translate for you in such a way as to make you as inconspicuous as possible. You, in turn, must do your part. You must not ask direct questions, and certainly have as few direct requests as possible. Ideally, you should make yourself one of a group. Wait until someone else suggests or asks. You should recognize the natural leaders, the aggressive, outgoing people. Move with one of them. He, being more self-assertive, will be more interested in himself and will tend not to remember you. He will also be more noticed, so that even with such a man, you must manage to stay on the fringes. . . .

Here he was now, and there were no rules covering what he proposed to do. That he would be barred from any future Time-car trip did not concern him. What did frighten him was that he had cut the reasonable bonds of carefulness and prudence imposed on him by men of his own time. Methodically, he was separating himself from his century. It occurred to him that few people any more visited the times in history where great decisions were made and great crises passed. Of course, these things went by fashion, partly. It was the East one year and 1415 the next, but people didn't go to Pompeii 79 any more or to the Siege of Salamis or to Pearl Harbor, 1941, or, indeed, to the Crucifixion. Feinberg, to his sorrow, to his great sorrow, now knew why. In the defeats of the things one held dear, there was the agony of reliving, like a nightmare, an act that rolled inevitably toward its awful end in loss, in death, in defeat. As for the victories, one often saw at what secret price, never counted by the historians, those victories were won. The heroes of one's childhood became, seen in reality, time-bound sharers in humanity: ugly, brutal, even dull, and, oh, alas for the heroines! An ardent admirer, seeking the Trojan Helen came back weeping tears of regret; and the first Catholic who had gone, reverently, lovingly, into the great Aquinas' study beheld there, to his horror, a man who used neither a fork nor a handkerchief. In history it makes no matter how long Erasmus wore an undershirt, but those who sit with him in Time say that it does.

"And here I am," thought Feinberg, "and what will I say to this man who cannot know that in five-hundred years his name will be a curse on everyone's lips and a word of approbrium, the very name for traitor. . . ."

A secretary approached. "Name and business," he said.

"I am Abraham ben Solomon," Feinberg said, aided by the equifier, "and I come today on an urgent matter of policy whose exact nature I am not at liberty to divulge to you on this occasion." Listening to himself say the words Feinberg thought: So, officialese is officialese, Praetorium or Pentagon.

The secretary was obviously impressed by this, which made Feinberg sure that the man would rise no higher in the government service, though for this insight he did not need an equifier. In a moment the secretary returned and was guiding Feinberg into the room of the Governor.

Of the two, if anyone had asked Feinberg: "Which man could be the Prophet?" Feinberg, from the dental and hygiene-minded twenty-first century, would have chosen Pilate. He was muscular and clean-looking and his teeth were straight and white; his carriage was one of dignity and manliness.

A whisper from the equifier, and Feinberg made his obeisances, going according to custom. In that manner he began to make his point indirectly. Since Pilate expected this, he waited, answering the trivial questions with pleasant good humor. But the pressure of time, the terrible pressure of the Cross hurried Feinberg along faster and faster until he stopped in mid-sentence and looked directly at Pilate. (Never look directly into the eyes of anyone, his travel instructions had told him.)

"Your Excellency, the Crucifixion of the heretic must be stopped."

"My dear man, if you had heard me speak outside, you would have known that I asked three times that the people suppress him themselves, and they would not. I had no choice but to sentence him. The man is an enemy of the state!"

"Your Excellency, I cannot appeal to you on logical grounds. You have done what you could, but—let me say this: I have traveled very widely over," and here Feinberg smiled slightly, "many years. I am sure you know, in all honesty, that Rome is sick with many sicknesses. One of these sicknesses is this very land over which you are now Governor. Daily, cults rise and fall, seeing answers to man's despair at God's rejection and at Rome. Some preach peace and some war. I must warn you against persecuting this particular sect. They preach humility, but they proudly assure themselves of heaven. They preach patience, but they are convinced of the imminent end of the world. They preach resignation, but they are full of the energy of the eagerly doomed in life. Dying for the Jews, this man is a heretic; dying for his own followers, he will die a symbol, martyr, and, fantastic as it sounds, his very accoutrements of death—his cross, nails, crown of thorns—will become the symbols of his new religion. That religion will call you heathens, will call you his murderers."

"Everything is possible," Pilate said urbanely. "Where were his disciples this morning? Why was no voice raised to save him?"

"Exactly, Excellency. The disciples will come now. Disciples will be made by his death." It sounded absurd even to Feinberg, the backward-seeing wiseman.

Pilate merely said, "Ridiculous! Even you Orientals are not so degenerate that you would worship ugliness, disfigurement, and death—not when Rome's reasonable rule is offered in its place."

"I have not the knowledge nor the wit to convince you. I have only my plea. I beg you to substitute imprisonment instead. This man may demand sacrifice. He knows the value of sacrifice. Your Excellency, you are not a Jew. You do not have the idea of atonement, but he does, and his people do. I beg of you . . ."

"To you it may seem simple, but only a fool acts so as to compromise his authority."

"If I can convince the council of Rabbis to guarantee his suppression?"

"If you can do that, I will take the matter under advisement."

"Will you stop the Crucifixion? There is so little time!"

"I said, I will take the matter under advisement! Farewell!" The Governor turned to his table and his other business.

Feinberg made obeisance to the top of Pilate's head and left.

As he stepped into the sunlight of the square, his mind was lumbering against possibilities, like a large, frightened animal in the dark. If the Rabbis would grant some sort of stay, he could get the elements of dissension working to bog down a decision, to forestall. Feinberg knew enough of the bureaucracy of his own day to wish that he could deal directly with the head of each official faction, if he only had the time! Ideally, the

way to work would be to learn where each man's passion, pres-
tige, and principle lay; to get to each one, and work toward
where his private desire joined a public reason to lean away from
punishment of the stripped and threatening heretic.

But there was no time. There was only time for pleading with
anyone who might be in a position to stop the oncoming of a
thousand years in this small hour. The Rabbi's council was still
in the Temple, but it was the end of their day of judging and
they were beginning to rise from their seats for the rites of
dismissal. Sabbath preparations had to be made.

Feinberg entered the sanctuary with all of the piety and love
of which his soul was capable. This Lilly of Jerusalem, this
Heart of his people—did they even guess how soon it would be
trampled, would stop beating? How many Jews would wander
the earth, and only after . . . He put the thought out of his mind
and tried to fill his eyes instead with the ancient glory that
would never again return. It was not all as the older Bible had
pictured it, not all that the Rabbis of his own day had pictured
it; but enough was here to set the soul singing inside the body,
to put tears in the eyes and a tremble in the mind. Again the
psalms of reverence and praise came to him and he whispered them in the forgotten tongue. Then he made his way to
the room where the judgments were given and the laws dis-
puted.

The Rabbis looked up as they stood or sat at ease, readying
themselves to close their proceedings and return to their homes.
Seeing the cut of his garment, they veiled their impatience and
greeted him respectfully. Abram Feinberg made obeisance to
his ancestors, his countrymen in soul if not in location, his past.
His love of his tradition made him painfully wish to do everything right, and he wanted them to believe him, but his eagerness made him stumble. It was so important and he knew that
they could not see. After a few of the civilities which he had
known were to be given even in his own Best of All Possible
Times, he found himself at a loss.

"Honored Elders and Priests," he began, "I have come to
you from afar on a matter of extreme urgency and import. I
must state my business quickly, the more quickly to have it
happily resolved."

Their silence was favorable, inviting. He thanked his equifier
from the bottom of his heart, if one can thank a brain which is

no brain but only the indirect mechanical contrivance of a thousand gathered brains.

"I refer," he continued, "to the disposition of the affair of one Jesus of Nazareth, heretic."

Immediately the looks changed.

"I know that he is, by your lights, a blasphemer and heretic. I am not here to argue the justice of the case, which I presume you have pondered more deeply than I. I am here to give you a practical argument against your approval of his crucifixion. Give him any fate you wish: exile, prison, any punishment short of death!"

The faces looked at him questioningly, in anger, in apprehension. "We have only judged. We have no desire to see him killed. We have only judged that he is a heretic. Why should we change our opinion for you or in that matter, for him? You are a stranger and he is a heretic and gets only the death accorded by Rome for enemies of its state."

"I do not presume to be his judge," said Feinberg, "I want only to save him out of a terrible selfishness. I am . . . much traveled, but surely you see it too, that Rome's troubles are ours also, that as she falls we will break bones. . . ."

Their faces were so hard and blank that he burst from his legal and rational and sane desire to deal with them on their own terms and in their own history.

"This man's cult will grow and spread beneath the horrible sun of persecution, and we, good Elders, will be called his murderers. For the two thousand years of which I am sure, our people will die horrible deaths in his name. Agonies undreamed of in this time will be our portion, and places beyond the rims of this world will be the scenes of our martyrdom for his sake. Of heresy he may be guilty, but of this he is not guilty, and it must not come to pass. Let your names not be remembered with sorrow by Jews dying a thousand years from now. If only I could show you," he said to the closed faces, "show you our dying, by fire, by sword, by rocks, by boiling water, by steel bits called bullets, and by bigger bits called bombs, die abjuring our faith and die confirming it and die by millions unless you save this one man now! Guarantee his suppression to save his life!"

In the buzz-drone silence he stood, listening to the flies and men breathing, the sudden wrench of bereavement for Ruth took him. Ruth lay in the earth with her generation, a host not to be numbered if a man counted day and night for all of his lifetime, a host whose grandfathers had numbers on their arms and their teeth mined for gold. He began to strain to see his picture in all of its horror, as if by this vision they might see it also. He looked at their faces. They had seen nothing. He had lost.

The second man looked at Feinberg's clothes again as if reassuring himself that it was not a waste of time to speak to him. He said quietly, "Have you any proof of your prophesy?"

"I have no proof, no orders written, no credentials. The proof of my words will come when your children's children and theirs and theirs are in the earth together, and before my children have been born."

Another looked up at him. "How do you know that it is this man's influence which will bring these things to pass? Every day heretics and blasphemers cry. Not only do they win converts to many causes which are mad, but their words, deriving from our own holy books debase those books to the unknowing. Now, more than any other time, we have need of unity, and the dissension of these heretics will destroy us if we do not act. He is, at any rate, the state's criminal, not ours.

"What if this man were truly a great teacher, what then? Surely many of his words are wise. He speaks of love and forgiveness. Would you want it said of you that another Isaiah was brought to the world only to be killed by his own?" Feinberg knew that here, as everywhere, there were secular men sitting, atheists, perhaps, whose view of their calling was expedient and political. He had spoken to them first and perhaps had lost his case thereby, for among the believers who believed as more than an occupation a murmur of anger rose.

"Who dares refer to himself as a messiah, let him raise the yoke from the necks of his people."

Feinberg faced the man who had jumped erect and cried out with the full passion of his faith. He had risen wildly, but the rest followed in their dignity and allowed him to lead them from the room. On the way an older man touched his sleeve.

"The issue of piety or heresy changes with each man's belief," he said. "Who knows, after all, but God? To make eternity takes eternity. You know why this is, don't you, this inaction? We cannot afford to lose that single crumb of authority that falls to us from Pilate's tables. If we do not obey our own tests and laws we lose the respect of our people; if we do not take authority we lose all authority. He dies by Rome; we cannot plead for him. There is no other way." He patted Feinberg's arm like a friend, and left the room.

He was getting very tired and he hesitated to go out again into that murderous sunlight to which he was so unused. Resting in the cool portico, he faced the innermost sacred place where the priests had gone. "If only you could see what I have seen."

"What if I could see it?" a voice said beside him. It was one of the elders who had been sitting most quietly and whose eyes had shown for a moment a flicker of belief. Feinberg turned toward him gratefully to begin to speak again, but the man cut him off. "It's of no matter, but I believe that your vision may be true. It is possible that you do bear between your two eyes the history of our people, but even believing what you say, I do not agree with your actions. All that I hear from you is what I have always heard: that we endure. New weapons are forged against us, but we endure; new agonies and new lands, but yet we endure. As persecution, you say, will exalt this new prophet, I believe so will it do to us until we are our own masters. As far as your vision can see, do we reach that far?"

"Yes," said Feinberg, weeping because this day was breaking his hope as it turned.

"And you speak of years in thousands?"

"Yes."

"I had not expected so much," he said, smiling a little. "I had arbors that I had thought to abandon this year because I had felt a kind of tremor in the motion of things. Because of what you have seen, I will prune them and gather up the bracken that has fallen around them."

The light caught him again about the head and he was dizzy and had to wait until he could see clearly and not stumble. Where was there to go now? Jesus' time of mockery at the Praetorium would be over by this time; the soldiers would have stripped him and done their indignities. He would be somewhere on the final road.

Feinberg asked a man who was sitting by the side of his house, "Which way is the way to Golgotha?"

The man pointed with the knife he had been using to pare his nails.

"Back away, it is," he said. "After the first turn though, you'll see it."

Feinberg walked on rapidly until he came to the crowd. Up the hill he could see the images of history. Jesus had already fallen, and the big farmer, whom the Bible would call Simon, was hefting his crosspiece upon his shoulder. Feinberg ran up the hill until he was at the edges of the crowd and alongside the guards. Softly, as he followed the closing of the spectacle, he pleaded with them, begging them to stop. He offered money and jewels, but they paid no attention to him. Sometimes it happened that a wealthy man might go mad and do such things, and so they did not handle him roughly but permitted him to run along beside them like a child, and they jested and bantered with him as one does with a child.

At the top of the hill they stopped, and the crowd—it was smaller than he had come to envision it—disposed itself for the view. The soldiers readied their scaffoldings and the condemned lay upon their beams. Because of his age, his rank and his madness, they let Feinberg go near the soldier with his hammer. He moved close to his pale ancestor.

"Please," he said, "for the sake of generations dying in no less pain than yours, for the sake of all the evils and horrors which will be done in your name, recant what you have said!"

In the noise of the hammers and cries of the tormented, he was not heard.

"If you must die, only do not let your dying make you a god. There are those who will say that you are sanctified and mankind's salvation by viture of this death!"

The man had not heard him; he was attempting to pray.

"You are not finished praying!" Feinberg shouted at him over the hammers and the stir of people. "What you will yet say and what you have said will move men to kill and hate one another for generations undreamed of by you, and the worst part of it will be that it will not be your words which will symbolize your life and your glory but your death. Even your way of death will be re-enacted as a holy thing, and more holy than what you said or taught. They will call you the Christ and themselves Christians and the Jews will be heretics to them."

The crowd closed in and bore him away. He swam against them desperately trying to be heard. "Ages hence your name will be a battleground. Men will wrangle from childhood to dotage over the interpretation of your single word. All your wisdoms will be only passwords to this or that portion of the battleground. If you love your mission, your hopes, your God, you will not let your teachings be covered by this cross!"

He pushed closer again. People stood back to enjoy him.

"Your true sons will be only a few, crying, crying in the wilderness!"

A man standing near said an obscene thing.

"The symbol of your teaching will be a cross! People will venerate this wood and use bits of it instead of goodness to exalt their lives. People will suffer on it to be like you!"

Jesus took a breath; turned his head away.

"No! no!" Feinberg shouted at last, "you have no right to remain innocent of what you are beginning!"

The soldiers had finished their work at the uprights. The other two offenders had already submitted themselves.

As the soldiers stepped foreward to raise the third, Feinberg threw himself at their leader. "Take me!" he cried, "take me instead! He must not die!"

Deftly and not too roughly, the Captain loosened himself from the madman's grip and let him fall to the ground. The madman was crying and sobbing, "My people! My people!"

The captain left him and attended to the raising of the man. The small knot of onlookers left Feinberg as he lay face down in the dirt and moved closer to the crosses on which the three were now raised. The jeering started. Weakly, Feinberg looked up. Above him stood a tall, powerful man, dressed exactly as he was himself, even to the pattern of the hem of his robe.

"Get up," the man said. He spoke English, the English that Feinberg had left in the Time-car.

Feinberg rose shakily. He turned to look at the crosses, but the other man blocked his view.

"Come along!" the man said curtly. Feinberg could scarcely walk. "The car is right over here. You will take it immediately and I will go for yours. I don't know if the agency will bring suit against you, but I can assure you that you will not be permitted to do this again!

The man guided Feinberg behind a large rock on the hill where the car waited. They got in, the man pushed the buttons, and left the car, closing the doors. In a moment everything dimmed again. When Feinberg woke, after the same period of somnolence, and emerged from the car he was back in the Time-car station and an attendant was helping him out. The attendant was apologetic.

"I'm sorry, Mr. Feinberg, we had to send Mr. Barbella after you, but we got the destinations mixed. Poor Dr. Simmons here nearly went to ancient Jerusalem!" He explained how these errors happen sometimes, don't they, and how the agency was not responsible for unforseen mishaps, especially when the contractee did not follow instructions. . . . "Now we do wish to fulfill our contract. We will send you on your way as if nothing had happened. . . ."

And before the astonished Feinberg could utter a word, the door of the Time-car had closed again and the darkness was returning. When the light came again and Feinberg opened the door, he looked at once into the welcoming face of Chaim Isaacstein.

As Isaacstein saw the expression on his friend's face, his smile faded, and a mixture of love and concern took its place on the large features. "Abe, what's the matter? You look like a golem!"

Feinberg stumbled from the Time-car and threw his arms about his friend's shoulders, and burst into tears.

THE
LENGTH

People used to tell me how dangerous it was to be hated by Lillian Felden; she was cruel and clever. Her life had been hard and it had hardened her, as nature hardens its wild animals; they have no guilt that they are pitiless. I don't know why she hated me, but it was obvious from the first time we met, and over the years there was no lessening of it, only a quieting, a deepening, as it submerged to sleep between her life and mine. Lillian hated with fidelity, but apparently she didn't love to the same depth. There were few friends to mourn her when she died. I suppose this was why her possessions had to be left to people who were only slight acquaintances. Surely I didn't expect to be remembered in her will, and that was why I was so surprised that she left me a treasured family heirloom. I was already married, and a mother, yet the will specified that I was to have as remembrance of her "the entire length of white bridal silk." I knew it was generations old. It was a treasure. Why to me? She had always hated me.

"She couldn't really have been such an enemy then, could she?" my husband said. "Maybe she was a little ashamed after all. . . ."

We were sitting at our slightly creaky table, wondering if I

should accept this benefice. It had been a bad year for us, but
no worse than some—Lewis' accident, his mother's funeral, my
broken toe, and the boys' sicknesses—we had the righteous,
slightly self-righteous pride of feeling that we deserved what
cost us nothing.

The will said that bequests were to be given from Lillian's
home. I hated to go there in dowdy clothes, as if I were begging
her executors for what she had left. I decided to wear my very
best dress and to have my hair done, so that I might look like
someone who didn't *need* an inheritance. As I left the apartment to begin my exciting day, I noticed that the paint had
peeled away from the window frame in the living room and a
tiny leak under the sash had left a single trail, like a tear streak,
to the floor. The landlord was always putting off the repairs we
needed. Perhaps we could sell the silk and do at last, at long
last, some of the things that had to be done.

I suppose I felt a little guilty, bringing the box home like a
prize for having outlived her. I tried to think that I might have
misjudged Lillian, but the memory of too many hurts still left a
bitter aura in my mind. When I got home I went into the
bedroom immediately and laid the box on the bed. The baseball
game in the street had degenerated into a screaming brawl. I
went and closed the rattling window against the din. Then I
went back to the box and opened it.

The white length of silk lay in its fold upon fold as if it had
floated there. It was soft, as closely woven as if it were living
stuff, and its iridescent sheen made it more beautiful than any
material I had ever seen.

Lewis came home tired and hot that evening. The kids were
filthy from playing in the street. Chris had gotten a nosebleed
and wiped the blood all over his shirt. Somehow it bothered me
more than usual, the sleaziness of everything. Our rooms were
worn and dingy, our clothes gray and shabby, our manners
were careless. We didn't take any pride in ourselves. Lewis
changed into his "lounging" things and sat sprawled out with
the paper after supper, and for the first time I noticed how
unkempt he looked. I wanted to tell him, and the world, I
suppose, the way we had planned to live. It was not what our
dreams were like or the people we were in our own minds. The
kids began to argue. Had I let their language and manners get
so coarse? I stopped them, but I knew that coarseness was what

they were used to. Inside, in a box in the bedroom was my judge, and a part of the soft, strong texture of my dreams. Somewhere, even in this city, women wore clothes cut from such lengths of silk, folded themselves in silences and fragrant scents, were delicate and treasured. Such people walked about, but their shoes were never muddied with the world. I loved my family; we were healthy and happy with our lives together; and I knew that I did not really want a *life* of dancing. Anyway, gentility and silence would be butchered on this street. We had to be unsheltered in order to toughen, to endure. Reality would shame me for self-pity.

The year that Lewis was out of work, the time that Robbie fell and the doctors thought there would be brain damage— how I prayed then to be as I was now. But something had made me see that we were poor, that I was getting old; and when I went to put away my treasure, I could not bear to let the children see it and mark their dirty fingers on it. I thought with a strange new kind of sorrow that there was no place I could put the tissue-wrapped piece of silk where it would belong. It lay like a beautiful stranger among the familiar, dingy winter storage of the closet.

When we had first moved here it was only temporary, and I'd had a thousand ideas about fixing things up. Now, after all this time, I saw how I had let things slide. I began to struggle again for the old picture I had of myself, which I seemed to have put away for storage also, only waiting to get old enough so that I could throw it out at last without apology. I cleaned and painted and waxed and buffed. I punished the kids for their dirt and noise and threw away Lewis' comfortable rags in the incinerator. I had my hair fixed and went on a diet and did my nails, but the more I did, the more it all seemed a kind of makeshift carnival of action and not real at all. My dime-store redecoration was as sleazy as a circus-owner's dream of kings and queens, as a whore's vision of respectability, and I suddenly realized one rainy day in the middle of a sigh, bending to scrub the seamed, uneven floor, that Lillian Felden in her grave was still my enemy.

She had seen me in love, unconscious of poverty, laughing. She had seen me proud and joyful with my husband, fighting sickness, job layoffs, all of it—and she had hated me. To destroy with bullets is murder, with words slander, with silk—

charity. What would I do with her treasured length? Redecorate and make everything else we possessed look even shabbier? Fashion a ballgown for an affair to which I would never go? She knew we had no daughters to dream about graduation dresses or their weddings. I went to the closet and looked at the box which held the marvelous cloth. Let her hate me. I would have my life and the silk also. I would outwit her by being joyful in my inheritance. I looked at the hot walls of the room on which the paint was cracked and blistered, and I tried to find beyond their outer surfaces to the fact of our family love, of the honor in our house. For an instant, the life of the silk gleamed a bit less brightly than the life of word, bread, and love.

The weeks went slowly by, and my battle with the silken length tightened and loosened the way a strong fish is pulled and loosened on the line that torments him. Sometimes I would look up from a magazine that pictured the Spacious Country Home of Mrs. Desire or Mrs. Dream, with her Immaculate Dream Children; and the surroundings of my life would make me shiver with despair. Sometimes a boy's momentary gentleness would strengthen me, until I turned inside myself again to realize that my sons would never learn to know what quality was, here in this wilderness of beauty. The battles continued into the night, weakening me in sleep with dreams of flowing silk dresses and a renewing youth in which I danced with shining hair, shimmering in white silk through the dark June nights. On wakening, the walls would hang about me with their crusted paint like a death cell.

I finally lost my temper—I don't remember why, now, but knowing how life builds its deceits by accretion, I suspect that it was something like a shoe squeaking on the floor or a towel damp against the face from someone else's using or the spot on a bedspread. Whatever it was, it was suddenly too much; I was no longer irritated, I was despairing. I rushed to the closet and hurled the box off the shelf. It flew open. That enraged me. I grabbed the long, white, rustling length of silk and ran from the room out the door and down the hall and to the incinerator. At the blackened door I cursed, pulled it open so hard it shuddered. Then I shoved the soft handfuls of the silk down into its burn-smelling maw. As it fell into the blackness it scraped against the sides of the door where the daily garbage of a dozen families had smeared, stained, and slid away. When it left my hands it was already smirched with coffee grounds and soot. Ugly. Anger was still feeding on that silk. I shouted after it, banging the heavy door shut, and beat my fists against it; and suddenly a distant thought came through the curtain of anger like a small light. Now it's gone, now all the beauty is gone. . . .

I went back to the apartment and closed the door, and I said to the four ugly walls, "That's that!"

That was the way she won, Lillian Felden, my clever enemy. She gave me a length of silk and for days I smelled its delicate little scent in the box that held it. She gave me a symbol, imperishable and conquering. I had never been aware of the beauty I could never have, the cool, fragile silence that would never surround me. My love for Lewis and the boys is suddenly blurred and bitter. I am unfaithful to them, in this feeling of poverty and loss. The rain is falling dully outside our room, and it is cold and sour-looking inside. I can see Lewis lying in our bed and I cannot help thinking that he looks as if he belonged here, tousled and old and dull. The window is rattling, and there is a fine trail of water building on the floor beneath it where the sash fits too loosely. My mind goes to its picture—a haunting, secret, voluptuous picture that cuckolds Lewis in so much more than his sex. . . .

The rain is falling outside, but the deep carpet makes the room seem safe and protected. It is warm and there is a black vase with roses, whose scent is cool and delicate in the darkened room. A light breeze comes into the room, but no rain is with it. It comes silently, freshening, billowing gently the long, white standing folds of the silk curtains. There is a brushing-by of the folds as they are blown before one another, a sound delicate, gentle, and comforting—and the voice of the silk is like the voice of the rain. . . .

SURVIVOR

"Mr. Levy, the heart is the center of a man. If the heart is sick—if the heart is hurt, the man, he is not any longer a man."

Tell him it's nonsense, Harry thought, but he won't believe it. Candido's politeness is like his coat; it has holes in it and the simple truth shows through. This *mala del corazon* is a gringo disease to him, a thing of the gringos of cities.

"There's a man, Vasquez," the voice went on, "from Los Pinos, where we came from, an' I asked him, an' Mr. Levy, he don't remember ever, all the sicknesses he heard of, there wasn't anybody down there that got this thing."

A gringo disease. Tell him it doesn't destroy him as a man, but he won't believe it, Harry thought. Then there's the one about how his people are statistically free of this disease, but he would never stand for being "statistical," and he would punch me in the mouth for saying he was illegitimate, not of his people. Harry sighed and gave Candido congratulations on finishing his training. "I'll start looking for some good job leads."

After Candido left, Harry got out the telephone book and started looking up numbers. Candido was a good man. He had been Harry's client for about a year and a half, since the heart attack. He had come to the rehabilitation agency where Harry worked after the doctor told him that he wouldn't be able to work as a roofer any more. Harry had tried to calm the man's terror at finding no future ahead of him and no present as a whole being, a whole man. He had tested Candido when he could, and found amazing dexterity and a good eye. Also, miracle of miracles for an Indio County Mexican, his client had a high-school diploma. They had agreed on watch repair and had gotten to know one another in many sessions during the two-year course. Now he was ready for a job.

Harry called about four places and got some interest, but number five looked like the one they wanted. He told the woman who answered who he was and why he was calling, and got about two sentences into Candido's talents when she stopped him.

"The state? What's wrong?"

He looked down at the name again. Castle's jewelry store. She must be the wife of the owner, and she was afraid of a "state" call because state means government and government means trouble. She had a thick accent and spoke breathlessly and quickly, as if she were afraid of being struck mute tomorrow.

"There's nothing wrong with our taxes; the store is inspected always. . . ." And she muttered something in Yiddish, so he spoke in his crude, Americanized street-Yiddish to calm her. "Don't turn yourself, don't toil yourself; it's no dark matter. . . ." There was a sigh of relief from the other end of the line, and then he went on in English to explain Candido's training in watch repair, explaining briefly, as the state required, the gringo heart.

"My husband was looking for a man to come—you are who?"

"Harold Levy, Department of Rehabilitation." And he smiled into the phone because he knew what she would say and in what order and by what precise intonation.

"You're a Jewish boy."

"Yes, ma'am, but now I'm trying to . . ."

"Imagine, a Jewish boy. Until now I don't know anybody Levy that works in the state. You're a college man, a doctor for this work?"

"Well, you see . . ."

"It pays good? It must pay good; there's no bad seasons, and nothing you stock it the styles change." Her laugh started high and descended over the phone easily and happily; why not, with one of the friending, familiar beings, understanding and understood. He tried to get back to Candido.

"It's a shame, a young man with a heart," she said. "So, I'll talk to my husband and maybe you bring in the boy and he'll fix the watches. Also, it don't hurt, you should get another one to put on your record."

He checked with Mr. Castle the next day and was told to bring the client in, but not before they had gone through some of the subtle fugue of wages and hours. ("What's a matter, he's a deaf-mute, he can't talk for himself?" —"I won't recommend a job to a trained man if the wages aren't good." —"I'll raise him if I like his work.")

Another call to the candy store around the corner from where Candido lived. The man had once thought to explain to him how all the neighbors used that phone and the boy who carried the messages was dependable if only the small wait was not disturbing. He never dreamed how familiar it was to Harry, the same but for the accent of the voices. Calls used to come to his father "by Mr. Rollnick" at *their* candy store in *their* neighborhood not far from the one he was calling. The old neighborhood was dissolved now, half under the Lawrence Highway, half incorporated into the Negro ghetto that was all the way up on Van Allen street when he was a kid. Suddenly, he thought, "our" neighborhood was anywhere; we are free. You don't *have* to live on Orange or Patrick or West Aberdeen (Vest Gaberdine, remember?). Now the agony of separation and its bittersweet joy, too, was for the Mexicans and Negroes. Now, a certain Spanish-American candy-store owner is sending out his little son. "Quick! a man is calling for Chavez, Candido, about a steady job."

Candido was waiting on the corner the next morning when Harry went to pick him up, and they rode over to the store without speaking. He had the very pale, very neat look of a desperate man enduring the anguish of hope.

Harry tried to make him relax. "We have some fairly good leads, and if one doesn't work out, another will."

He nodded, looking straight ahead, and they pulled up at Castle's.

It was a nice looking store with the usual display of watches, jewelry, and gifts in the window, solid, conventional silver tea services that you put on the sideboard and never use. They went in, Candido insisting that Harry go first. It was quite early and no one else was in the store, so Mr. Castle stepped forward, immediately enchanted with them for a moment until he realized that they weren't customers. He was wearing a sport's shirt open at the neck.

In back of the store, his wife was getting ready to begin the day. She was dressed more formally, and Harry guessed that she must wait on the customers while he did the repairs in back. He held out his hand, introducing himself, and Mr. Castle held out his and tried not to look disappointed. As his wrist turned for the handshake, Harry saw the tattooed blue numbers. There was even the funny cross-hatched seven that Germans make. He wasn't ready for the numbers. He had seen them before, of course, but never without being ready for them somehow; and he couldn't help staring at them until he made himself stop, flustered, and forgetting what he was going to say.

"Oh, yes, Levy, from that agency"; and the jeweler stepped forward and Harry stepped back to bring Candido forward and introduce him.

Mr. Castle was staring. "How come you didn't say you're bringing one of *his* kind in here?"

Harry began a hurried, desperate scrambling to remember what he had said over the phone about Candido, and to erase the numbers, and the special proof of the funny, crossed seven so punctiliously made. Surely he'd given Candido's name. All he could think of was his own plea: Don't hurt him, not *you*, not *you*. The thought carried a kind of panic that Harry didn't understand. Then he remembered trying to touch Mrs. Castle's fear with the comfort he could give her in the crude patched-up Yiddish he had learned once and tried once to forget. Over the phone each of them had assumed that the other was a friend because of those words. My people, he thought, with a certain shocked amusement at himself, my people, and therefore generous and humane, of course.

"Well," Mr. Castle said, "are you going to get him out of here?"

"If you'll just wait . . ."

"Nope, no. Mexes I don't take."

His wife had come from the back of the store, wondering perhaps why there was such sharpness in his tone and such stiffness in their postures as they stood pulling back from one another. She walked warily.

"Just wait a minute," Harry said to the jeweler, and then he turned to Candido to tell him to go to the car while they argued.

"Listen, I'll tell you," and Mr. Castle made the familiar Come-Let-Us-Reason-Together gesture that Harry had grown up with and was therefore almost a password between them. His complete denial of Candido's presence infuriated Harry.

"Mr. Chavez, why don't you go out to the car for a few minutes, I'll be right out."

When Candido disappeared into the early morning glare, Harry took a breath to begin, not about Candido but about himself, Jew, citizen, ghetto-born boy, free man. "When a man is trained and competent . . ."

The reasonable face only hardened a little. "I don't take 'em. They're not our *kind*, Levy, they—they . . ." Words failed him.

But the numbers, the numbers, Harry's mind kept insisting. He has to understand because of the numbers! It was all he could think of, suddenly, those numbers creeping up that arm, and among them the slatted seven. There was a letter, the camp, then the hundred-thousand decimal place, the ten thousand, the thousand, the hundred, the ten, the one. "Don't you see!" he said, louder than he should have, "it's what they said about you, about us. They put you in a camp by the same logic . . ."

"They told lies about us . . ."

"Yes, yes!" Harry whispered.

"What they said was a lie!" Castle said stiffly. His body was rigid now, his face rigid, the muscles twitching in his cheek. "Lies!"

"Yes!" Harry whispered in a hiss, and the whispered hiss carried to the woman so that she flinched and her hand came up to her lips, and they remembered her there. Did she have numbers too, and a place in her memory that she kept open only at the risk of losing her present comprehension of the world? Harry saw the reasons standing simple and understandable before him. Castle saw into the darkness from which he had come. Harry couldn't stop. The man was killing his heritage, or whatever a Jew is supposed to remember with If I Forget Thee, O Jerusalem . . .

"The numbers meant that you weren't even hated for yourself; you were no different from any other Jew, the murderer and the exalted man, the honored rabbi and the poor idiot, no good or bad, no single, separate, private qualities to differentiate you from the best—or the worst. When they numbered you, not by what you were but only by how many, didn't that anger you?"

He was a standing corpse among the silver and shining glass of the showcase windows. Candido had gone and the three of them stood in the silence of 1939, barely sifting the present hush with their breathing. Castle's face was pale and Harry reached out a hand to touch him, but the anger came again and he could no more stop himself than he could stop the deaths that had been and gone. "Didn't you *learn* anything in that damn camp?"

It struck in. Castle sucked in his breath, alive with the wound. "What do you know, smart guy that didn't see *nothing!* Yes, we were herded, animals! Scars I still got from them. They took everything from me. I came here with nothing, *nothing!* This store you see right here is my answer to them and what they called me and what they made me do like an animal! The "Garbage" got a store. The "Garbage" sits and walks and lives with fine silver, with good merchandise—quality, every piece. No junk. AND THERE AIN'T GONNA BE NO MEX IN MY STORE!"

Harry left, having murmured good-bye to the pale, shocked people. Candido was waiting outside in the car. He went around to the driver's side and got in and sat fumbling with his key until he could say, "I'm sorry, Mr. Chavez."

Candido shrugged and answered with a look. It's all right; a family quarrel, I know how it is.

Harry thought wryly that Candido was sensitive about family things, as sensitive and knowing as he and Mrs. Castle had been with one another. He rammed the key into the ignition and stamped the gas pedal without making sure the car was in neutral, so she jumped and stalled and rocked back and he gritted his teeth, cursing, rammed for neutral, danced brake-to-clutch-to-gas and hove out with a dare. Luckily it was early and no one was there to collide with his anger. "Well," he said, "we'll go on to the next one." His head began to pound.

Candido leaned over and said very gently, "Don't feel bad, Mr. Levy, people say things; it's not your fault. You Spanish, you get use to hearin' that stuff." The anger that had been opened in Harry turned toward Candido. "Did I tell you, I called Montoyas yesterday? You know what they said—No Spanish. We don't want to get a reputation for being just a Spanish place."

Candido looked down. "Everybody got his own troubles, Mr. Levy." Another apology.

They stopped at a drive-in place and had coffee before they went on, and Harry thought to himself, as he drank it, that all this time he had been sifting and re-sifting the ashes of his people's holocaust for something that could be saved, some valuable thing that could be learned and kept. (Does degradation ennoble? No, but *my* people, surely *my* people are generous and humane, of course . . .)

"Candido, do you know why I was arguing with Castle?"

"You got too angry. It's not too good to get so angry. It makes the other one get angry back, see."

"Do you know many Jewish people?"

"Jewish? No! Madre, I heard they aren' even Christians!"

"Harry, a call came in for you today. Mr. Chavez? He said you would know about it. 'Tell him I am hired at Felshers to start Monday.' Okay?"

"It's good news. I wonder if I should call the candy store and tell him *mazel-tov*. What's *mazel-tov* in Spanish?"

VIRTUOSO

She was tutoring Stephen out of pity, because his clothes were someone else's, because doors banged in his face and broke his glasses, because what should have been his moment of glory was vaudeville and he had done it himself.

By now it defined him; laughter came with his appearance and followed after him in the halls. It had started with Miss Percy, looking to him to bring the anguish of Soviet Dictatorship before the slumbering afternoon of her sophomore civics class. "Perhaps Stephen will tell us about the regime in Poland, and how he escaped."

The expected speech raised a groan behind the stolid faces of the class. Most of the students could think of nothing but the April hunger they were suffering. They waited dully for his soporific gratitude-platitude, his unintentional complacency in telling them they didn't know how lucky they were, his embarrassing lie about *wishing* to die for freedom. The words were too familiar, the passions too much a part of the rhetoric of firecracker Fourths. The class waited for the standard echoes. Stephen took a breath, and, suddenly, weird and eager, all hands, like a deaf man arguing, the boy was chopping out disjointed idiocies about a wrong brother, a passport with a beard, and then something that sounded like "belted with two girls in big bubble-mine." Then he gave a stiff bow and said, "Thank you."

The class' roar scattered all the sleep.

Miss Percy tried to fake being reasonable. She said, "Well, I see . . ." She didn't see, and the class knew it and laughed louder. They couldn't help themselves. Stephen was standing stupidly lost, knowing he had said it wrong. His lips were moving with the effort of pulling all those words back desperately through the mazes of translation. Miss Percy tried a last time. She cleared her throat. "How did you happen to escape to the West?"

"Oh," he said amicably, "holding hands."

"I beg your pardon?"

"The mine," he said, having found the deceiving, treacherous hole in the words, "*in* the mine, *rubber* bubbles."

He stood in the fame that followed, his smile coming and going because he knew he was being laughed at but not why. The sophomore advisor asked Renata, who was a quiet, studious girl, to help him with his English. It was embarrassing for everyone, giving asylum to such a madman—rubber bubble-mines!

Stephen learned quickly, sawing through words with his hands and impaling them on his fingers. His gestures and comically open face fooled the people who didn't know him into thinking that he was stupid or a natural clown, and Renata began to see him setting that open trustfulness on his face as he went into the school, the room, the day of loneliness. She began to walk with him in the halls, trying to protect him from the popular and ephemeral code phrases that the popular and ephemeral leaders took up and rejected without warning. She came to hate those special phrases in which he invested the intense, trusting foreigner's loyalty—a week too late.

She knew she didn't understand Stephen very well herself. Beyond his unpredictable words, there were times when she wondered if he was laughing at her or being serious, times when his lightnesses seemed weird and his darknesses eccentric and overdrawn. And he could be sententious in a way that made her cringe. She couldn't tell him that this manner was more intolerable to Americans than stealing; he wouldn't have known where it was or how to cover it with a little lightness or self-deprecation—poses that were made to be seen through.

She wondered if his strangeness was his own or a part of his people, familiar and shared somewhere else. That would have made it better somehow. She thought about it when he asked her if she would go with him to meet his friends. "They laugh at me when I tell them I speak Polish no more. I bring you. They see me a Yankee; I make them speak English too."

She smiled and accepted.

As the day for the visit came closer, Stephen began to wall her in with conditions. "Some of my friends don't know American girl too good. If you wear low dress, they think a wrong thing." "—In Poland, girl not argue what a man says." "—Better you don't tell them you not Catholic; they don't understand."

She got angry and told him she didn't want to go after all. He answered that he had told his friends about her, that to bring her was a source of pride to him, and that he didn't want to be embarrassed. She told him it was too bad; he had spoiled the day by trying to change her to suit his friends. He turned on his heel and left her standing in the hall outside the classroom while a ring of curious students entertained themselves with the argument. She was amazed and angry when he appeared at her house at nine-thirty on Sunday morning, jacket and tie and glazed shoes, asking her mother if she was ready.

"Look at me! I'm in hiding in my own house. Tell him I'm not dressed, and not going!"

"I can't tell him that. He's out in the living room all clean and shined and eager. Maybe he didn't *understand*."

So Renata dressed, muttering, and went out to meet him.

"Oh," he said approvingly, "You look nice, *very* nice."

She was wary, and didn't smile back.

They went toward Selkirk Boulevard, into a neighborhood of discount stores and saloons whose customers did not drink for pleasure. All the stores blazed with desperation. *Everything marked down!* FIRE SALE! GIGANTIC DISCOUNT. GOING OUT OF BUSINESS 20% OFF! The streets were hung with drastic remedies in the red-letter print of panic.

Stephen saw her sadden at the mood of desperation and transience. "This," he said, "never change. Business of going out of business very good. Sometimes I think my friend—I mean Polish friends—to be like that. All ready to die, but not now; still one more day, one more plan."

She wondered if the similarity wasn't just that he (he only or Poles?) was used to saying one thing and meaning another.

He led her to a small door between the fear-gaping mouths of two stores (Open Sunday, Buy and Save!), and they went inside and up three flights of narrow stairs. At the top they heard laughter from behind one of the doors, and Stephen said, "They are here already." A tightness made his voice sound strange.

She looked at him. He was frightened! He had escaped from fearful enemies, yet what kind of friends could make him so nervous. There was even a rime of sweat blurring his upper lip. He looked like the poor-but-honest suitor in an old movie, taking a breath and knocking at the door. The laughter inside stopped, and in the long silence before the door was opened, she wished she had held her ground and not come.

He whispered to her, "You see, there is a rumor—only a rumor—it is possible Fedke comes today."

Then the door opened and laughter and voices came again in the foreign tongue. She smiled above the handshakes. "How do you do." And then they all sat down and folded their hands to sweat and wait in the hot room. Fits of polite conversation.

"You go to school with Stefan?"

"Yes, we're in the same class."

"In Poland would be in university now, Stefan."

"He is learning English very quickly."

A grunt. "You cook Polish?"

"No."

"You mother, father Polish?"

"No, our people came from Sweden."

"Well, can't all be Polish."

And they laughed and then they sat aging. She could feel her fingers beginning to ache with tension as she held them in her lap. Suddenly, at no signal she could name, the room exploded in a cacophony of incomprehensible sound. She sat smiling vaguely while the uprooted strangers around her plunged into their own true, honest, sounding, nourishing, signifying tongue. They were radiant, all hands and mouths, pulling strength from the immediacy of give and take that would—that had to—keep them patient and willing for another week among the multitude of strangers and the unreliable, distant new words. The talk was peppered with the name of Fedke, which Stephen had mentioned at the door.

At last, an older man wrenched himself from the true tongue to be polite to her. "You must be hoping meet Fedke today." She said she was. "Stefan bring you. Proud. He has not see Fedke." He said it with a meaningful look, as if she must know how important it was. Then he laughed abruptly. "I see Fedke, surprise, once on street. I have no job—sick—no shave. I look across street. Is Fedke! I quick look in store window, try look like Chinaman so he don't see me." His look suddenly changed. "You not *tell* Fedke." She said she wouldn't, and he bounded up. "I want if Fedke come, we have drink."

Everyone was talking and laughing, so no one heard the knock until it was given a second or third time. Then the hush came again and this time she could see the friends counting themselves off, and the whispered realization that they were all here, so it must be Fedke himself. There was a sudden shyness, and some of the men smoothed back their overlong hair. Nervous adulation always brought out the worst in her. She had a sudden, maddeningly irreverent thought: They will open the door to the Archangel Michael dressed as the Pretender to the Throne of Poland and panting from the climb. . . .

Someone opened the door.

The man standing there was a hymn to nonentity. His face was bland, without texture or feature, sandy, receding hair. It was hard to see where either flesh or hair began or ended: a man worn by his clothes, shabbily. He came with a thin smile, wavering, blinking into the light of their welcome. And the room rang with cheers and greetings. A woman beside Renata turned, beaming. "Is Fedke. Here."

Stephen came up, too nervous and too eager. "Come, I want you to introduce. Proud day for me." He had been leading her to where the molelike man stood blinking, with his equivocating smile. "Fedke, is honor to produce my friend Renata, from my school." He bowed slightly and offered her forward. Fedke presented her with a flaccid hand. When he opened his mouth to speak, the room stilled so that his utterance might be given attention. "How-do-you-do," he said.

Renata bit her lip. Voltaire, to the fingertips!

Karol, the man who had spoken to her before, ventured a comment from the hush. "Well, Fedke, you don't see girls like that in grocery business!" Uproarious laughter. The sound flowed out the windows, bowed the walls.

Fedke stood in the cauldron of sound, half-smile, while it rose and broke. He hadn't moved. Renata fell under the illusion that if she spoke, she would somehow understand. "Oh, are you in the grocery business?"

Laughter multiplied. People whooping with it, holding their sides, weakened with laughter. The host began to move among them with sustaining whiskey. Everyone took a makeshift olive glass or chipped cup or coffee mug, leaving the single whiskey glass for Fedke. A man stood tall and raised his glass. "I stand to salute Colonel Fedke, Commander!" Another surge of laughter. "To Dr. Fedke!" The other side of the room was answering, ceremonially. "Great medical success!" The laughter this time bore a haze of the most powerful whiskey Renata had ever tasted. The toasts and drinks went on. "To Professor Fedke!" "To Fedke, Master Artist!" More laughter. Then she saw Stephen, alight with triumph, raising his glass, "To Fedke, Geological Engineer!" They applauded the sumptuous title, fitting from one who was receiving an American education. The laughter was so intense that it was pain.

Renata's head was very light; she wasn't used to drinking, but she knew she wanted to go home. Whatever this Fedke was, it wasn't what they were toasting. It must be that this shabby, sorry bunch of expatriates had chosen a scapegoat, a pitiful nobody, obviously dull, and probably feeble-minded on whom to smear and ridicule their vain hopes, so that by laughing, they could endure hopelessness. They laughed at Fedke's ludicrous posture as he accepted the overblown tributes. The ceremony of it disgusted her. Stephen's friends would never be professor or doctor or colonel and so they tried to cheapen those things. She looked around her at the gesticulating people. Her eye caught the kindly man who had sacrificed five whole minutes of his soul-nourishing language to speak with her. How had he used it? Simply to tell her how ashamed he was at once seeing Fedke, Fedke of all people, on a day when he was looking seedy and ill. Why not? There are all kinds of pride—prince on throne and fly on dung hill—anything to be superior to a Fedke who was still smiling in his borrowed titles. She went unsteadily to Stephen who was talking to another man. "I have to go home now; it's getting late." He looked at her and smiled graciously. "Oh, yes, Renata, I have trouble to be from here, where is old language."

In the hour or so they had been there, his accent had thickened, his grammar had slipped. One of the bunch, she thought. They began to move toward the door. She knew he would probably want her to say good-bye to the Doctor, the Professor, the Colonel. She might as well make it right; she wouldn't be coming back. Fedke didn't seem to be in the room. She asked a woman by the door, trying to sound casual.

"Oh," the woman answered, smiling, "He go just now when we were laugh. A few minutes Fedke is enough."

A few minutes Fedke was more than enough. By the time Stephen tore himself away and they had walked the three flights to the sidewalk, terrible with banners, Renata's head was clearer.

"They like you, my friends," he said warmly, "you come back next week, we teach you song."

"A song would have been better than watching what you did to that man, that Fedke," she said. He looked so amiable and satisfied that she lost her temper. "Oh, Stephen, what *for!*"

He answered, as she knew he would, in his defensive, slightly sententious way. "Renata, is hard to understand other people ways. Always to try to be patient is good. Many of your ways seem to me most strange, but I am tolerating person, always patient to understand."

"It was disgusting," she said.

Then he looked at her and seemed to be thinking, trying to remember what could justify so bad a word. "I see," he said. "It sound too—too like carnival to you. I see now how it must sound. It hurts you that we are not honest, not humble men enough to call him what is his true name—thief, murderer, liar. We must make up fancy title so we do not show to him and to ourselves, what thing he is, what thing he does."

"I don't know what you are talking about."

"I see you with Karol; I think he tells you about Fedke. I cannot find way to tell it; I ask him to help." She shook her head slowly. "Invite me coffee, then," he said. "I am broke."

They got to a wretched hamburger place, and she laughed and asked him if sacrifice should go so far. "Tell me all about it now. From the beginning."

"From the beginning is too long, too much," he said, but it was only because he didn't know where to begin. "Fedke does not look to you like hero, like man who is sentenced to die all over Poland, but Fedke is modern man with special trade. Fedke is thief, special thief. Fedke steals people." He smiled slightly at her wonder. "All people you meet today—they are people Fedke has steal and bring across the borders and help to come in America. My brother, he was going to come, but then he die. I come in his place. The miracle is Fedke. You see, Renata, if a boy is not at school or sick in clinic or in home, police come. To fix this is part of Fedke's great—clever . . ."

"Skill?"

"Yes, skill. You remember a man call Fedke, Grocer?"

"Yes, why did everybody laugh?"

"Fedke is grocer, Fedke is not grocer; Fedke make plan to sell eggs to army, gets from army flour which fills quota of state flour man, who then fixes books of other man. Three favors owed to Fedke. If man who buys and sells food is grocer, Fedke is grocer. The man who calls him Doctor is man whose passport does not look like him. Passport is one favor. Fedke gives him pill that swells him until his mother will not know him. A medical report, also by Fedke, explains very serious bad disease. Ugh! At border they let him quick over the line to go to special hospital. Colonel Fedke—well—he has bribe so many soldiers, a man figures out it is enough to make into a regiment."

"I can't believe it; I just can't."

He told her gently that she was fortunate to be unequipped to believe such deceits and risks. Actually, what she didn't believe concerned Fedke himself. She couldn't reconcile the blinking, smile-watering rabbit of a man with the sharp-witted, resourceful hero of Stephen's escape, of everyone's escape. There must have been thirty people in that room. "You mean that Fedke really brought all of those people out?"

Stephen nodded.

"All right, what about what Karol told me, about seeing Fedke on the street when Karol was sick and out of a job."

"He was ashamed, Renata."

It hadn't been pride then, but shame, a guilt that Fedke should think his risks were wasted on such a failure.

Stephen pursed his lips and then laughed. "Even today, you see Karol making as if he is big success, tie and wristwatch. He all the time stick out his stomach so he will look fat, like man who eats all he wants."

"I didn't notice," she said.

"It is a small thing, just a little funny."

"Stephen, tell me about Fedke and you."

"He is hero to me."

"Why did you drink to him as an engineer. Did he turn engineer for you?"

"They laugh in school, my escape."

"I won't laugh."

"We go in old mine," he said. "We breath from bubbles— you know, little children rubber bubbles with special piece for the mouth. These filled with oxygen to get through gas pocket."

"Children rubber bubb—*balloons*, you mean *balloons!*" She saw him filing it in his mind, filling the —oons with air to help him remember.

"Fedke is more than this," he said. "I say Fedke have skill. I think not skill, art. Fedke has *art*."

It was outlandish to speak of that man in that way. As Stephen explained him, Renata kept losing the features of the featureless man to whom she had been introduced.

"I say art," he was continuing in his pedantic "public" way. "I say art because artist make sacrifice, much sacrifice, and Fedke sacrifice all—all."

"You mean that he sacrificed having a home and family, because of the risks . . ."

He shook his head slowly, looking at her in sorrow and wonder. "You don't understand nothing! What did you see today, bunch of stupids laughing at little man?" She began to get up and he waved her back impatiently. "No, fault is mine, Renata. I want to praise someone—when I am happy, I forget you are not from my country, then I get angry when you do not see. How can you see?" He stopped speaking, and his hands moved restlessly while he searched his mind for a way to show her an image that she could understand. It came to him. "Renata, make description of Fedke. Quickly, come. Tell me how Fedke looks. You saw him half-hour."

"He doesn't look like anything. He's . . ."

Stephen's smile broke wide and changed his face. "This is the art, Renata, this is the sacrifice. To walk away from home, from tongue, from all memories—this everyone does who leaves his country. To go from love and hope is big sacrifice. To go from *man's own self*," he struck the words against his chest with the flat of his hand, "is to sacrifice all. This Fedke does for his art."

"What art?"

"Art of modern time: to steal what enemy needs without his knowing. This is art. To lie always and still be trust by everyone; this is art. To *live* as Fedke—an art."

"Do you mean that he develops that, that he makes himself —*not?*"

He said, "Yes," and took a drink and winced at the taste of the coffee. "Renata, if a man loves, he will be caught; if he hates, he will be caught; if he has even little hunger for money or be famous or to be scholar or to be peaceful, he will be caught. Even to like his coffee or not to like. If a man has hunger to be *his* self, special, to be remember, he will be caught. Fedke has make such sacrifice for his art."

He had said that Fedke was his hero. The face he wore in school, that compliant, half-smile-face was Fedke's face. He was trying to master Fedke's art. "Is it so hard in school," she said. "I'm sorry, I just recognized something, and it was as if I had seen the face before, the face you put on for school. . . ."

"I do not have his greatness to do this. If I could be Fedke, pain does not come so near me, to be alone and funny fellow *by nature*. When he was with us today, Renata, I keep thinking that to me it would be pain to see others who have self, laughing and speaking and everything, because of me, who has none. Fedke likes to come to see us. Maybe our special, our laughing, our big success makes art what he does. I think, sometimes, if we are not rich, smart, happy men, most successful, then what Fedke does is only bus driver, taking people to this place, that place. I try, Renata, but I do not have such talent. Fedke *likes* to come to see us. I tell you secret; for some of us is failure in Poland, is failure here also. We do not let Fedke find this out. Even he must have little, little bit of pride. All Pole have pride. Pole is strong people; Pole is proud people."

She said, "Here we go again," and smiled into the sour coffee.

THE
LAUGHING
FIONA

It was morning and Clara was a stranger, coming into Edinburgh in a downpour, tired after the all-night train ride from London, where she sat up in the coach able only to listen. The others had been talking about their experiences in the bombing of London. It would have been callous, somehow, to sleep, so she was meeting the unfamiliar city heavy-eyed, and it was raining.

The bright-faced boys going to school and the tight-lipped men hurrying to their work made her feel perverse as well as strange. She hefted the bulky luggage again and boarded the bus to which she had been directed. It was supposed to take her to Glaves Crescent Road. (Lodgings: Students—clean and reasonable, which she had seen on the university bulletin board.) She sat down and the bus droned past street after identical street, while she looked out of its rain-spattered windows in surprise. Clara's idea of poverty was what she had seen in the littered alleys of American, Italian, and Spanish tenement slums; and it expressed itself, oddly enough, in excesses. Poverty had always meant too many people, a din of noise, mountains of trash, stench (which might only be too many smells crossing one another), and the overflow of everything into everything else—garbage, rubble, and undecaying decaying wreckage that rusted and hid rats. She wasn't prepared for the kind of poverty through which the bus was moving now. It was utterly bare—there were no fire escapes festooned with forgotten rags, no litter; only row on row of buildings, all four stories high, all gray in dreary stone sameness. There wasn't one scrap of color to mark any of the vacant-eyed windows; and people walked by dressed in gray like the houses, and pulling their gray to themselves, shivering.

At last the bus stopped at Glaves Crescent Hill, one like all the rest, it seemed, and Clara got off, clumsy with weariness, juggling baggage. She began to curse the books she had brought from London, weighing and weighing in those suitcases. After a walk that seemed longer than it was, and soaked to the skin, she finally came to a door that said 18.

It was a heavy door, solid. Its polished wood was smooth with generations of waxings, and gleaming on it was a brass knocker in the shape of a lion's head—mellow and classic. Clara stood looking at it, relieved in spite of the rain. It promised more than its own beauty. Such doors open on crackling fires, glasses of sherry, old silver, old wood, old leather, and the slow, deep, and measured tones of Scottish speech. She lifted the lion's head and let it fall, all the satisfying metal presence of it, into the waiting cup. There was no sound from inside, and after a while she let the lion fall again; then stood and listened, being rained on like a patient beast of burden. The third time. There was a sound and then the loud grate of unlocking and a voice, pitched high and strident, breaking a crack in the door.

"What d'ye want!"

"Glaves Crescent Lodging House?"

"It is!"

"I'm just off the train from London," she said. "Your card was on the university bulletin board . . ." She was having trouble, in her tiredness, understanding why she was still standing outside while the rain was finding new ways, smaller and smaller, inside her clothes.

"Weel?" the woman said.

"Have you a room?" Clara asked at last.

The door opened a little wider and a small, strange face looked out suspiciously. "Twelve shillings a day, bed, breakfast, and tea!" like an accusation.

Clara took a deep breath, wondering why she couldn't seem to make herself understood. "May I come in?"

The women was guarded against this wild intrusion. "Weel, if you must, but mind ye keep ye'er dirty feet off the fleors. Walk on the rubber mat!"

Clara walked in. Why was the house no warmer than the rain?

"How long are ye gooin' to stay?" the woman demanded.

"I had planned to stay in Edinburgh for three days and have a day in Dunfermline . . ."

"Well, ye'll pay by the day then!" she said, and held out her hand.

After wrestling like Laöcoon with the luggage and the contents of her purse, Clara managed to produce twelve shillings.

Then the woman led her down a long, dark hall to a room, her high, rasping voice going with her in a perpetual filing back and forth across the senses. "The lodging is paid in advance. No reum is to be locked. Ye check out at ten. If ye *must* use arti-fi-cial light in the reum, ye'll sign fer it in the beuk; it's tuppence a five-day week, thruppence a seven. The house is not responsible for per-so-nal property. Lights are out at ten at night. Ye'll not sit on the beds!"

The room was as bleak as a detention cell. Four beds stood in it and the woman pointed at one of them. Suddenly, Clara was exhausted. She dropped her luggage at the foot of the bed, stepped out of her sopping shoes, shook off the wet jacket and sank down on the bed, sounding down for sanctuary in a green darkness.

"This is a re-spec-table lodging-house, young woman!" cried the receding world. "We're not put on this earth to sleep the day away—and ye're on the spread! Guests are not permitted . . ." And the deep closed over.

It was about two in the afternoon. The rain had slowed to a drizzle and Clara stretched, feeling a new thrill of excitement at being rested and coming alive again in a strange old city with echoes she had wanted to hear for so long—Burns and Scott and the kilted men of clans. She was determined to see the city in spite of all the cold and rain, to clear her mind of the bleakness of her penitential room, so that it wouldn't touch the way she wanted to experience this place. She had come so far to see it on the short holiday from school. An old city—so much to see and do. It would be a good idea to get a map first. She got up and into a raincoat, slipping on the wet shoes again with a groan. Damn D.H. Lawrence had come to Edinburgh in her luggage instead of overshoes. As she went down the dark hall, someone passed, quick, black wraith, like a bird beating 150 heartbeats a minute.

"Hello," Clara said to it.

It fluttered a little white wing-hand, and was gone.

Clara went to the door and reached out for the knob and was impaled by the point of the voice of the Matron.

"Late tea is served at six, so ye'll know not to be late!"

The shaft had come from a black place off the dark hallway. She nodded indiscriminately to the dimness and left.

The Castle and the High Street, the usual walks; but the grim bareness of the city and the falling of that interminable rain left her more with Burke & Hare than with Scott and Burns. Grim people, she kept thinking over and over, grim houses, cold year after cold year. No wonder they had Calvinism and demons. You need something to differentiate life from death. Her mind hung morbidly on the "resurrectionists," and by the time she returned to the chilly house behind that magnificent, deceiving door, she was almost feeling stared after.

At ten of six she changed clothes, and when a bell rang, went down the hall to one of the rooms that now burned its grudging twenty watts against the darkness. Twelve or fifteen women, some of them young and pretty, were drinking tea and talking in whispers to one another. There she recognized the little bird-girl who had passed her in the hall; so, hungry for some kind of human warmth in all the dampness and chill, she went over quietly and started a conversation. Bird-girl was shy at first, and in her black dress with a pale, almost bluish skin, she looked like someone who was existing somewhere between the stroke and the fall. The Grim Reaper's scythe—death images (Stop it!) . . . She went resolutely on with the talk. It was in the middle of one of these mind-spinning, mouth-warming sentences, that she realized with a kind of nervous anguish that all the others were deathly still and that the Matron was glaring angrily at her, and that no one had a cup any more. She stood like a thief, caught, overpossessed of one cup, one saucer, one spoon, and one cookie, and, paradoxically, naked. Bird-girl motioned with her eyes and she gave up the offending teaware with a clatter that was magnified in the silence, like coarse laughter in the county morgue. Death again.

"We'el read!" said the Matron, looking pointedly at Clara, "from the Epistle of St. James." Then she took a breath and attacked.

During the reading, Clara got a chance to look at the Matron steadily for the first time. She was small and very thin, and her hair was dyed with henna and gathered tightly to her skull. Clara had a feeling that it was a wig, serving convention, of course, and for health, and never for vanity; she could almost hear it being explained. The woman could have been fifty. Droning. ". . . a restless evil, full of deadly poison."

Clara breathed a sigh of relief as the voice dropped and the Bible was closed, but no one stirred.

"Let us pray!" the Matron demanded. "Oh, merciful Lord, we have sinned against Thee, miserable offenders, miserable offenders all. In our deeds and acts, yea, even in our most secret thoughts, we have sinned against Thee, our Father. Set our feet from that road, from iniquity, and our souls from evil! Shield us from the ever-present temp-*ta*-tion of lustful pleasures and un-natural desires, the ruin that is everywhere!" And then, as an afterthought, "Through Christ Jesus, Amen!"

As she ended, letting the last words chop vainly at the silence, Clara wondered who, among all these hushed shadows, had ever known any rustling silken garment to covet it; or any bare, warm flesh, lips, warm eyes, or strong arms to lust after them; or any small, single perverse or heretical thought's temptation to want it. The Matron rose and pursed her lips.

"Lights go out at ten. Those who wish to use up the electricity *in their reums* will sign the beuk! Good evening!"

"Good evening, ma'am," they chirped, and a few curtsied; and Clara was left with the sudden, wild belief that she had stumbled inadvertently into a house of correction.

The spirits drifted apart and disappeared. A few of them gathered in the library under another recklessly improvident twenty watts of power. In Americà, it would have been all right to joke: Handy having the heat and light furnished by the same bulb . . . But she was a stranger, and her country one of stupendous wealth and wattage with neither let or limit. She contented herself with whispered questions, and their whispered, hurried answers. This was a rooming house after all, one which catered to girls from farms and small towns ("moral and decent females of modest circumstances," the rules read), who had come to Edinburgh to get work. Some of the girls clerked in a factory, two were waitresses, and the rest students at the university medical school. They paid a special monthly fee for the lights they burned in study.

Literacy was a rigor also. The library was high-walled and cold. In a bookcase against the wall there were rows of worn and "edifying" volumes marshaled against the living.

"Does one read the books there?"

"Oh, yes," the whispering informant assured her. "Those are na' forbidden. They are inspirational beuks. There is much wisdom in beuks." She blushed, and Clara suddenly felt it all getting the better of her.

"I have books too, in my luggage," she said, "*Sex & Temperament in Three Primitive Societies, Sons and Lovers* . . . I even have a Revised Standard Version of the Bible . . ." She stopped. No good shocking the inmates. It wasn't the inmates who were to blame; it was the rain.

It had begun in earnest and she knew that if it hadn't been raining so hard, she could at least have left and gone down the street and stuck her head in a letterbox and told a dirty joke. As it was, she contented herself with a selection from the shelf, *Blossoms in the Garden of Virtue*, and a hard chair. *Blossoms* was a collection of spiritual exercises in verse form, especially for young ladies. Virtue, she found out, has chapter divisions, and she had finished "Modesty," "Piety," "Bravery," and "Prudence," when she realized that the cadence of the rain was putting her to sleep. Lacking the courage and optimism to ask about hot water for a bath, she washed at the sink's single cold tap and got into the icy bed. There she lay awake, rigid with cold.

It must have been about a quarter to ten when she heard the sound. It made her forget the cold and how hard it is to wait for sleep. She jumped out of bed and went to the door. It was the sound of laughter. Someone was laughing. The sound of it was rich and warm, joyful and womanly. It was about summer, about all the warm, generous things that one remembers of freedom and summer. It was beautiful. She had to go out and see. She pulled her jacket over her nightdress and hurried out to find the single soul in that house of the dead who knew what living was.

By the time she reached the dim library, the summer had gone. The library was empty; but across the hall, in a room behind a door of frosted glass, Clara saw a figure move. She waited like a spy, and at the last moment before the house's signal for the automatic ending of its day, someone opened the door and stepped out into the hall against the light.

The girl had brilliant red hair; it was the first thing that struck one, the heavy, rich mass of her hair, gleaming like old copper. Her face was plain, a "good" face, composed and pleasant, and she was in the shapeless dress that seemed to be inmate issue.

Clara said, "Hello."

"Oh," the girl said, "you're the one from America."

"Yes, my name is Clara. I'm on holiday from London."

"I am Fiona," she said.

"Was it you, laughing in here just now?"

"It was I," Fiona said serenely, and then before Clara could ask another question, she turned and said, "The lights will go soon. Good night."

Never had Clara been so conscious of her loneliness as when she thought it might end. In the morning, with the cold rain still falling, the bell sounded and the penitents filed into the front room for breakfast. Looking around for Fiona, Clara saw her standing behind a chair at one of the window tables. As she started to go back and join her, the Matron came up and took her by the arm.

"Leuking for the choice seat, were ye? Weel, that's reserved for the per-manent guests. Ye'll sit over here!" and she led Clara to a chair on the darker side of the room.

"Oh, Lord God," and again they were reminded of their Fall, even with Eve. Eventually the prayer ended, and Clara got even by eating as heartily as the rules permitted. Waste not, want not.

During breakfast whispers, she asked about Fiona.

"Oh, she is one of the girls at the medical school," her companion said. "She is in the second year."

"Oh, the work is very hard there," another one confided. "Fiona has nothing but drill and study. She has even made special arrangements. They let her burn her lights before sun-up to study."

They, Clara thought, they. A little woman in a black sweater was sitting across the table. She took up the subject with eager malice. "Fiona is a favorite." What Byzantine splendors that privilege must confer! Maybe so much as another half-up in her teapot, maybe the extravagance of another blanket. Clara realized that a full day of the ascetic's rain and half of *Blossoms in the Garden of Virtue* had done her very little good. Still, it was surprising, really. Fiona's spirit was in her face. She had laughed, had admitted laughing. It was against every thing that the House and its Matron stood for. Even the thick red hair was an insult to the wearer of that hideous henna wig.

At the end of breakfast another bell rang, and everyone rose, toast or no, to leave. Clara started to make her way over to where Fiona had her place, but the privileged ones left first and she was gone. The day was a grim tourist's nightmare, "doing" the points of interest in the downpour, cursing with all her heart a city which had not been made, as Seville had, and Padua, at least a little bit for the poor. With only one more day she couldn't spare any time looking for another rooming house that was as reasonable as the Burke & Hare. So, she was caught, like Sin under the iron hell of Virtue. At last, because warmth is as strong a need as food or water, she was forced to go to one of the exclusive hotels for tea, and to be embarrassed, feeling poorer than she ever had in London. In the great carpeted lobby of the hotel, the warmth was as voluptuous as satin after sackcloth. Then, when the clerks began to look at her a little fishily, there was nothing to do but grind down the stones a little more before returning to the Burke & Hare.

On that evening her silence at late tea was exemplary, neither did her cup rattle, and she held her head down for something out of the Book of Job. She also learned that it was only with its refreshments that the House dealt its piety, and that those wealthy enough to eat somewhere else could also buy themselves free of reminders of their unworthiness, which were dispensed so lavishly to the captive poor. But guilt-free gormandizing in Edinburgh could make her student life in London insupportable, and the fare had eaten away more than she could really afford. She decided to spend the final day in the city as she had been doing. Dunfermline was out anyway.

It cleared briefly in the evening, and Clara saw, looking out into the deserted, shiny streets, warmed with a twilit mellowness, that this city did have a kind of beauty in its gray, grave formality. But the darkness came, and with it the damp and oppressive cold of the House. It seemed now as if she had never been dry or warm. It seemed now as if to be dry and warm was more of a desperate need than the need to breathe or blink. As the evening dragged on, she huddled in the bed, and her mind seized again on what was almost second nature to it in these surroundings: thoughts of horror. In the foreigners' darkness, with its smells of ancient, damp linen, its sounds of muffled steps, creaking walls, its atmosphere of poverty without humor, and despair without even the easing thought that it was undeserved, nothing could ease her fear. Ugly pictures bloomed in her mind: the grave-robbers again, then the vampire, the Black Hag—Socttish history merged horrifyingly with Scottish legend. She was staring through the night toward a shadow like something her mind groped to name when she heard the laughter again. Fiona was laughing.

For a moment it seemed to be part of a half-waking dream, and Clara was brought up from it gasping. Then she remembered where she was and that the elusive Fiona was laughing, and that she was more lonely that she had ever been in her life.

She was almost dressed because of the cold. It was only a few steps out of the room and down to the frosted glass door. Then she knocked.

"What is it?" Fiona's low voice said.

"It's Clara, the American. May I talk to you for a moment?"

The door opened. Fiona had a genial, surprised look; and Clara took a deep breath, because she knew she had to leave this place tomorrow or sicken with its sick ghosts; and it was now or never if she ever hoped to learn how anyone could stay alive in such a place. "Uh—you were laughing again. I see now that it wasn't because something struck you funny last night, was it? It's a—a ceremony." The words were abrupt, impertinent and poorly put, but there was only this last night. "How can anyone *laugh* in this place . . . ?"

"I am in the medical school," Fiona said, in her slow, grave way, "and there they give the first year students a brief lecture on how best to succeed in the medical school. One of the things that they emphasized to us was that we must guard our own health; we must get the proper exercise and suitable recreation. I get my exercise by walking from the lecture hall, and this, that you have heard, is my recreation."

Clara saw that she wasn't being arch. Her voice was level and her face held its usual expression. Somehow that only made it all the more impossible. "Great God Almighty!" Clara blurted, "if a cup of tea and a piece of toast can be called breakfast, and if this palace of grim night can be called a living place, I suppose that a laugh behind closed doors at a quarter-of-ten can be called recreation!"

"Mrs. Leukie, the landlady takes getting used to," Fiona said quietly. "But during my first year she did a great deal to help me. I feel that it is a duty of mine—in some small way—to repay her."

"How can you talk about repaying someone who doesn't even understand the currency?"

"Oh, I do not think that she takes any frivolous pleasure from the laughter that is in her house, pleasure as one ordinarily thinks of it; but this—activity of mine is—salubrious. The laughter that is my recreation also serves the purpose of being needful and beneficial to her as well."

Clara looked at Fiona and teetered on the edge of a torrent of laughter herself. The Scottish sense of humor—dry, cut on an odd bias. How delicately she was being taken! Then she realized that Fiona simply meant just what she said. Nobody could fake a laugh like that, therapy or no therapy. That laughter wasn't decided by some dutiful and efficient clock-watcher for her "five-minutes uplift." It was only Fiona's language that was betraying her, the stilted, old-time pedagogical musty-closet diction that might be an emblem on the banner of a "moral and decent female" from the villages, now a scholar in a country which took everything so damn seriously.

"Has she ever mentioned it?"

"She has never spoken of it, but I am sure it is good for her health, as they recommend pleasant surroundings. It is something I can do for her."

Pleasant surroundings. Clara wanted to ask what Fiona thought of to free such good, wide-open torrents in these cold, awful rooms. She couldn't ask; Fiona probably wouldn't have answered anyway. Didn't Fiona know that she couldn't stay forever in this miserable place without the laughter becoming a lie? Didn't she know that she couldn't lie and not have the lie destroy something good and fragile in her? Such things couldn't be asked, much less spoken as warnings; so Clara just stood and looked at Fiona, and at all that rich, womanly red hair.

"You see," said Fiona, in the inflection of ten professors, "it is both a duty and a privilege, and to satisfy these, the means will always be found."

The bell rang and they bade one another a quiet, formal good night; and the heavy rain took up its beat again, and it continued to fall.

L'OLAM
AND
WHITE SHELL WOMAN

I was broke and there was a Tribal Fair looming ahead, so the Window Rock Reservation Restaurant & Coffee Shop took me on as its first "Anglo" waitress. We started work at seven in the morning and finished with the last coffee customer, around eight or nine at night. We got fifty cents an hour and hypothetical tips. It wasn't bad the first week. I got up early and walked to work in iridescent morning light; we would serve a few customers and then sit idly and watch fat flies fighting and making love through the siesta noons, a few more customers and we would close up right after Mr. Coombs came in for his eight o'clock coffee. There was time to walk in the evening cool, enjoying the vibrating clarity of the air, feeling tired and pleasantly philosophical in all that immense desert darkness, because of having a job there, in a sense, belonging.

The other waitresses were Navaho girls who had learned their English sketchily, as a second language. I jumped at the chance to learn some Navaho. (In the catalogue of accomplishments, the exceptional ones are valued out of all proportion to their usefulness.) It would be a wonderful tongue to "lapse into" at school. It was disappointing to learn that Navaho is as tonal as Chinese, as inflected as Greek, as glottal as Hottentot;

a language without tenses, nouns, or verbs as English knew them; without objective meaning as English practised it. In the end I had to be content just waiting table. Alas for the hope of the scent of sagebrush blowing over the groves of academe.

By the end of the week, Navaho were beginning to drift in from the back country, and there were tourists stopping for sandwiches and coffee. The Indians would come in pairs, tall, potbellied men dressed in a Woolworth Western style, which they made theirs by wearing velveteen shirts—rust, peacock, and orchid—weighed with rows of dimes and quarters that were sewn in decorative patterns across their chests, huge turquoise belts, and long hair tied in the "butterfly" bun. They would come to us and speak their English word gravely, "Petsi." They never stopped to talk to the girls or to look around. They gave their money, drank their Pepsi's, and left, to disappear, even as I tried to follow them with my eyes, into the endless, empty landscape. Generations had lived this way in the desert, the descendants of those who had fled from the Spanish, their rich, rapacious conquerers, into the places where no one could follow them and survive. They got the horse and the sheep and the art of silver from that Spaniard and took his gifts into the desert to wed to their way. Bessie Tsosie, who had the tables by the window, told me that the People had always had these things, and this land. She couldn't imagine the People without sheep, horses, turquoise, or silver—things "ancestral."

In the early mornings, and at night after closing, I sometimes walked down the road toward Fort Defiance. It amazed me that people could live in a land where so little grew. Sheep are as rapacious as conquistadores. I soon learned that the Navaho wander by single families over hundreds of miles, moving often, to keep those sheeps' bellies full. Alice Yazzi told me that children spend the years of their childhoods alone, watching the family flocks which they drive to graze the mesas and the dry washes. "All time alone," she said. The earth and sky I saw were so overpowering that I pitied the little child who had to pass between them all alone; and I did see them occasionally, walking by in the distance, straight little figures between the great everlastings, with a stick against coyotes and their father's twenty sheep.

I'd forgotten that the idea of childhood as a separate time was not a universal idea. When a kid came in one day with his fly gaping wide and no underwear, I laughed to Alice about it, and then said half-jokingly, "Somebody should tell him to zip up before he falls out." She looked at me in wonder. "Are *his*." (His pants, his parts—if he had wanted them another he would have put them another way.) They called themselves The People, after all.

Other Indians barely existed for them, and the Anglo was a pale fanatic who walked around killing sheep to save the herd. But the Anglo and his Second World War had been powerful enough to deal a death blow to the Old Way. Husbands and sons had come back from training camps and battlefields transformed by the white enemy-brother, and had begun to agitate for electricity, English, and the germ theory. I had forgotten about the Christian church.

We were clearing off the big table one afternoon when the radio that had been blaring its standard rockabilly whine suddenly went into syncopated, tremulous machine-gun sounds, —Navaho. After some talk there was a song, a haunting, warping, Oriental-sounding song in half-pitches. I was sure I'd heard it somewhere before, but that was impossible. When it came to me, I burst out laughing. It was "The Old Rugged Cross!" It sounded Oriental because in Navaho, tone dictates meaning, whether a melody will or no. I tried to stop laughing at the impossible sound of that hymn, to tell them that the laughter meant no disrespect, but with every try I would get the giggles. When I finally coughed out an apology, Alice only shrugged. "Anyway, I am not Christian," she said.

"Not me too," Bessie echoed.

Lita and the two cooks who had come out to watch me laugh, shook their heads. I had to laugh again.

"Well," I said, "neither am I."

"You ain' no Navaho." And the girl looked at me as though I had stained something borrowed. The People and the Enemy, brother or stranger.

I couldn't let things stay that simple for them. "No," I said, "and not Tewa or Zuni. I'm something else, something called a Brooklyn Jew."

"I never heard of that tribe," Alice answered skeptically.

I looked out the window over the dry reaches of the land. "Our two people would have understood one another. My people once came from a land like this, and they herded sheep too. You name everything on your land for some event in the past, a miracle or wonder that happened there. My fathers did that too. Navaho don't disappear into the people of the pueblos or the white man. My fathers kept their ways too." They were quiet, still skeptical.

Then one of the cooks said, "You Anglo; you talk Anglo."

So I rared back and hit them with the "Shema," and then "Kol Nidre," which was what came to mind.

They listened in complete silence and, afterward, Bessie Tsosie said, "That sound like Tewa."

The fat cook snorted. "I speak Tewa, and that ain't Tewa."

"What did you say them people was?"

"In the beginning, Israelites, then Hebrews, then Jews."

I saw a sharp glance go between Alice and Bessie, and the two cooks were looking at one another. Having more than one name meant something to them. I was about to ask about it, but a bunch of tourists on their way to Fort Defiance came in, and we were busy all the rest of the afternoon.

When the last dinner customer left, I saw the girls whispering together, and when I walked up to them, they stopped. "What's up?" I asked. My voice sounded tired.

Alice said, "We was goin' to ask, could you an' Lita close up, cause we want to go to the Squaw Dance."

I'd wanted them to ask me to a Squaw Dance so much I had almost hinted at it. To the big Navaho socials came people from way back in the hills, the little scattered families and bands who were summering their sheep west of us. Many of them would travel for days to meet friends, eat, make love, trade horses, and dance and sing all night. The hosts laid in tremendous stores of mutton and fried bread and Anglo coffee. I knew that few Anglos had ever been invited to a Squaw Dance, and it would be ruinous to try to crash one, even though it spread out to seven acres of ground, with trucks and horses parked beyond and the courting strung out beyond that. But it was their dance, after all, so I agreed to close. As soon as I said yes, they turned and left.

Lita and I stood in the middle of the floor and looked at the nothing that was swept off, mopped up, put away. It took us until after ten to get things straight.

We left together, exhausted. Outside the air was cool, thin, and trembling, like glass. The night was black, the sky busy with all its stars; there were clouds of them—clustered, spilled, spread. There were more stars than I had ever seen before. Eastward from where we stood, and miles away, we saw the faint glow of reflected light from Gallup, and in the night wind, now faint, now clear, a series of rippled sobs: the sound of the chanting of the Squaw Dance. I tried to ask Lita why I couldn't see it; there was no light, no sign of movement over the great plain that barely rose and dipped away from us. Her English wasn't up to my question, so I finally just asked, "Where is the dance?"

"Ah," and she pointed with her lower lip, the Navaho way, out where it was, where I saw nothing but stars and the huge night overhead, brush, rock, and sand below. There wasn't even a sign of their smoke, although I knew that they would be building high fires by now. Lita could bear her separation no longer. With a quiet sound to free herself of me politely, she began to walk out into the emptiness to which she had pointed, and in a moment she had disappeared. I was alone, looking up at the crowded sky, wondering if my ancient fathers, Jacob or David, pursued in deserts and wise in the nomad way, didn't also camp so as to be invisible, lighting fires for their feast of mutton without even a wisp of betraying smoke coming between their pursuers and the friendly stars.

The next day we were up and running, the Fair gaining on us. Tourists and concessionaires and Indians from many tribes were setting up just outside the administration area. All of them wanted coffee and hot cakes and sausages and eggs cooked four minutes precisely. More coffee. More eggs.

"Hey, miss, these cakes is cold!"

"Hey, waitress, where's that order of beans and steak!"

"Hey, waitress!"

"Hey, wait-RESS!" The usual 1:30 slackening disappeared in a sea of soda, coffee, and "petsi." None of us were really good waitresses, but the girls who had spent all night at the Squaw Dance were particularly lead-footed under the pressure: endless nontipping Navaho; hot dogs: two with, three without; side of French fries; the troupe of a carnival comedy act asked for eight double orders of tomato juice with raw egg and Worcestershire. Campbell's soup calmly boiling over (cause-and-effect) to run all the way down the back counter. Five malteds. How do you make a malted? Grandma at her first Anglo restaurant and fifteen minutes of grunting and lip thrusts before I found out she wanted Alice to serve her, avoiding ritual pollution at my hand. I went and got Alice. ("I'm really Navaho or else they're really Jews, a stubborn, stiff-necked, lost tribe of Jews! Over the Bering Strait and the Mezzuzah fell in the water!")

What is graceful and natural at 7:30 in the morning and in no particular hurry, is misery at 2:00 in the afternoon with Bessie backing out, and three tables waiting, and the cook cursing the world in Navaho.

By 4:00 it's catastrophe. Alice was breaking dishes and I had gotten so far behind that customers were leaving, and the owner, working cash register during the rush, was glowering at me. The work kept building as the supper people began to come. The dinners got fancier, the table settings more elaborate, and I began to feel like the innocent bystander in an old Laurel and Hardy movie, someone suddenly caught up in a pandemonium he hadn't made and didn't understand. All this, and in the din you couldn't hear yourself think. Our customers were not city people used to living in low voices; and, of course, there was the radio. (Blood and Whiskey—eight choruses.) We closed at 10:30. Nobody said good night, and I didn't remember making it to my bed.

The next day was worse, a dish-clattering, spoon-dropping madhouse, a nightmare treadmill of noise and anger. When we got in one another's way, we growled, and the courtesy we had erected to save ourselves from one another fell away. Somebody got the idea that Bessie was taking tips off the other tables. God knows, there were few enough tippers in the crowd, and nobody had actually seen her; but the suspicion was planted; it grew and twisted in our tired minds until we found ourselves "covering" our tables against a thief, suddenly wary and unreasoning in exhaustion. The Fair was a week long and I'd wanted to see it, but we were closing late each night and I was too tired to go after work. As it was, I wondered if I could make it through the week.

And then it rained. It was a bitter thing to learn that the desert's rain was as brutal as its drought. A baked ground has no power to absorb its gift of moisture. The water rose in each little low place until it was in flood. It beat against the adobe earth; it fell sheeting solidly; exploding drops stung like shot;

and I learned with my own arms and shoulders how the hard rock ridges could have been tunneled down into arroyos, the arroyos into incredible canyons. There was water flowing away to loss everywhere. The rain-eaten gullies poured water in torrents, but it was spilling away uselessly, all that needed water in the dry land, a tragic waste. We barely made it to work that morning without falling in the ruts that hadn't been there the night before. We opened late and served a couple of cowmen and a family whose car was bogged in a low spot. Later there were some Indian agents, but no one else, so after lunch hour we all went into the kitchen to see what the cooks had for us.

"Surprise for you girls," the fat cook said. "Right here."

It was "their" treat: fried bread and chili. The bread was a crisp-edged, edible platter of deep-fried dough, and the girls spread it thickly with green chili.

Alice turned to me. "You was tellin' about them people liven somewhere like us . . ."

"You mean the Hebrews?"

"Yeah, what they eat?"

"Well, they had mutton and prickly pear like yours, but more varieties of fruit . . ." And I bit with scholar's confidence into my bread covered with chili, chewed, swallowed. I had eaten fire. Fire erupted inside me. I felt my face go red, tears sprang from my eyes, searing heat traced paths into my head and down the whole track of my throat. Through tears running freely, I saw Alice and Bessie and Lita and the cooks rocking with laughter.

Then someone put a cup of hot coffee in my hand and said, "Drink."

"No," I gasped, "water."

The voice said, "Coffee, now. Hot. Water don' work."

I drank, and for a moment the heat of it only brightened the scalding pain of the chili, but then the burning leveled, then it lowered. I was still flowing tears: nose, eyes, mouth. "That was very good," I said, feeling foolish. It set us off again until we were all in tears.

"Your tribe," Alice said, "I don' know what they eat; I know what they don' eat."

I laughed wetly and held my coffee cup and looked out the window into the grim rain. There we were, enjoying my Anglo anguish while the urgent, vital, earth-feeding gift, all of it, was draining away. I looked back at their faces, calmed and healed by the laughter, and I was wondering how I could have missed the single quality in my fathers which must have been the ground-tone of their lives: patience—with hunger and drought and such wasted plenty as this rain. We stood around quietly, eating and listening to it sound over our heads, more at peace with one another now that there was a chance to rest.

What a strange beauty the desert had. I liked it best at night. The Psalmist says God's greatness is from Everlasting to Everlasting. It was only a beautifully meaningless thought at home, because the world at home was man's creation and even time stood for a certain rate of depreciation. Here, there was Everlasting in any direction, as far as the eye could see; and through it, cutting it into east and west, north and south, a man-sized man might come, leading his sheep to where the grass was young and there was water. Abraham and Isaac knew the desert's beauty and tyranny, capriciousness and cruelty. I was learning an admiration for the strength a people must have who would wrest their lives from it. My Abraham and Isaac were American Navaho, who had never seen a Jew before.

In the late afternoon the rain stopped, and two hours later it was impossible to tell that it had fallen. Only a fresh scent hung in the air. The ground was dry; the brush was dry; the torrents that had flooded and poured downland to some distant river were gone. People were all around, putting out their heads and folding up their raincoats to go on where the rain had stopped them. There must have been a hundred people in the supper rush, and we didn't close till ten.

At quitting time I asked Alice if the Squaw Dance was still going on.

"No, they be one before end of grass here; soon people start south, away from high place, cold."

I was still hoping for that invitation, but I was afraid to press it, so I asked her what the steps looked like. She searched me for ridicule. None was there. "Here," she said, "I make it for you. . . ." And she showed me, but it wasn't much: a shuffle back and a shuffle forward, widening to the left so as to move very slowly in a circle. As she did the step she looked as embarrassed as Navaho permit themselves to look. "Step. This *step*. *Step* isn' *dance* . . ." Wrestling with the impossible Anglo words to try to tell me what I could never know from my world of dances with *steps*. She had been forced for the first time to consider the poverty of her "step."

I said, "I can see that. I know a dance that looks like that. The joy in it is that the people are all together, stepping together and coming down with both feet on the same place as the person before them, and the dance grows in layers. The dancers make the layers together, as if they were saying: All together we make one."

"A dance of your tribe?" she asked.

"One of them."

"And you are not Indian?"

"No."

"Soun' like Indian to me."

The question of identity was put on the day before the end of the Tribal Fair. Because of overtime I would be able to get back to school in time for registration. I could leave when the Fair ended, hitch to Gallup, Gallup to Denver to New York— and no money spent staying over. As the Fair edged off, the crowds in the restaurant slackened, and on the last two nights we closed at nine.

There was a full moon. The Navaho God in charge of such things had lit my night, and I was grateful. We stood around outside and talked, waiting for the cooks to come out. There was supposed to be another Squaw Dance over near Fort Defiance, but the girls were too tired to walk. The plan was to wait near the highway for a ride, and I guess I was hanging around hoping to be invited along when the car showed up. Their talk was the mixture of Navaho and English that they used when they were together. I was only half-listening.

"Who was shearing in the Fair for—" (the last lost to Navaho and to me).

"Johnny Begay an' his uncle, who—"

"Who was singin'?

"They got—"

It reminded me of the Yiddish-English stew I spoke with my grandfather.

Lita put out her lip toward me after a while. "Her tribe— sheep—if they got song like . . ."

Navaho are a reticent people, and while the ancient Hebrews may have been reticent also, it's not noticeably present in modern Jews. I was amused while I listened to them, and curious enough to speak first.

"Did you say sheep? Funny, I know a song about a lamb . . ."

They smiled, yes, in the moonlight; and I smiled, yes, took a breath and broke free. I sang "Chad Gadyo," and then translated it verse by verse, from the dog and the little lamb to God's battle with the Angel of Death. Singing got me drunk at this altitude, maybe; maybe freedom and the full moon; but I was loose-limbed and happy, and, before I knew it, we were all dancing a hora in the American desert to the very uneven strains of "El Yivneh Hagalil." They countered with two shepherd's songs.

I tried to feel them as a Navaho, but I couldn't. The trembling lifts and lowerings of their melody reminded me of a good cantor, hovering proudly, gently over his best notes. The songs were quiet, trembling, but clear; melody rising from the small voices between illimitable earth and illimitable sky might be the cry of my own people, reminding God, however gently and reverently, that One-and-Omniscient must still be instructed by man in the agonies that only man knows: mortality, imperfection, being so ceaselessly changed, and so quickly ended. I sang them a Psalm. Egypt had not yet taught us whips and slavery; Babylon had not yet made us dwellers in cities; ghettos had not yet walled us in. Afterward, we traded song for song.

Alice said, "In them songs, it's still singin' for God. You don' tell which God you singin' about."

"We were nomads," I said. "We couldn't take much with us, roaming the world. After a while we even had to leave our languages behind, and our dreams. We took our God. One God. Only One."

"Oh," she said, pitying me my poverty. "We got different song, different Spirit."

"I've heard a little about Changing Woman," I said, "and White Shell Woman, and Born of Water . . ."

"Well, White Shell Woman is Changing Woman, only change . . ."

"No," Bessie said, "White Shell Woman different. Song say," and they took the discussion away from me again.

Theology. I hoped I wasn't giving them revenge for the green chili. If I want disputations, I thought, I'll go home. Then, for no reason, I remembered the kid with the open fly and no underwear. Blessed are the poor; they have the most stupendous pride. If you are poor and have a long history too, the pride gets perfected under the eyes of countless conquering armies.

Lita said, "Your tribe—make sand picture, like us?"

It's cold in the desert at night; I hadn't felt it before. Now I was getting dizzy looking at the stars—And I will multiply your seed as the stars in heaven . . . Well, that had been a different night and another land. I said, "My tribe wasn't like Navaho in some ways. We have one God, a spirit we believe is too great to name or picture. Names and pictures define things, limit them. He has no limit for us, no edge, no boundary. The only visible thing—is a book."

Two lights broke over the small hill to the south. It was a car on the way to Fort Defiance. It came up the road and stopped before the subtle signal of Lita's arm lifting only a degree from her side as they walked to the highway and I followed. I knew that I had been included without having to be told. I was learning. Now I could tell a silent affirmative when I heard or, rather, didn't hear one. We all got in the car and moved down the road.

I asked, "Who is giving the dance; I want to leave something."

"I take you," Bessie said.

So we went a distance, and then stopped and got out of the car in the middle of Everlasting, and we walked off the roadbed and into the desert. I stumbled over everything: white hummocks, ruts, stones. They walked easily. I was an Anglo, all right, a stranger.

In the American city of my birth I was a stranger too. I learned the city's ways until I passed, "assimilated" but for the strange intonations of my prayers, out of the ghetto. I never regretted the passage. Beyond that ghetto there are a thousand worlds to see. I was often lonely for the security of the "separated," but loneliness is a small price to pay, and the pain of it would have as much easing as I could give it. This night was such an easing. I didn't know the Navaho, not their language or beliefs. They didn't know Abraham or Isaac, but I wasn't lonely, stumbling over what they knew and expected. Why should I be; it was the biggest ghetto I had ever seen.

We went over a little rise in the land I thought was level and saw the big fires and the trucks—all of it in the downwind silence.

"Can Anglo understand Squaw Dance?" Bessie asked.

I smiled. "The tenements of the old ghetto teem with people, shriek, noise, and stench," I answered. "Washlines scar the sky between the houses. The streets shine with rotting fish skins. A man lives his swarming, impacted life without seeing one green thing growing from the ground. With such similarities, how could I miss?"

SUMMERING

There was a farm owned by the friend of some distant relative, and I was sent there for a summer with admonitions to eat vegetables and rise early and breathe deeply. After I unpacked and changed, I went out through the back of the house, closing the door quietly, shy in strangeness, to pursue the dutiful, mournful occupation of pulling air into my lungs and pushing it out again. There was a path leading from the back door to the dairy shed and a small stream and some outbuildings of the farm, and behind them the great rising heap of a mountain. At first sight and ever after, the greatness of it was like a chorale with many voices, or like a great Mass, so in my mind I called it Kyrie Mountain. It lifted in the Kyrie's three folds: pine groves to rising meadows to summit, strong unison, bare rock like an altar. I stood for a long time listening to it, and faltering to explain it to myself, the sound of something seen. All the voices, and each voice moved in the counterpoint of rise on rising hills.

The door opened behind me and a girl came out carrying a pail and walking past me to the dairy house. She kept her eyes straight ahead, except for a quick flip of the glance over me and no change on her face at all. Then a woman came out and

Summering

waited on the small back porch, calling, "Justine, don't you just get them eggs, and don't you hurry! I got no cake just waitin' for them eggs!"

I smiled at the elliptical speech, and I could hear Justine in the dairy shed, muttering in her own thread of theme, "Damn woman—lay your own eggs, or what's the cackle for!"

After a while she returned from the dark doorway, holding the eggs and keeping the straight-worn path from the shed to the back steps of the house. Her muttering, as if she were engine-driven, kept a steady undertone; and I realized, as she mounted the steps and went inside, that she hadn't stopped to look around her, not even to the great lift of mountain or a glance to the white clouds above us or even one at me. She walked as if she were wearing blinders: the packed-earth path, the steps, and up, and in, and gone, leaving only the bang of the screen door behind her and then silence.

After a while I went in myself; the mountain was making me dizzy with its grandeur and the girl confusing me with her blindness in the face of it. I went up the steps, closing the screen door quietly because of that presence standing behind me. The dark hall led past the kitchen, and I heard two women's voices and the creak, coming and going, of a rocker. Mrs. Van Riper and the older hired woman were resting before they started supper.

"Summerin'," one said, and the long creak.

"You seen her?"

"No, I ain't." (Creak.)

"Skinny-lookin', rat tails of braids—she's loony, you know." (Creak.)

"What's she do?"

(Cre—eak, and a laugh.) "Don't have to *do* anything. Why, Cina, country girls go to the city to work, but city folks send their girls to summer away only when they got TB or they're loony." (Creak.) "That water boiled yet?"

I was wild with delight. The longer I thought about it, the happier I felt. They thought me important enough to be mad! What a tribute! In a great leap of joy and awe, almost as great as at the first sight of the mountain, I beheld my freedom in this lie of madness. It stretched as wide before me as the summer itself, and seeing it opened out from the first day, it seemed to be more than the delight of saying and doing what I wished. I had always been hesitant with people and engulfed by change. Now I was not to be hindered; there was no need to see both sides of an issue, to stand before circumstances like a muddled scholar toiling over a pun in a dead language. Madwomen took all the binding little bits of daily duties and trifles and bore up from them and pulled free. Laughing, I snatched the twisted, snaggled rubber bands from my braids and undid them. My hair was straight and dry, full of electricity so that it lifted away around my head. It was wonderful hair for madness. For a while I leapt around, posing the gestures, but soon I remembered that if I feigned "loony," I would be doing no more than changing one disguise for another. I did a few more crouches artistically, in the corner, and then re-combed and re-braided my hair and went outside again to listen to my mountain.

In those first weeks I was bitterly, ridiculously possessive of the whole great hill. Every inch of land over which I passed, I claimed; walking west into the birch groves, I was jealous for the east, at dawn for sunset, at sunset for midnight. This first love was as pure a greed as any ancient despot nourished, and I sacrificed even my wish to be let alone, let free, to besiege the stolid Justine with questions about the mountain's winters. Had she ever seen the northern lights there, or noticed the winter sunrise or the autumn stars? What she had seen was little; what she could describe even less. The stars were pretty; the snow was deep; and no more. When I tried to ask how deep, how pretty; she would shrug and grunt about some chore, and hurry off in bewilderment. Justine was a summer hired girl who lived in town nearby. I learned later that she had once beaten an attacking wolf to death with a shovel, and that she was quick and utterly fearless in the face of danger, yet before the simplest of my questions concerning the birch grove she was reduced to the numbness of a frightened child.

And I showed off my mountain even as I was jealous of anyone's knowledge of it. I bragged to Mrs. Van Riper about the berry groves that I alone had discovered high above the pine slopes, even above the great rock thrust crowning the mountain. She always nodded and said wasn't that nice, which angered me so that I went out the back door, muttering along the via dolorosa to the dairy shed. "Isn't that nice! Moses off the mountain; God written down and notarized in his hands.

Looking and smiling. Ten thousand Van Ripers, 'Isn't that nice!' "

Pausing at the black threshold of the dairy shed, I would think that it perhaps wasn't proper to be so angered at her lack of feeling for nature. I was moving toward the very quiet, very cool corner where she kept the tub of new butter. I would scrape a curl of it discreetly from the tub. In the secrecy and darkness it tasted like sunlight. It tasted like the flowers on Kyrie Mountain.

II

On the first fold of the slope there had been a farm. The ruins lay eastward and couldn't be seen from where we were, but once the front of the three rises was climbed, faint old paths began the subtle work of leading a walker, almost against his will, to the deserted place. The house was now a heap of fallen boards and the weed-grown holes of cellar and storage pit. The barn was still standing; and though it leaned heavily in the way of the wind, it still reminded anyone of cattle and people and tilled soil. I had announced to my amazed parents that I was tired of the human race and that I wanted peace from all the family noise; but I found myself going out of my way to pass the deserted house and to question the ghosts—how they came and how they left.

Now, it was full summer. The days were hot; and before noon the heat would water up from the earth and the sky; and the hills would blaze yellow. Going up one morning, later than usual, I began to get dizzy with the heat and the climb. My heart was pounding. Although there were trees down the sides of the hill and a big maple near the ruins of the house, the sun at height had driven the shade from them, so as soon as I came to the barn I went unsteadily through the gaping door into the dimness. Outside the crickets sang with a hot, crackling buzz, as though the world was frying in its own heat. I closed my eyes and let the trembling dizziness pass, and then I rested, smelling the agedness of the place—rats, cobwebs, and a shadow of sweet-smelling grass that was stored here once.

After a while I got up and went out into the oven of the noon. I stirred idly in the wreck of the house, finding blue bits of old glass which the sun had darkened. Above the house and to the right there was a little patch marked off with stones that had been her kitchen and herb garden. Weeds had taken it over and some of the herbs had gone wild and were strange to me, but some were still mine to know, and I walked looking, building to the unknown lives facts of a table and a cool pantry and a medicine shelf. There was mint and camomile, fennel and wild onion, dill weed and flax. The sun was making me dizzy again, so I went down to the path past the house to the barn like an owner, having gone so boldly to the intimacies of cupboards and drawers. I was at the barn door, one hand on the doorpost and one foot rising for a step, when I saw him coming out, a hard, burned-leather face with two pale and wild eyes and a tangle of hair. We had come from nowhere, both of us, to stand so close so suddenly. His clothes were ragged and brown —face and hair and clothes all of one color. The body beneath the tatters as lithe and fierce as an animal. My terror broke. I turned and tore away down the hill toward Van Ripers', hearing him follow with awful ease in the long grass behind me.

He would play with me, let me hope to reach the bottom first without stumbling and falling. I was too busy watching my footing to notice that I was running toward a great island of shackleweed. Suddenly I was on it and I knew I could never get past. The long vines would trap me, slow me, clinging to my feet; and he would wait, grinning. He would watch my struggle and my defeat. I couldn't bear the thought of my own stupidity and humiliation. I could see myself becoming frantic; I could hear his breathing. I stopped short of the green tangle and straightened up. I would turn with what dignity was left to confront him.

The hill behind me was utterly bare and still. All the way up to the farm the long grass weltered in the heat, but there was no one there. For the first time since I had seen Kyrie Mountain and named it for its chorale, I was frightened of it and eager to be back to Van Ripers'. It was unsteady walking down the last way, feeling watched and knowing that I was not, feeling betrayed and knowing that I had only been foolish. I went into the house by the formal front door and to my room without being seen, and for the first time without turning and a small wink or a head tilt toward the beloved hill.

At supper I wondered if I still looked pale, but if so, it wasn't noted. Mr. Van Riper was discussing his trip to town and I, needing to feel more natural at their table, was helping to serve and take plates. Summer was heavy with work; there was usually no lingering over coffee; but this evening scandals and feed-grain prices kept Mr. Van Riper at his place, his expression more alive with his telling than I had ever seen it; and I noticed all of us as we sat, and how the light was falling and how there was a little spill of sugar by the bowl. Sugar always spills a little, and that's familiar. I had been forced to run toward the familiar; I was grateful, even moved that there was a here to run to when mountains bred their apparitions. I had raged at my want of freedom, hated the stupid and stultifying bonds that held a person to his groups and clans and parents' expectations; and I had forgotten or never known how cold the world was and how dark outside the rooms of lighted windows, in one of which I sat now at first humbling, glad that someone knew me and would be moved to search if I were missing.

The next day I wandered around the farm, and in the afternoon drifted into the kitchen where Cina and Justine were laying out the canning things. As we worked, it was almost easy to mention coming on the mad-looking stranger. I was standing in that ordinary place in the middle of a common task, but Cina answered with a wild whoop of laughter, putting her towel down and throwing back her head, and she laughed in a long flood of sound. I would have been angry or ashamed, except that listening to her was a joy in itself.

When she could, she grabbed the towel again and flapped the bewildered Justine on the head with it, crying, "Don't you see. Don't you see what it was?" Her eyes were wet with laughing. "Oh, my soul!" and she sputtered and laughed again, fighting to tell us. "Lord . . . Glory! I ain't seen old Word in a couple of years, and except if you know him, he must look like you said, all wild and dirt-color. But he ain't no one to fear. He used to work on that old farm up there. Went to the war, and when he come back, the folks had gone away somewhere. He took to roaming the hills all these years, but he stays around here; and ever so often he goes there, where he worked when he was a boy. He ain't got *no* harm to him. . . . Now, what's funny . . ."

And off she went into a ripple of giggles, and I laughed too, with relief and gratitude. "What's funny, is that he come running down *here* yesterday, from the western side he come, and run in here just a-cryin scart, an' says, 'I was comin' out of the barn when I seen a ghost at the barn door—a witch—tall as a man and skinny, an' it was pale as the buried dead!' It took me near an hour to quiet him, and I just lay it to loneliness, because I didn't think of you being there at all!"

We all laughed together and remembered the expressions we must have had, and laughed again; and my paleness from the heat, and laughed again; and how we must have run by different ways past the wind but not our fear, and laughed again; a ghost and a witch, and laughed again; but toward the end it came to me that we might be too much alike, old Word and me, not to have been afraid, that maybe Word was my soul twenty years from now.

That evening I sat by the dairy shed and watched my mountain and listened to its night-chant of rising and falling tones, up into darkness. If old Word walked the hills I might meet him again. We wouldn't laugh. I said to Kyrie, "My mountain. Even if I owned you, he would be there. You can never be owned." It was a bitter knowledge so soon in loving. How long ago had Word learned it, that he could witness and endure and no more?

A few days later, Cina took me aside, smiling, and said, "I let on at the store for him to come. He's here in the kitchen, that old Word, and you go in, see him, show him you ain't no witch."

I went in slowly, finding him in the room, staring at him, overwhelmed at my own powers with phantasy and fear. He was short now, almost small, and though his body was agile, he was very slender. In the hard light of the kitchen he was much older than I had imagined. As he looked at me, his eyes widened with terror and made the hurried equation of his place and mine and the door. Then he looked at me again in the ordinariness of the kitchen—stove, wall calendar, light chain dangling—and we just stood for a long time.

Then I said, "I'm summering here. How do you do?" And held out my hand. The sound came very small and quavering, but the effect, though I had not planned it, was right. I saw him relax, and when he looked up again at me the hardness of his look was that of a recluse to a strange young girl, not mortal to ghost.

"Good afternoon, ma'am," he said, disdaining my outstretched hand, a travesty in a woman, that male gesture. The shamed hand retreated to me.

We talked about our mountain, and I was careful to show surprise and interest when he told me that the pine grove had once burned down and was starting again a little southward of its fathering stand. I mentioned the bee tree I had found.

"I never go there no more," he said. "Snake bit me there once and I shied clear after that."

We gave and took little scraps of fact and recognition, but the talk was clumsy in a kitchen whose whole purpose was standing against Word's nature and my dream. Our strangeness increased instead of diminishing, but we both knew why, and it helped.

I was honored when the old man, turning to leave, said, "You seen the stream begin, up over by the high rock?"

I had, of course, but something kept me from telling him so. He said he would show it to me, and the old mining trail to Woman Mountain, too. All his treasures. I knew then that he would give me everything he could, every knowledge. It was a greater generosity than I would ever be capable of, and he had humbled me with his modesty in it. He said good-bye and I watched him go down the road and walk toward town, knowing that once out of sight he would cut off the road and begin to climb. His delicacy was such in this thing he so understood that he would never let me see him climbing "his" mountain, sure and knowing and steady. Such a thing spoke intolerably of ownership. His deftness was a gesture of courtly grace from the old lover to the new.

III

If the first month of my mountain was like a meeting, a love and courtship, the second was like the beginning of a marriage. I began to walk to town; I worked with Cina; ran errands and hung the wash; holding to myself the sureness that Kyrie Mountain was always there to think of, to run to, a secret source of power and love. I saw Word now and then, and he showed me trails and caves and told me about the people who had had the farm. The very joy of my love gave me a surge toward the world. It began with Justine.

On that first day I had seen her stolid and unaware; and later, all closed and mute against my questioning, it seemed to me that Justine was just dull. Having measured her in that way I stopped thinking about her. Then, one evening when supper was almost over, I heard the sound of girls singing. The sound was clear and sweet, coming down the road toward the farm. I was about to ask what it was when from the kitchen a starched and pressed and beribboned Justine flew, quick behind her eyes and glowing with delight, to answer it. Gone was the flat-footed walk, as if it had never been.

I smiled because of it. "Who are those girls?"

She answered, "It's the girls from the laundry. We're all going to the picture show in Nillis Gorbal's truck!" And then to Mrs. Van Riper, "May I have my money, ma'am, please?"

I got up to go to the porch in order to look at them, but I caught a glimpse of Justine's face as she passed me. She did not want me there. I repaid Word then by paying Justine; I went to the parlor and contented myself with looking through the crocheted curtain at them. There were eight of them, about two years older than I was, and they looked so happy and friendly in their starched skirts and tumbling hair, laughing and practising steps in the road, that I repented me of having wished mankind to end forever as recently as a month ago. I went in to my room quietly and read one of my books, knowing even with the little sting of envy that, anyway, not a single one of those gay, pretty, singing girls would know the name of what I was reading, although it was a famous work.

After a few hours I got tired and went out to stretch in the open night. The full moon was as close as I had ever seen it. On the arm of Kyrie Mountain the aspen grove was silver, and my shadow was black on silver, and I began to walk down the road to the highway, turning around again and again to see the great mass of mountain pulling away into the darkness all its ridges and peaks. Now Woman Mountain to the north seemed to be ascendant, and I saw, or rather heard and saw, how ringing my chorale would have to be to encompass all of the great range of hills. I lifted my arms to greet it in its magnificence, when I sensed someone close to me, sitting off the road in the tall grass or against a tree perhaps, and watching. It was not fear at first but anger that made me call out, "Who is it?" hating whomever

Summering

it was who always seemed to be standing between me and my moments of singleness in the world.

A voice answered from a tree. "It's just me—Mary Emerald." The voice was good and firm, but dry, like Word's, and she hesitated before dropping down from one of the low branches where she had been sitting. "I'm Mary Emerald Wrather."

I had to puzzle out the words in moonlight which had wrought so many changes on the world. She sat down under the tree and I saw her frilly blouse and patterned skirt. She had a well-made solidness to her body and a plain face, even in this moonlight, and I said, "Were you one of the girls with Justine tonight?"

"Justine an' them went on over to one of their houses. I guess they'll be goin' on till morning."

I walked closer, wondering if she had chosen the great silence instead of the lights and noise and gaiety of the "night out." If she hadn't, she would be laughing at me.

"Why didn't you go with them?"

"I don't know," she said evenly.

I groaned to myself. Another Justine.

Then she looked up at me for a while and said, "You're the one stayin' up to Van Riper's, supposed to be crazy, ain't you?"

I said I was.

"I had a aunt once like that, but she was locked up. I went to see her once. It was awful there."

"Why?" I asked.

"No trees. Lots of people, stone walls, people laughin' an' screamin'. No trees." She shuddered. "I never want to be where there's no trees." Her voice, like Word's, carried no emotion with the language, but the dryness of it conveyed a feeling that was somehow even deeper than if they had been said with some sort of flourish, such as I would have used. Suddenly she laughed shortly. "It's all over town about you and Word met up to the barn. Cina's come to tell it like 'amen' in to church."

"I hope nobody's been laughing at Word about it," I said, knowing that they must have been, and being grateful again for his delicacy and gallantry that he had said nothing to me or let it change the clumsy deference of his half-man to my half-woman. We were both quiet for a time, looking at the glowing space between the road and the mountains, an air that was visible in moonlight.

"I think I should tell you," I said, "I mean about being crazy. The truth is that I'm not really. People here figure it because—well—because I'm here. I used to think I'd like to be, but I'm not." We stood quietly to watch the night and the blades of the wind cutting in the aspen grove.

Finally Mary Emerald said, "You ever been to the lake? That's the best place to go on nights like this."

Across the highway and down a small hill, closer than Kyrie, and I had never seen it. It was covered on one side by the shadows of tall trees, so that the half of it that wasn't glinting silver was as black as ink. Without having to decide, we shed our clothes, suddenly heavy as duty, and leaped into the water.

Two loud splashes, the moon in every drop, and then we were quiet. We didn't joke or laugh but made trails with our bodies in the water to see how the moon would stumble on the roughened paths. We dove down, silently, sounding, and then came up under the top sheet of the water to see how far the light reached down; we floated on our backs against the stars, secretly part of the water as it was of us.

Suddenly Mary Emerald turned her head toward me, putting her hand up so that I swam to her, making no sound.

"I heard a truck stop!" she whispered.

We waited, and I was almost ready to say, "See, it was nothing," when I heard a titter of laughter and a guffaw and a girl saying, "He does too!" And more laughter.

"It's them!" Mary Emerald hissed. "It's Justine and them and that Nillis Gorbal!"

We hurried out as quietly as we could. Suddenly we were very vulnerable and alone, standing naked on the edge, and Mary Emerald turned. "Hurry up. We can dress under the trees!" with an urgency that was almost fear.

We grabbed our clothes and ran to the shelter of the dark grove, I following her with long strides, just alike in our nudity, the fragment of a Greek vase gone mad. We dressed, listening to the laughter and horseplay on the shore which we had left. Two young men were trying to persuade eight laughing girls that if they all went in and came out together, no one would have time for peeping. The girls seemed to waiver; the warmth of the night and the others, the sky and water were urging them; and finally they gave in, exacting an absurd promise of blindness from the boys and the more real threat that if anyone looked, all of them would beat the offender senseless and leave him at the garbage dump as an example. I heard Justine's voice and it surprised me, it was so light and young, answering a joke, and someone saying loudly (unless it was the pain speaking in us that made it seem so), "old Mary Emerald is probably home right now, Nillis, dreamin' about you all bare-naked!"

Everyone laughed and there were some more jokes about Mary Emerald. Two hours had been a long time. Here I was, angry at them for her, and we now allies against them; her friends would henceforth be mine, and her enemies also, and all of it as naturally as if I did not hate the world.

When we were dressed, we crept away carefully; and I wondered for a moment why so carefully. When we were up on the highway, I said, "You know, we could have had our evens on them for taking the lake away from us. Once we were dressed, we could have gone right up to them and shamed them to a fine, cold sweat."

"You don't think I thought of that!" I heard bitterness in her voice. "Look, the way you are, you don't care maybe; but if eight walk the road together an' one takes the hill trail, it ain't the road-walkers got to explain, even though there's cars and stink an' all, but the one gone by the trail has got to say, 'well, I'd take the road, but I promised Gram I'd get her some wild rye, or Sinai Ellis pitched a fit for the trail till I had to take him'." She remembered. "Sinai Ellis is my brother." I heard her anger at the unfairness and at the many times she must have begged pardon for herself and been only half-forgiven, for the shaded truths by which she had excused herself for no sin.

She would never lie, certainly never wildly, eloquently, as I had done, framing grotesque and outlandish fantasies that were my form of rebellion at the questions and the cornering. Mary Emerald thought I didn't know these hard facts of the difference between road and trail; I knew them to the bone, scored in to me through a hundred parties and a thousand lapses of preference and ten thousand "pleasurable" activities, which had no pleasure in them but which had burned into leisure and privacy like fire into paper. But she had said these things, stood up and declared them; and I was full of admiration for her.

It was only in the paleness of very early day that I remembered that our singleness, hers and mine, was only that of a smaller group, that the very finding of one another was, in part, a mirror of the joyful Justine flying to her own in a rush of starched skirts and ribbons, found at last.

IV

With the urgency of girls who, with so much less reason than the old, feel that they might die tomorrow, we began to pour ourselves into one another. We knew, even then, that we were not the usual friends, but that we understood one another and could share what had been hidden in ourselves for so long—not the knowledge that a mountain could sound like Lassus, Byrd, or Beethoven, of whom Mary Emerald had never heard, but that it could sound at all. I could only guess at the cruelty of those who peopled Mary Emerald's life, but I could understand with ease how the saddest word in her vocabulary was "treeless."

One day she came up to the abandoned farm. She and Word knew that I liked to be by myself, but when I was there, it was because I liked to be with them too. Then sometimes they came up or called to me and we would sit in the ruins and talk. That day she said, "We was finished early today over to the laundry, and I come up to ask you about what I was thinkin'." Her face didn't change, but there was something in her manner that made me sense the struggle—wish for something, fear I would laugh—her own consciousness of my knowledge made her fumble. She used the voice I had first heard—low, dry, and expressionless. "I want to have us a Slumber Party an' set up in our pajamas an' drink cokes an' that."

All in the level voice, profoundly serious eyes above the words. I had to push my laughter back until it threatened to choke me. One day, who knows how many years ago, some young, curly-haired cheerleader in town must have picked up the idea and parlance from a magazine and tortured the import into the rigid mold of this mountain town. The Wrathers were poor and crowded, and Mary Emerald was a strange one and unwelcome in the pleasant and party-giving houses in town. At last she saw a chance for the "amenities" to come to her own place—something genteel, even if it was only the name, to give a glow to the years about to come. We were fourteen. Here beginneth Romeo and Juliet, the proms and the pressed roses and violin music, boxes of love letters, diaries and lipstick, and lace and La Bohème. It would come to me, and I might scorn it because I was plain; but Mary Emerald, wish or no, would never have a single moment of it, and she knew it. There was only her Slumber Party, cokes and all.

I said, "How do they usually invite people? Do they just ask them?"

"No, they call up on the phone or they send out those little cards with pictures of cats wearin' pajamas or girls swingin' ribbons."

I said, "Oh, then you'd better send me one of those, I guess." I was being flippant because the whole ridiculous thing was in such dead earnest. I was half through when I saw how wrong it was. "Maybe we'd better both choose the cards and send them to everybody who is going to be there."

Her face eased. "I been lookin' for a while now, an' thinkin' about it, and there's ideas I got about the best ones to get." She sat down very intently and began to work out our guest list. "You never invite the mothers, and Mom'll be sleepin' over to Shires' anyway 'till after the fruit harvest. Mary Virgin 'ud love to come, but Frank wants her to home. They just been married last year. The boys don't get one, so that lets them out. The rest are all to home. Mary Opal would just laugh and Micah La-France and Sinai Ellis are boys, and Mary Pearl is too small, so none of them need any. Now—" (She had gone over this for a long time, I knew, the figuring was only for me). "Now Gram is old and she won't come, but maybe we should send her one in case she's got a mind to come or maybe just to know we're giving it."

I said I thought it was a good idea.

From her spark, the glimmer of such a small dream, Mary Emerald was coming to brightness. She looked at me again for asking, but she was surer now. "The hardware store's got cards, but they ain't nothin' to what's over to Cricket Lake." She knew I would agree.

We went down the hill, borrowed a dollar from Justine, walked the nine and three-quarter miles to Cricket Lake, and there purchased three party invitations and three bottles of

coke for our Slumber Party. Mary Emerald wouldn't let me pay
for the cokes. We thumbed a ride back on a vegetable truck,
and as I rested against the burning, rattling metal side, I was
delighted with myself and with my hostess, who had borrowed
a whole dollar—ten cards' worth—and said nothing to Justine
about getting only three. It was early evening when we got
home, and Mary Emerald left me at the road to Van Ripers.

"When do you think we ought to have our Slumber Party?"

"I think we should have it next week," I said.

"I'm off on Thursday, so why don't we make it for Wednesday night."

I paused, thinking and planning. I knew that she wanted me
to act as she must have seen it at school, the pretty and well-
dressed popular ones, pausing to find place in their heavily
mortgaged days and evenings for this party or that. Finally I
said, "Yes, I think I can make it on Wednesday."

She nodded gravely, and we turned and went our ways. Two
days later the invitation arrived in the mail. I knew that the
smaller Wrather kids would be at home, although Mary Emerald was working, so I wrote a little note of acceptance and took
it over.

The older Wrather boys had married and gone, but their
ruins still lay rusting in the front yard—two gutted cars and
some parts, filled by the last rain. The house was weatherbeaten
and old, but the rib-sprung, rust-eaten mound of junk in front
of it made it look more dilapidated than it really was. Behind
the house and at the sides, pine trees sang in the light wind.
The time-grayed place could have belonged to its land—enduring in the same rule as the rock and the pine tree—but that
junk heap seemed to make the Wrathers intruders there
and not inhabitants. I walked around the tangled maze of an
old bedspring that had been hurled over some car-guts. The
Wrathers' poverty was a parody of conspicuous consumption.

Mary Pearl, the youngest, came around the side of the house
holding a broken pitcher. She turned her cool, poised glance at
me, standing there, and I saw one hand slowly leave the pitcher
and go to an old tire that was leaning against a tree and rest
there, familiar without the use of sight. The ruins, then, were
not for possession but for barricade, against man and nature.
I'd been to the house before with Mary Emerald at night, and
had met the children all dimmed with sleep. Now recognition

came, and the little girl turned and went into the house and soon they were all out on the porch, shy and wary, with the same grave, level look—the Wrather look. Mary Emerald had told me that her father had died three years ago. Now Micah LaFrance, man of the family, said in his child's voice, "Mary Emrald ain't to home."

I said the words as I heard her say them, to give them something familiar. "Don't mind, just see this note to her." Then I turned, a difficult thing with all their eyes on me, and walked back down the path.

In the days between I walked high Kyrie's stands of trees and berry meadows. The mountain was in full summer and its ripening weighed the rising air with dusty, warm fruit smells. I gathered berries for the farm and Mary Emerald. It seemed that there weren't buckets enough to hold the plenty. I left great potsful at the abandoned farm for Word, until he told me in an agony of embarrassment that they "laid on his stomach," after which he turned and fled into the aspen grove.

On Wednesday evening I went to Mary Emerald's house with a pair of pajamas, a toothbrush, and clean underwear in a paper bag, and a silk scarf for Mary Emerald. I had come early; there was to be no moon that night and it was just about sundown. In the long, slanting golden light that came through two windows, the cowed and wide-eyed children stood pressed around the walls. I wondered what threats Mary Emerald had held to them to insure their manners on our "occasion." After a long, strained silence, she excused herself and left the house, and at her going a great sigh, easing, went up in the darkening room, and Sinai Ellis piped up in a wonderful voice of awe.

"She's gone to the backhouse. She made us clean the whole floor. She made us burn the whole trash. She even made us to wash the windows!"

The doors of their discretion were unlocked. Everyone but Mary Opal, the loyal lieutenant, had strange and wonderful things to tell. Mary Pearl told how there was no time to wash and iron all the clothes, and everyone giggled and looked importantly at the wardrobe in the corner. Micah LaFrance pointed out the stacks of draining dishes. It was darkening. On the wall the faces of the silent dead left us for shadow. The set, scared face of Mary Emerald's father departed in peace. The kerosene lamps were lit and put out on the table, and a whisper at my ear said, "See—even the lamp glasses, an' she made us dry them too!"

I thought I heard a light knock at the door, so I went and opened it. A young woman stood delicate and hesitating in the outside evening. Twilight is a flatterer, but as she stood there I thought she was the most beautiful person I had ever seen. Behind me the joyful recognition came.

"It's Mary Virgin! Mary Virgin's come to visit!"

I said, "Oh, come in." The name shattered my composure. "Please, Mary Emerald will be back soon—uh—I'm her friend." I couldn't make myself say her name.

As she moved into the room I saw that she was really beautiful. Her face was clear and serene, the features perfect. Later, as I saw her—and I kept looking because she was so beautiful —I thought her face lacked a certain vigor or liveliness, but at first sight the sweetness of her look and the almost luminous clarity of her skin and eyes made me feel an awe of her, so that I stood away a little to look at her. She had been wearing a light, loose coat; and as she shook it off, I saw that she was far advanced in pregnancy. She looked about, knowing the chairs in the house, until she found a steady one and half-sat on it carefully, so timid and so careful as if she did not trust her whole self's weight anywhere.

"Gram told me about Mary Emerald's party and I just got to longing . . . Oh, the house is so clean." She was looking around at everything. "It's so pretty for the party." Her eyes came back to herself and her rounded body. "Frank just let me come to see. I got to be back afore long, truly."

In the stillness between the little tentative whisps of her sentences, we heard Mary Emerald coming around the outside of the house. Somehow, in Mary Virgin's presence, the noise of her sister's big feet and strong, solid weight was rude and intrusive. When she came in, banging the door, there was silence, so that she looked around quickly, at one and another, to see if anything was wrong. Mary Virgin was sitting very still, waiting and smiling. When Mary Emerald saw her there, she jumped high and hit the floor hard with both loud feet, letting out a yell of pleasure, and the house shook.

Again the soft, even voice—shine of delight, but no abandon —"Congratulations on your Slumber Party, Mary Emerald. I wisht I could stay, but Frank wants me to home. He's waiting over to Territ's."

"You walked from Territ's," I said, trying to sound interested but not surprised. Territ's was a bar on the edge of town and a good three miles away. That would be six miles, three of them in heavy darkness. She got up, a little more heavily now, and hesitating.

"Can't you stay an' have a coke with us?" Mary Emerald asked.

"No, I better be starting."

"Do you have a light?"

"I have a little lantern, but it needs kersene."

A whisper, but Micah LaFrance sped for the kerosene; Mary Opal for the match; Mary Pearl and Sinai Ellis to hold the lantern and stand at the door. Mary Virgin had a special kind of wonder for all of them more than her name or her mysterious life away from them or her pregnancy. Perhaps it was her beauty, so rare and special a thing for them—something valued. Whatever magical thing her presence was, Mary Virgin had come the long way to bestow it, and now we all belonged to the Slumber Party.

"Frank'll laugh sure when I tell him how you took on, seein' me settin' by," she said. Then good night to each one, and they to her. There were no nicknames; there seemed to be a pride in the possession of two names and the time to use them, and they looked at me with pity because I only had one. I had asked Mary Opal why all the girls' first names were the same, and she had answered that Mary was the best name and why should one girl be luckier than the others? When Mary Virgin's lantern was ready, she took it out into what was now full night, murmuring from the door her last hushed sounds of good-bye.

". . . I wisht I could have stayed . . . Have a good time . . . . . . your party . . ."

After a while we opened the cokes, carefully pouring the six portions. Micah LaFrance, who was a part-time errand boy in town, gave us hilarious portrayals of his boss and some town people; he had a good eye for the little pretensions and airs he saw around him. He was ten or so, and he had the freedom to see; but I knew it would go before long, vanishing somehow into the muteness of the men in these parts. Even with his wit and lightness, a sense of the ceremonial hung over our evening.

Mary Virgin's little shining had saddened us all somehow; in the light of the kerosene lamps we all looked wise and solemn. Soon it was time to sleep. Since there were only three beds in the two back rooms and we wanted to be by ourselves, adult and confiding, Mary Emerald and I unrolled old quilts on the front-room floor and fell asleep in the heavy, breathing darkness.

V

Now the summer was aging on Kyrie Mountain. Maples and the stands of aspen in the groves wore layers of dust on their leaves; the colors were dark and the veins protruded from their coarsened skins like old men's hands. At the farm I had taken over some of Justine's jobs and was proud of my success. I wrote a letter home describing in detail the round of the day and what I had learned to do, and with the puzzled response knew that Mary Emerald, Word, and the mountain itself could never be told. The letter put a film of disappointment between me and the world. I knew that I was a stranger here, but the letter made me remember that I was more of a stranger at home. Where the joy was, I did not belong; and where I belonged, was no joy for me. The only cure for sadness that I could think of was Kyrie. I was going to cut into the wild plum grove and ride on my eyes up the hip of Woman Mountain until I found myself on the top and looking across at the great rhyming surges beyond. Walking the highway I was so down-eyed that I didn't even see Mary Emerald coming toward me.

I was almost face to face with her when she said, "Cinder searchin'?"

I jumped, startled. I had been too vulnerable, but she was a friend, so I laughed.

"I'm goin' to cheer you," she said. "Mary Virgin an' me—we want you to eat dinner up to her and Frank's house."

I had planned to climb to where I could spend a while with my sorrows, going through them room by room, glorying a little in all the small sensibilities, the real and the studied. "Does she live in town?" I asked.

"Oh, no. Frank and his brothers are building them a house near to Yarrow Crossing."

It turned the decision for me. "When do we go?'

"We're gone now." She laughed.

We stopped off to hang Mary Emerald's basket in a tree to wait.

We walked until a sign said Beaumarchais. Mary Emerald corrected me to Bowmarches. To the south the land gentled from rock and pine to hills and long meadows bordered with great leafing trees. In one long vista, over the pull of a hill, a double row of poplars were standing alone, and we caught our breaths with the beauty of them.

As we were held, looking, she said softly, "Seems a wrong, don't it, sayin' pretty trees an' pretty dresses an' pretty shoes—all like it was the same. I once knew a girl said God was swell, an' the priest heard her an' he got mad, but people put all kinds of things to one word an' nobody says nothing about it."

We walked on, as if looking were drinking and we could pull the sight to satiety, but we were not sated when we left the poplars behind a rise in the land.

After Beaumarchais came water. Creeks and ponds and streams, still water and falling water opened one after another. We crossed many bridges and the sound of water was always with us.

"Yarrow's not too far," Mary Emerald said, as we left the town. Behind us a car honked, and when the noise seemed too persistent for flattery, we turned. "It's Frank; he'll give us a lift maybe."

Both Mary Emerald and Mary Virgin had spoken of Frank with a kind of fear and awe in their voices, and I half-expected to see forked lightning sitting harnessed behind the wheel of the car. But as I looked, I saw an ordinary man with a thin, unexpressive face. He was milling on some gum. Mary Emerald went hesitantly to the car, her natural stride all crimped and stilted and her voice strained.

"Hello, Frank." And then, "Are you set for home?"

His answer was slow and his smile almost as stilted as hers. "Yea, I'll take you—an' your friend, too."

I said, "Hello, Frank, I'm pleased to meet you." And we started off.

Frank asked about the family, and Mary Emerald answered

politely, too reserved, I thought, for a sister-in-law. When we came in sight of the raw-looking clapboard house standing on a bald knoll, Mary Emerald praised the building elaborately, and the strength and perseverance of Frank and his brothers. I listened to the undertone in her voice. I didn't want to, but it sounded and sounded under the words. It was fear—a strong, abiding fear—and I looked away, wondering if Frank heard it or understood. Under the words—Will a man take me away one day, by some drawing force that I do not know, defenseless, to a barren, treeless knoll to bear children and cook for him and be bound to his sins and faults forever? Sitting in the old car with Mary Virgin's husband, Mary Emerald and I shuddered together.

The car stopped at the bottom of the hill and we got out, looking up at the house. Mary Virgin was out, moving gingerly over the wooden planks and building things in the yard.

"She's gettin' on to her time," Frank said, smiling with embarrassment, and I hated the smile because I couldn't determine whether it was for himself or because of her swollen body.

"Are you all ready?" Mary Emerald asked tightly.

"Oh, we ain't havin' no midwife; she got her head set on the hospital care." He breathed out heavily; money, I knew, and I hated him for that too, because I was intolerant of the weight he bore, a money weight, a worry weight, the weight of another's possessions gathering weekly in his house.

Shyly, Mary Virgin was waiting for us as we walked up the hill. She arranged the folds of her dress and apron, her hands always moving to hide, moving to hide across the middle. When we got to the house, Mary Emerald again repeated the praises about its splendor that she had just poured on Frank, and for a while Mary Virgin walked with us, showing this feature and that, saying where she would set out some plants next year and where the baby would play in the sun. Then the two of us were sent down to the stream with buckets for water, because the well wasn't finished. Talk of water in the house made Mary Emerald perk up, and she fluttered her fingers (ideas of a lady), but as we went down from the knoll to where the stream flowed hard and cold against the scoured rocks of its channel, she said, "If there's no need to go into the cold, when the stars freeze like to burn you, then you don't. Then you miss the stars and the cold smell that the air has."

I nodded, walking into the stream and getting the sick shock of icy cold running up from my feet and ankles. We stood together, filling our buckets, blue-lipped with cold, and in her worry for Mary Virgin and fear for herself, since the world was colder than the stream sometimes, Mary Emerald said, "Frank's a good man. He ain't one to get drunk or beat up or take after other girls, but Mary Virgin loves trees near as much as me, an' there ain't but wind going to blow on that place years—an' years."

I heard again in my mind, against a night lit with a lantern, the timorous breath of Mary Virgin's good night—"Frank wants me to home." And the widening of her eyes as she said it.

Mary Emerald looked at me with the water running over her bucket. "She says she likes bein' married, but she don't come an' see us much any more." I knew she had felt the little wind of her own loneliness blowing, so we took our buckets and went back up the hill to the house without speaking.

I guessed that Micah LaFrance and Mary Opal, Sinai Ellis and Mary Pearl would turn up for dinner, and I was right. We had big dishes of potatoes, bread, corn jonnies, and venison canned from last fall's hunting. There was little talk while we ate, but every word or grunt from Frank was greeted with the reverent attention due a nugget of Socrates. When he took his toothpick and went out to sit by the car, we all relaxed and felt free again, and by the time the water for the dishes had heated, we were laughing and joking.

When we had finished and were putting things away, I said, "It's a pity Frank isn't here to laugh at that one!"

"Oh, you don't tell Frank!" Mary Emerald hid her mouth with her hand. She should have hidden her eyes instead, for the little look of fear that ran across them.

"Oh, not Frank!" Mary Virgin said, laughing too.

"Good night, listening to you two makes me think you're scared of Frank," I said, wishing I could ask and be told really.

Surprisingly, Mary Virgin's face did grow graver and she turned her head up a little, like a puzzled child. "Men's ways are different." There wasn't a sound in the room. "Yes—I am afraid. Frank is everything in the whole world, an' he don't

know it. If he takes a notion—even some quick—it could be
my whole life changed forever. And maybe, maybe in the middle of the notion—to die . . ."

I remembered seeing it in a new way, the picture of
Mr. Wrather on the wall of Mary Emerald's cabin. It was of
him Mary Virgin was speaking now, and she was in another
time, standing with the towel in her kitchen; she was possessing
the body and sorrow of another year. Frank was one of that
powerful race, that notional race, one with her father.

Matthew Wrather had died and left his family with half the
winter still to endure. Hunger, misery, and loneliness had taken
his place. He had fathered eight and had favored his first
daughter above the others, and he had died. Now there was
another of that race who was a universe and who was mortal.
The thirteen-year-old Mary Virgin came back into the waiting
mother of seventeen, and took up the calm, ethereal look her
older face had in repose.

When it was dark, Frank said he would drive us home. We
thanked him again and again.

VI

On the shoulder of the mountain three trees had gone a
brilliant yellow. Suddenly I saw that the time which I had dared
myself to spend freely and without stint was running into its
last days, and that I was not ready. I walked through every
grove and keeled every ridge, to fill my eyes and complete a
vision that would stay with me forever. I asked Word questions
too. Did men know they were the world? Why wasn't everyone
here a poet or a saint, living with such sweeps of sky and
silence? When I finished the question he searched me for
scorn, but there was no scorn. I was looking at the swells of
land falling down and away forever from where we stood and
waited.

He said abruptly, "Ready for a climb? I been wantin' to
show you somethin' an' this is as good a time as any."

I said I was, and we began making for the crown of the
mountain.

"You asked me about men knowin' they're everything. I
think they do—them down there, maybe even me. We do know

we're everything, but we know it one way. When we get older, we know it another way, but the words ain't changed. It's almost a whole other way of feelin', but the words to put to it ain't changed." He looked back at me. "Do you understand that?" Almost like an attack.

I said I understood.

"It's why I give up a lot of the words." And he waved his hand off to show me the valley and the world. "Second thing is maybe this: the hills ain't responsible, and they bear men is patient an' not angels. Hill folk ain't city-great; they're hill-great. Maybe what educated folks call eye for beauty is nothin', but the sick man takin' his own pulse all day—how do I feel and how hard am I sweatin'." He looked a little hopeless and cornered, the "Justine" look. "Well, you comin'?"

We walked to the top of the whole beautiful Kyrie Mountain, and I kept wondering where he could take me that I didn't already know. To cap it, he said by way of reassurance, "Just whatever happens, don't get frighted."

We crossed over the summit of bramble-covered rock and went down the southwest side through long, wind-winnowed grasses into the tree grove, the ancient and dried-up spillway of what had once been a waterfall. As the wind blew across the trees, Word gestured with his finger and whispered, "Hear that? Sounds like water, don't it? It ain't, though; it's the wind up-cuttin' the rocks to the far side. It blows across there. Our knowin' what was here once is givin' us that sound. It's the memory of water."

I had often seen the spillway and the dark chasm, but Word said, "Come on. We're goin' to walk it now."

I had never dared it. It was a fearful, dangerous climb down, on water-smooth rocks that seemed to hang over yards of air to the brutal fall. When a rock slipped under Word's foot and hit—clunk—clunk—clunk—all the long way down; I heard the sound like breaking bones. At last we came to easier going, and Word threw back his head and shouted, "Eloy! Eloy!" There was no answer. We kept going down, and "Eloy! Eloy!" again; and then Word grated my rib with an elbow and pointed to a stand of three scrub pine a hundred feet or so further in the chasm.

I saw nothing. "Where?"

"There—there, over by the tree."

Against his background the man was almost invisible and I had to pick him out, a bit of him at a time. I'd seen the same kind of brownness in Word himself, and it had frightened me at first. Now the surprise was not that the man seemed to merge with the rocks and the earth but that he was standing, wary and still, with a great heavy rifle aimed straight at us.

Word edged closer to me to whisper, "Can't but admire him. Blind as a bat, born blind; but he's too proud to admit even to the ones knows him." He called out, "Oh, Eloy, put your gun up. I brung a lady to you an' she's like to faint now, you gone scared her!" There was no word spoken, only a moment of silence and the shattering sound of the gunshot. "Eloy!" and then the second shot, a terrible sound in that deep well of rock. Cursing, Word scrambled up the canyon side, I following, too terrified to make a sound. Fear made me clumsy; I stumbled several times, wakening little stones and earth from my footholds and expecting each misstep to bring a shot in reprisal. After a while Word said, "We're out of his range, now." We were both panting heavily. "I guess it's just Eloy's way," he said simply. "If he'd wanted us, he wouldn't 'uv shot."

"But why, with a gun—when—he could—have told—us?" I panted.

"Well, men's born blind and men's come blind. Eloy, he's both. Man don't know he's blind less someone tells him so. When Eloy found out, he got so mad he come down here an' stayed ever since. Now he's a hard man, but that's his pride. I don't know what got to him to do that way." I saw that Word was a little annoyed for me. "I been goin' down there years now, but he gets notions."

As I got my breath I suddenly found myself trembling. These were the virtues I had always hungered for, and I had recognized them well enough now in Eloy: independence, bluntness, hatred of bonds, sharp will, scorn of "manners." All my loudest wishes, and here they were mirrored, and I was not pleased with them. I wondered if even Word didn't question Elroy's "notions" now. Word had once said to me that he was lonely some, but no more than he ought to be. It had seemed a virtue to be lonely, once.

When we reached the top of the chasm and stood in our own lands again, we looked out over the fall; and Word, mistaking my look and probably my paleness, tried to comfort me with something, anything he could think of. "Uh—I come to wonder on that question of yours, how there ain't more poets. I don't know much about them, but I wonder now how there ain't more preachers and prophets like there used to be. Uh—they always did laugh at me over to town, you know, seein' I hate hunting. Hereabouts boys grow up shootin' just like part of their nature. Now I started to think about when I was with two boys right over there on Woman Mountain. I was still in the way where I was tryin' to fight myself for what I ought to like or let alone. Abraham LaForet spotted him a buck deer an' he shot an' hit it, an' the buck come turning in a big leap that was a beauty to see, but it landed dyin', all spraddled out an' wrong, breakin' its legs because it'ad stopped living in the middle of that leap. When we got to him, I just looked, an' it was like a drawing that the school kids make; the buck lookin' so stupid with its eyes gone hard and dryin' up in the wind. It was changed; it made me start to shake. Just then, old Alonzo LaForet, Abraham's grandpap, showed up, an' them boys started to go on—ain't it beautiful, an' all. I didn't say nothin', just stood by an' tried to forgit I was there. Someone took up that I wasn't sayin' nothin', so they start—What does Word think; say somethin' now; an' ain't it a beauty, Word? You know, Eloy found out he was blind on a day like that day was for me; but Eloy went off, an' I had to stay there, knowin' from then on that whatever it was I was supposed to have in me, I just didn't have it. I said, 'Word says it looks like a dead cow. It's big and it's dead and it's meat; and that's all you can say for it now. All the good got left behind in that leap.' Their mouths just hung like they was broke, an' Abraham started to double him up a fist for a fight; but old Alonzo came in an said—I'll never forget the words of it—'Can't help the difference between you boys; it's the eyes you brung to this.' Then they took up the deer and headed home."

The light was beginning to go. It held in the yellow trees of the aspen grove and drew brightness in narrowing lines through the nets of the pines. The summer wind, with its smell of the sun-warmed rock and the berry thickets, was gone. This wind was cold and clear and from the west. It was an autumn wind, from which even we had to turn for shelter. For the first time Word and I walked together down the mountain, and the dark came on behind us.

VII

Mary Emerald was at the abandoned farm the next day. She let me come close before she spoke, as if the secret was so deep that she had to whisper it. "Mary Virgin's time come this morning. She's gone to the hospital now an' we got to wait for Ma to come an' for Frank to tell us anything."

We walked down the hill. It was afternoon. I had spent all day walking up the northern side of the mountain.

"We'll go home and wait," Mary Emerald said. "I got to *do* something."

We went to Wrathers' and waited. Night came.

"We'll need a lantern, and when Frank comes, we got to go tell Gram and Gramps."

I wondered how far it was to where they lived. The cards for the Slumber Party were a good ten miles. We were sitting in the dark in the cold front room. She had said it was no use making a fire if they'd have to leave. The kids were at Shires, and there was nothing to do.

Finally, she said, "If news comes, I want to get something to take to Gram."

We took the lantern out behind the house and walked up a little rise. It was pitch dark. Mary Emerald hung the lantern on a tree and then bent down and began to pick stalks of wild rye. She showed me how to pull the strawlike stalks with their heavy heads of seeds. Gram baked them into bread, and I had eaten it at Wrathers'. The wild seeds had a special taste. I started chewing a few in the cold, dark night, waiting to hear about Mary Virgin, tired and groping out of the dim circle of lantern light to pick the straws. Fresh, cold, sleepy, an astringent taste in the mouth, a funny . . . The laughter built in me until it shot out of my mouth, and I threw myself on the ground full length and let it break. I laughed until I howled, my lungs heaving for breath; and Mary Emerald was soon laughing with me, puzzled, but consenting.

I caught a gasp to explain. "Not moonlight—picking rye by moonlight is romantic, but with a lantern. . . !" And I was off again, arms and laughter wide under the sky.

We gathered a good sheaf before the car drove up, and when Mary Emerald saw it, bumping over the footpath, she snatched

the light and we both went running and stumbling to the front
of the house to show that we were there. It was Frank, and
Mary Emerald took a step back when she saw him, awed by
someone so heavy in power that he could cause this anguish.
He was part of Mary Virgin's fear and glory, and all he could
do was say, "Well, she's borned us a little girl."

We let out our breaths as if thanking him for having spared
his wife.

Mary Emerald said in her low voice, "Is she good? We're
agoing to tell Gram and Gramps now."

"She seemed okay when I was by. You tell them an' I'll go
get somethin' to eat now," Frank said. He turned the motor
over and it shivered and grunted into an idle. "Your ma's with
Mary Virgin, but she'll be back to Shires."

"Do you need cookin' or washin'—uh—there?" Mary Emerald asked.

"No, my sisters been seein' to me." And the foolish man
turned his car and rode away.

She had tensed beside me, and if there had been light, I
would have seen the short whip of muscle tighten on both sides
of the impassive face. Frank never realized that to Mary Emerald his sisters were interlopers in her sister's kitchen. If only
he'd said that he was fine and gone his way! I cursed him rudely
in my mind because he was stupid and would never know it; his
women would keep it from him.

We started out for Gram and Gramps, and I was about to
ask how far it was, pitying myself beforehand, when Mary
Emerald turned and pointed out the light of a cabin no more
than five hundred feet down the path on which we were walking. I'd often passed the place going down the highway and
seeing it through the trees, thinking it was deserted. It was an
old, weathered place with a sagging porch, and bare as the
Wrathers' was barricaded. I never dreamed that anyone was
living in it; even seeing the light made me think of some old
tramp sleeping his single night on the warped plank floor and
cursing his ill-fitting bones; but as we came up to the house I
saw that it was sturdier than it appeared. Mary Emerald
warned me about the porch. When we were up on the crying,
swaying layers, she smiled, knowing them, and then knocked at
the door and shouted. After a while the door did really open
and my eyes hurried ahead inside to a warm, well-lighted room,

full of knickknack clutter, far from the bareness I expected. The woman was very old; the man seemed older; and we came in very quietly because of it.

In a small, whispy voice I was greeted. They were very shy until I sat down and said some small thing, and then the old lady leaned forward and touched my arm.

"I heard about you an' Word scarin' each other up to the Marrenses place, out'n the barn," she said; and I laughed, by now a little mechanically. Was there nothing else that could draw me to their circle? I wouldn't have been surprised if the most remote of all the mountain kin had heard it to tell it back to me at the ends of the earth. Of course, she had to use it; there was nothing else.

Mary Emerald said, "Gram knowed Word when he was just a young 'un an' hired out to Marrens."

The old lady said, "I knowed Word when he were bare half-a-letter." And we all laughed at that, Gram holding her hand across her mouth daintily, while the tough gnarled cords of her neck stood out, giving a sadness to the delicate gesture. All the years of buckets and bearing and fighting winter, and still there had to be the delicacy.

"Gram," Mary Emerald said, "Mary Virgin had them a little girl."

The old lady looked satisfied. "I been expectin' it sooner than them doctors said. She done good, didn't she?"

"I don't know." Mary Emerald sounded echoing and lost, even in the comfort of the room. "Frank ain't one for much news."

They talked on for a while about babies and birthing, Gram with a sort of impersonal cheer that seemed strange to me. Perhaps there had been so many . . . I looked over at Gramps, sitting on the listing bed with his pipe materials spread out in front of him. Gram was telling a story about some long-dead woman's long-dead cousins. It went on for quite a time, and I waited for some point to it, half-listening for the drop in voice to mark the end. As she went on I looked at the room, going over the expected things and feeling comfortable. I had been right after all. There was the swollen-faced Madonna on the wall, gaudy calendar, dried palm fronds, souvenirs of Bridgeport, Conn., and sunny Boonesboro; but as I turned from that wall to the other, I saw Mary Emerald. Her eyes were hard on her grandmother, and she was straining for every word. Some thing was happening, something in the words of the old woman to her.

It was nothing so abstract as Gram's eyes loving or her hand that badgered and worried every now and then at Mary Emerald's arm. It was the words themselves. I wondered what could be so vital in the happenings of unknown people now dead and gone. She had stopped talking about Cousin Jane Tredway apparently, and was now busy with a "Clara that's daughter married a Sprue."

I stood up, listening, and after a while, found myself into a long history of which Mary Emerald was the present link. Letitia Bow-March and Cousin Jane, and Clara and Mary Emerald also, though Gram didn't say so, had all been left fatherless and poor, and thus motherless. They had all had older sisters whom they had taken to their souls as mothers and had lost again to marriage. They had all suffered—some wisely and some unwisely—but the anguish was valuable with Gram's telling. Grow in, it said, and grow over. For Mary Emerald the anguish was still red—marriage bed and child bed. I'd been too busy to see just how lonely and hungering she was, too new to know how long and how deep the pain had been carried.

"What happened to Clara when her sister's baby was borned?" Mary Emerald was asking.

"Well, you know that Clara was proud, and her sister some too proud. She left that cold house of ther'un with her great tall man, an' she never come back no more nor tried to keep them kids in mind. Them Bournes was all quiet folks. Clara never said nothin', nor made like she cared at all; but when the baby come, she left where she was and she run into their house an' snatched the baby right up out'n the midwife's hands an' held it like to hurt it. Well, Alice's great big tall man was no better'n a sick puppy, cryin' an' pleadin'. It was the midwife made Clara put the baby down, an' then that quiet Bourne girl throwed the biggest, longest screamin' fit was ever seen in the county. It was the start of daylight in her mind, an' Alice done some humblin', too, after that. Clara went an' married Stokes oldest boy later. Ha! He was the only one of all them Stokeses worth the dirt it took to bury 'em."

Gramps brought her a pipe which he had filled for her, and

she took a series of short gleeful puffs. He was shy of me. He asked after the family. He said he was going fishing this week, and would bring them something. He couldn't speak his mind in front of me, and it labored him to talk around me to Mary Emerald about things that were close to him, so I asked her to see me to the highway and I said good-bye. As I closed the door behind me, I could hear Gram saying, "I heered that girl was crazy."

"No, she ain't a bit," said Mary Emerald's voice.

"Figured she wasn't," Gram said.

I jumped down from the porch carefully, smiling.

There was a very quiet music from the great body of Kyrie Mountain as I came toward the farm. My eyes won the shapes of trees and road from the darkness, and with the music it seemed that this world was one at last in which I belonged. There was no longer need to ask the trees to name the generations of those whose vitals had suffered loneliness, or, when the brief times of peace and easement came to puzzle them, wondered with fear and awe how they could bear the thrust again.

VIII

One more week of grace, please, I wrote, not daring to add that I had things to finish and a mountain to seal inside myself forever and that I wanted to give Mary Emerald a gift. I knew what it was to be the first time I heard the kids talk about starting school again. I had seen their poverty naturally and casually, as they lived it during the summer, but when they spoke of school, ill-fitting clothes and uncut hair, worst of all, their shaming ignorance, I knew I had the one gift for Mary Emerald that I was born to give her and that she would never have without me. We were subdued, talking about winter and my leaving. Every moment that we sat talking, the mountain was changing around us. The wind had a fresh smell; and the quietness of its passage was sad after the bright, hot noise of cicadas and the ticking of a thousand insect lives of summer.

"Mary Emerald—what if I could come and visit you at school for a day. Just to see what it's like there?"

She said she would see, and we talked about other things, our eyes going over and over the whole mountain.

"Eloy told Word once that the earth reverences men just as much as they reverence it."

"I don't know," Mary Emerald said. "It don't seem that our pines or them poplar trees near Mary Virgin's reverence me."

I thought for a minute that I heard bitterness. Mary Emerald had found it enough simply to love before Mary Virgin had married and gone; now the yearning turned, however timidly, for answer.

The next day Mary Emerald hurried over to tell me that I could come to school with her. She had stored the eagerness until the wish could be made real; and this prudence, which I had once thought strange in people of a generous land, was now clear to me and seemed natural and good.

We walked to town in the early morning, and for Mary Emerald's sake, I humbled myself for that one irretrievable day to hate the cool blade of the wind. My hair was a glorious mass of curls. I sprouted ribbons; I crinkled and jingled: Mary Emerald's City Friend to Whom the Great Things of the World Are Commonplace. Let no brisk-handed mountain-born wind dare disarrange me. I was a confection.

We came to town and then passed it to where the Consolidated school brooded on its slaty hill. The building was modern, but dull as rote—square lines. I couldn't tell Mary Emerald that I thought it should have been named Ethan Frome high. It was only here, for the first time since I had left a city I hated, that I remembered part of it with joy: my school, and all the schools there, with their mad, pirated, and misfit-Byzantine, crenelated Woolworth, Hackensack-Ionic school buildings. I had gone to a school above whose cornerstone's mayor and dignitaries was a blue ceramic plaque: Joseph Runciman O'Callahan Hoc Me Fecit. I had loved O'Callahan; hated, feared, and gloried in him; but I had seldom been indifferent as these students were.

We began to walk up the squat hill to the squat building, playing our parts very deftly and smoothly, as if she had no one to introduce and I no one to impress. She introduced me to her home-room teacher; the bell rang; and we rose together, two as one, into destiny. Although I was plain and knew I could do nothing about that, I had fought it with curls; and I also let it be known during the course of the morning that I could joke in

Russian and Greek, spoke Urdu conversationally at home, had once been understudy to a child stage star, and thus knew Tony Perkins and Debbie Reynolds as "Perk" and "Dee Dee." I labored my humility too, admitting ruefully that I found both physics and Chinese difficult. Unplanned, undreamed glory: *Romeo and Juliet* was being read as if through morphine, in English class, and when I was asked if I wanted to share in the reading, I did so, of course, from memory. The suspense of waiting for me to step on Juliet's train kept everyone awake, and the teacher practically kissed me. Mary Emerald was shining as I had never seen her do in public, laughing and using all the tricks of feigned modesty that most girls learn young.

At lunch she let me know who had been kind to her and those were the few with whom I permitted myself to smile. I was working the point a little, I knew, but there was only one day to give Mary Emerald the Powerful Friend in the City that I wanted her to have. We laughed over secret jokes together and I managed to leave before my curls fell. Our day had been pure luck, a triumph. We never thanked each other, which would have meant touching the thing and marring it. I only wondered if, with all the nourishment the summer had given me, I had grown in any way. It didn't seem to me that I was any more competent or quick. I had known and loved Kyrie Mountain and was the ally of two people in its shadow, but this wasn't ancient Greece, where an enemy might see, standing behind his adversary, the mighty shadow of a protecting god. I wanted the whole summer for a crown, so that I could walk showing my crueler world the glory of what I loved.

On the last day I met Mary Emerald, knowing that when my parents came to take me back, I would have to show her to them and them to her, and that neither would ever know what the other meant. We stood looking up at the three waves of the mountain. The trees that changed were golden, and the wind blowing over them made their colors vibrate like sounds with overtones. I thought of how the air vibrated with the heat of summer, and how in moonlight, too, the dead spaces thrummed with life.

"We'll miss you when you're gone to the city," she said absently.

I turned to her and answered, "Well, at least you know that I didn't come to 'summer away' here because I was crazy. I have to admit that I heard you telling it to Gram."

"You must be laughin' how I fixed it so flat-out," she said, "lettin' you hear through the door like that; but there wasn't no ways to come up to you an' tell you, was there—only I wanted you to know."

It had been fake for fake. I smiled at her. Then we sat back and looked out again like fellow mourners at a funeral.

"What can I take with me?" I said.

She was thinking of the kids and Gram and Mary Virgin and the pain of loss and the end of summer and maybe of one night when there was fear, laughter, and comfort all together. She answered as if she were talking to herself. "The taste of wild rye."

I started to cry a little, hearing a car pull up in front of the farmhouse. When its engine stopped there was a fearful quietness.

I looked back at my mountain and said, "For He Who is mighty has done great things for me and Holy is His Name."

She turned with me to go to the car. "You always talk so nice."